WONDERS OF MAN

THE HAGUE

by Mark Greenberg

and the Editors
of the Newsweek Book Division

NEWSWEEK, New York

NEWSWEEK BOOK DIVISION

Edwin D. Bayrd, Jr.   *Editorial Director*
Mary Ann Joulwan   *Art Director*
Laurie P. Winfrey   *Picture Editor*
Eva Galan   *Assistant Editor*
Diane Raines Keim   *Picture Researcher*

Alvin Garfin   *Publisher*

WONDERS OF MAN
Milton Gendel   *Consulting Editor*

ENDSHEETS: *Dutch blueware tiles, painted in The Hague during the seventeenth century—the Golden Age of the Netherlands—depict the men and women of the newly independent Republic in varied seventeenth-century period costumes.*

TITLE PAGE: *Under a lowering—and typically Dutch—sky, several young Haguenaars play soccer on the Sweelinck Plein before a row of brightly lit façades characteristic of The Hague.*

OPPOSITE: Le Flâneur—*"The Stroller"—doffs his hat to passersby on the Lange Voorhout—a symbol of the geniality one encounters throughout The Hague.*

Library of Congress Cataloging in Publication Data

Greenberg, Mark.
  The Hague.

  (Wonders of man)
  Bibliography: p.
  Includes index.
    1. Hague (Netherlands)—History. 2. Hague (Netherlands)—Description. I. Newsweek, Inc. Book Division. II. Title. III. Series.

DJ411.H3357G73   1982   949.2'3   81-83746
ISBN 0-88225-310-7

Printed and bound in Japan

Contents

As a rule, swans dot the surface of the Hofvijver, the Court Lake that separates the government buildings of the Binnenhof from The Hague itself. But on those rare occasions when the Hofvijver does freeze over, local Hans Brinkers are quick to take to the ice with a puck.

10

Introduction

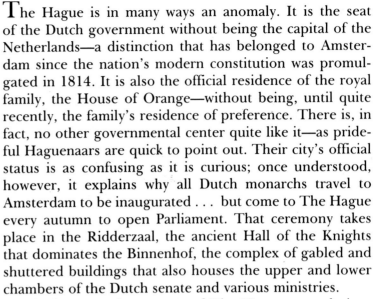

The Hague is in many ways an anomaly. It is the seat of the Dutch government without being the capital of the Netherlands—a distinction that has belonged to Amsterdam since the nation's modern constitution was promulgated in 1814. It is also the official residence of the royal family, the House of Orange—without being, until quite recently, the family's residence of preference. There is, in fact, no other governmental center quite like it—as prideful Haguenaars are quick to point out. Their city's official status is as confusing as it is curious; once understood, however, it explains why all Dutch monarchs travel to Amsterdam to be inaugurated . . . but come to The Hague every autumn to open Parliament. That ceremony takes place in the Ridderzaal, the ancient Hall of the Knights that dominates the Binnenhof, the complex of gabled and shuttered buildings that also houses the upper and lower chambers of the Dutch senate and various ministries.

It is the anomalous status of The Hague—not de jure the capital of the Netherlands, but certainly its capital de facto—that led one seventeenth-century visitor to label it "the mightiest village in Europe"—an epithet that Haguenaars have repeated, with varying degrees of pride, bemusement and irony, ever since. That same visitor identified The Hague as one of the most beautiful villages in Europe—and in that he was no less correct, for the same combination of circumstances that rendered The Hague mighty despite its size also rendered it wealthy quite out of proportion to its actual productivity.

Like thirteenth-century Venice, The Hague owed its vast wealth to the sea; and like fifteenth-century Florence, it used that wealth to attract the greatest convocation of artistic talent assembled anywhere since the High Renaissance. The so-called Golden Age of the Netherlands did in fact produce art and architecture of remarkable beauty, as even the most cursory walking tour of The Hague will reveal. Among the most elegant of the many buildings erected during this period is the severely classical *hôtel* of Johann-Maurits, count of Nassau-Siegen. The Mauritshuis collection, displayed in the mansion he build at the corner of the Binnenhof, includes the two exquisite Vermeers found on pages 70–71 and a dozen splendid Rembrandts, among them the three canvases on pages 58–59. A city of surprising "might" and surprising riches, The Hague is also a city of surprising charm. Never having lost its small-town ambience, even as it has grown to big-city size, it remains one of the most accessible of major political, social, and cultural centers.   THE EDITORS

THE
NETHERLANDS
IN
HISTORY

I

The Rise of the Netherlands

In about 1250 William II, count of Holland, set out toward the old hunting lodge of his father, Floris IV, in the westernmost part of his territories. He was in search of a site suitable for another home. In a land where one was hard put to distinguish the water from the bogs and the bogs from the mists, Count William was surely seeking something more than a pleasure spot. Holland was then, among the many Dutch counties, baronies, and bishoprics, the most aggressive province, and William, only recently named king of the Romans by the pope, was out to give substance and presence to his power by establishing a manor house appropriate to his stature and his ambitions.

The spot William finally chose was doubtless the most pleasant he could find in the area. It was blessed with game and potable water, and it was near the sea. On this land stood a hunting estate, built by the lords of Wassenaar, that William's father had repaired and rebuilt. The house that William constructed adjacent to this manor was known for centuries as the Old Hall, or the Hall of Rolls, and the complex itself was called 's-Gravenhage, "the count's hedge."

William's son, Floris V, had even greater ambitions, and to his father's manor house he added one of the largest rooms built in Europe during the thirteenth century—the Ridderzaal, or Hall of the Knights (see city plan, pages 164–65). The count's secretary, Gerard van Leiden, designed this monumental hall, where Floris could entertain the neighboring nobility in a manner intended to awe. Eventually an impressive series of buildings would be constructed in front of this hall and to either side, forming the Binnenhof, or "interior court," of 's-Gravenhage. The town that grew up around the Binnenhof took its name from the original structure, shortened to den Haag, or The Hague.

All this took time, of course, and for at least a century little stood on the site but Floris's imposing brick structure, the Old Hall, and the surrounding moats and walls. The Hofvijver, or Court Lake, protected the complex on one side, and alongside the lake were gardens and a summer house. The area beyond the gate—the Buitenhof, or "outer court"—contained the court farm, the stables, and the smithies. On the present-day Plein was a vegetable garden, sufficient in its day to supply the court as well as the small town surrounding it.

The power and prestige of Holland grew steadily after 1250, and three and a half centuries later, when the Netherlands had freed itself from foreign domination and declared itself a nation, its leaders returned to The Hague to hang the captured banners of their vanquished oppressor, Spain, from the Ridderzaal's beamed ceiling, proclaim their independence under its arch, and call this ancient home of the counts of Holland its capital.

The Ridderzaal still stands in the middle of the Binnenhof, perhaps not as vaulting and impressive as other Gothic structures of the same period, but certainly somber and imposing, with its great pointed roof flanked by two even taller towers. Here, on the third Tuesday of September, Queen Beatrix of the Netherlands delivers her speech from the throne, officially opening parliament, which meets

Rampant lions bracket a stork on the official crest of The Hague.

in an adjoining building. The ceremony begins with a procession, headed by the sovereign in her gilt state coach, that passes through the city center to the Binnenhof. For this occasion the Ridderzaal itself is banked with orange and white flowers—the royal colors—and hung with the national flag and the flags of all the Dutch provinces. The nation's past is thus remembered each year in this hall—built before anyone dreamed of a Dutch nation.

Holland's preeminence among the territories with which she would eventually unite may be traced, in part, to the struggles between the papacy and the Holy Roman Emperor that took place following Charlemagne's death in 814. Before Charlemagne became emperor in the year 800, what would become the Netherlands was inhabited by staunchly independent tribes of Frisians in the north and west, Saxons in the east and the center, and Franks south of the Meuse (see map, pages 164–65). Conversion to Christianity, which threatened tribal integrity, was constantly attempted by indefatigable monks, but the new religion was generally resisted. As early as 695, for instance, an English monk named Willibrord was appointed bishop of the Frisians by the pope, but only under Charlemagne did Christianity finally prevail. He subdued and converted the warring Saxons and Frisians, and thereby gave this part of the world the first peace it had known in centuries. When Charlemagne died, no one ruler proved able to master the empire he left, and in 843 it was divided up among his three grandsons. The Netherlands was assigned to Lothaire as part of the Middle Kingdom—which was, in turn, divided into East and

West Francia, with the Netherlands belonging to the so-called Eastern Kingdom.

What really mattered in the Low Countries after Charlemagne's death was not the sovereign, whose power there was largely theoretical, but the local vassal, nobleman—or, perhaps, monastic order—to whom land had been granted in fief in return for loyal service to the emperor. Far from the center of power, in a region where there were neither great landholdings nor serfs to farm them, these vassals' hereditary fiefs were seats of absolute power. By the year 1000, the Netherlands was thoroughly fragmented. In the western areas, autonomous regions were loosely controlled by the bishops of Utrecht, the dukes of Brabant and Gelderland, the count of Holland, and the count of Zeeland and Flanders. Farther east, power was even less centralized and local barons were practically sovereign within their own small boundaries.

The emperor had the power to appoint bishops, and, understandably, his appointments were generally guided by political rather than ecclesiastical considerations. The bishops of Utrecht, appointed by the emperor and supported by him militarily, were able to maintain control over vast territories in their diocese and keep their ambitious neighbors at bay. In 1076, when Pope Gregory VII attempted to reassert the church's right, surrendered centuries before, to appoint bishops, a fierce dispute broke out between secular and ecclesiastical authorities. While Emperor Henry IV was sojourning in Utrecht, Gregory announced his excommunication. From his pulpit the bishop of Utrecht denounced the ban as

unlawful—a not altogether surprising move, for Henry was, after all, the real source of the bishop's power and the guarantor of his independence. Both emperor and bishop lost, however: the Concordat of Worms, signed in 1122, gave the right of election to the clergy of the diocese, not to the emperor. Without imperial backing Utrecht could no longer withstand the advances of neighboring counts. To the south, Brabant and Lorraine extended their territories north to the river Meuse; the dukes of Gelderland consolidated the eastern territories; and the counts of Holland seized the entire western coast.

The crusades to free the Holy Land began during this period, and a great expansion of European trade took place. Because of its location at major estuaries, the Netherlands provinces, and especially Holland, were able to profit enormously from the new commercial opportunities. Holland competed fiercely and successfully for shipping with the Hanseatic League cities, and she established a highly lucrative trade with Prussia and Poland. To the south, Flanders prospered by obtaining raw materials from England for her weavers and then trading overland with the Hansa and the cities of northern Italy. The growth of trade encouraged the establishment of towns at or near important waterways, and Deventer, Zwolle, Kampen, Dordrecht, and Amsterdam all date from this period. Within these towns a new class of artisans and merchants was developing, a class sufficiently powerful that its members could demand—and receive—charters guaranteeing their independence from bishops, dukes, or counts. They owed nothing and felt no loyalty to the petty local

barons, who had all they could do to resist the growing power of the great nobles. The tendency toward centralization and consolidation was supported by the townspeople, and it was likewise supported in the countryside, which was also undergoing a dramatic transformation.

The Netherlands is really a broad delta, with large rivers that spread over a low, flat land. It has always been dangerously exposed to the sea, which periodically altered the land, sometimes flooding it completely, sometimes receding to create islands and lakes. The earliest large-scale attempt to control the sea and reclaim flooded land occurred around the year 1000, when dykes were built along the Zuyder Zee (now Lake Ijssel) and the West Friesland coast. Early in the thirteenth century, Count William I enclosed a major portion of southern Holland within a series of dykes. His program was far more successful than earlier attempts because it established an organized system of maintenance and repair. Officers appointed by the count oversaw each area that was protected by a dyke, and these officers were assisted by a "polder board" composed of the local nobles and peasants whose land was affected. This board undertook regular inspection and rebuilding. Throughout the eleventh and twelfth centuries, this system was maintained and expanded. Rich farm land was added as land hunger made these ventures profitable, and a new peasantry was created whose loyalty was to the count rather than the local baron. Thus, simultaneous with the growth of free towns, a free peasantry was born, and both groups looked to the count for protection. The pow-

The Ridderzaal, or Knights' Hall, is The Hague's oldest extant structure and one of the largest secular Gothic buildings in Europe. It served as the principal court of the counts of Holland, and Duke Philip of Burgundy twice held conclaves of his Knights of the Golden Fleece in the vast, vaulted hall (above). Although it suffered a long period of disuse—serving, for a time, as the national lottery headquarters—and briefly underwent a bizarre neo-Gothic "renovation," its restored façade (left) and brightly lit interior now recall Gerard van Leyden's original thirteenth-century designs. The Ridderzaal is used for ceremonial meetings of the Netherlands' legislature, and in September of each year the queen arrives at the hall in her golden coach (top left) to formally open parliament—a stately annual reminder of The Hague's regal past.

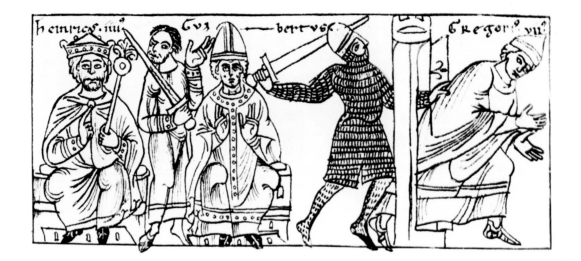

er of the local nobility was broken, laying the groundwork for a united Netherlands.

Unity was to come from the south, from France. During the fourteenth century the dukes of Burgundy, a cadet branch of the French royal house of Valois, succeeded through land purchase and marriage in extending their territory northward into Flanders, Brabant, Luxembourg, and Limburg. Holland was inherited by the counts of Hainault at the beginning of the fourteenth century and by the counts of Bavaria in about 1350. Around this time The Hague was again chosen as a capital of sorts. Albert of Bavaria, count of Holland, moved from Haarlem to The Hague, and he was followed by most of his court. For the first time a small but significant population began to gather around the count's home. Later dynastic changes, which transferred the center of power to Brussels, would temporarily reduce its importance, but The Hague was now firmly established as a town, and an aristocratic one at that. Not much is left of the construction that took place during this period, but in the Buitenhof—the exterior court of the Binnenhof complex—the Gevangenpoort, the former main gate of the castle, still stands. It is now a museum containing the instruments of torture with which "justice" was for so many years dispensed.

Count Albert's second wife, Margaret of Cleves, founded the Kloosterkerk, the church of the Dominican abbey and the first brick church in The Hague, on the Lange Voorhout in about 1397. The town itself was divided by a stream called the Beek. On one side were the count's castle and the homes

A woodcut from the Chronicle of Otto von Freising (left) depicts the feud between Pope Gregory VII and Emperor Henry IV over the appointment of bishops, a critical political issue in tenth-century Holland. The Gevangenpoort (lower left), which dates from the fourteenth century, is all that remains of what was once a prison—and thus its name, which means "prisoners' gate." Until 1923 the Gevangenpoort was the only entrance to the Buitenhof, the historical center of The Hague, but in that year the houses between it and the Hofvijver were demolished to make way for the Hofweg—a concession to the city's population boom and the popularity of the automobile. (See diagram, pages 164–65.) Today the Gevangenpoort houses a museum of torture instruments. The Kloosterkerk (right), once part of a Dominican monastery founded in the fifteenth century, escaped the destruction suffered by so many Catholic churches during the sixteenth century because it was adapted to secular uses, serving first as a stable and then as a foundry. Today The Hague's oldest church is a Protestant house of worship.

of such great lords as the Egmonds and Wassenaars. On the other side was the village itself, and there life centered around the Grote Kerk, the old St. Jacob's Kerk, which by the late fourteenth century was very nearly the size it is today. In 1395 it was reconstructed in brick, and after a fire in 1402 it was reconstructed again and on a larger scale. The six-sided tower was added in 1423. The Grote Kerk is a fine example of the Northern Gothic style, a "hall church" whose large and airy nave is paralleled by aisles of equal height. The choir, constructed around 1500, now contains the arms of Philip's Knights of the Golden Fleece, who attended a meeting there in 1456. The church burned again and was restored in 1539, and in 1565 the tower was furnished with the wooden spire that houses its bells.

As the population and importance of The Hague grew, commerce increased as well, albeit on a small scale. The Hague was connected to nearby Leiden, Delft, and Rotterdam by canals, and side canals were added to the Spui—The Hague's main waterway—so that produce from surrounding farms could be brought to market more easily. The Lange Voorhout was still largely pasture land, and muddy lanes led from the town center to the outlying farms. The nobility could still hunt in The Hague Woods, which, though not as dense as in former times, nevertheless contained fox and deer—and brigands.

A small weaving industry developed in The Hague, but this did not suffice to change its rural character. Silversmithing also became an important occupation, since both the wealthy Haguenaars and the church required fine silver plate; and though

smiths like Jan Thyrion acquired wide reputations, The Hague was never a commercial or industrial center. It was not part of the confederation of cities whose voice was heard at the meetings of the "estates"; indeed, it was never fully chartered as a town, and it was never fortified or enclosed by walls. It largely avoided commerce—and so, perhaps, it avoided trouble: The Hague was, for the most part, spared the terrible destruction visited on so many Dutch cities during the sixteenth-century wars of independence since its lack of fortifications made it an open city. In fact, the rival town of Delft petitioned William the Silent to destroy The Hague because it could not be defended against the Spanish. William replied, laconically, that it was "not advisable to burn down The Hague." Spared by both sides, the city was occupied frequently by one side or the other, and although it did not escape the plundering that accompanied these occupations, The Hague survived it all.

After three short marriages of state, Jacqueline of Bavaria, the last independent countess of Holland, decided finally to abandon her role as a pawn of Burgundian statecraft and marry for love. In order to do this she had to divest herself of her patrimony, an encumbrance when love and family interest clashed. She therefore made over the county of Holland to her cousin Philip of Burgundy in 1433. Philip, called "the good," ruled an empire that extended—thanks in part to Jacqueline—from Switzerland to the North Sea. His court was at Brussels, where, in fabled splendor, he ruled over his vast, if loosely knit, territory. Here he assembled the "es-

tates"—landowners, burghers, and, occasionally, free peasants—who could vote him "benevolences," or subsidies, whenever his own purse ran short. Malines, or Mechelen, was the seat of his law court. The Hague was chosen as the site of the council of Holland, and the *stadtholders*—who acted as Philip's lieutenants—visited it frequently.

As the Burgundian dukes sought to consolidate their power, they once again turned to The Hague, which they knew was still looked upon in Holland as the seat and symbol of its independence. Sometime before the close of the fourteenth century, the Bredero family had established itself as the most loyal supporters of the Bavarian counts—and thereby became the most wealthy. They built their mansion in The Hague, and it must have been splendid indeed, for the chroniclers refer to it as "the Court of the Brederoes." In any case, they unwisely chose to oppose Philip, and in about 1450 he requisitioned their property and turned it into The Hague's town hall. It was torn down a century later, but the cellars remain and can still be seen.

When the Bredero buildings were demolished in 1560, the construction of a new town hall was begun. It was designed in the Antwerp style—a square and sober building with the considered proportions of the new Renaissance style—but it was thoroughly northern in mood. This structure, which still stands, is gayer than Renaissance Italians would have thought appropriate, and it is as boisterous as were the nobles and burghers of the Netherlands. Its gables of brick and stone are ornately decorated. On the left side rises an octagonal tower that is some

seventy feet tall and even more fanciful than the principal façade. The loggia, resting on Ionic and Corinthian columns, contains sixty consoles and sculptures, and its base is richly decorated with sculptured reliefs. Two life-size figures guard it at either end: a woman holding a snake to represent strength and another holding handcuffs to represent justice. Above is a gable with the three female figures of hope, love, and belief. Below them is the national coat of arms, a rampant lion, which is surrounded by two others to form a unified group. Over the gable is a Latin motto, inscribed at the time of the building's construction, which sums up the eternal wisdom of municipal management: *Ne Jupiter quidem omnibus, Vigilate deo confidentes* (roughly: "Not even Jupiter can please everybody"). This town hall, the Oude Raadhuis, served as the principal municipal building until the early 1950s, when new quarters were built.

The dukes of Burgundy reigned toward the end of what we call the Middle Ages. The dukes' wealth derived, as did the wealth of all medieval rulers, from vast farm lands, but it came increasingly from trade and industry as well. In towns like Bruges, Antwerp, and Ghent, fortunes were being made in the weaving industry and the shipping and banking trades. The men who profited from these ventures, burghers with no ancient aristocratic titles or country seats, became more and more powerful at court. Their political goals clashed as much as did their tastes with those of the noblemen and knights, who still saw their rule as divinely sanctioned and their tastes as a reflection of this God-given order. Philip

the Good had devised a system of governance that allowed these new men some influence in state affairs. In a sense Philip was doing nothing more than accommodating to an altered reality, for in the meetings of the estates the voice of the burghers was powerful, often decisive—and in the towns they pretty much ran things. With their new status came a surer confidence and the desire to live as the nobility did—in splendor.

We see this reflected in the art produced during the Burgundian period in the Netherlands—a splendid art that decisively changed the way men looked at and thought about the world. In the generations before the towns of the Netherlands and their burghers could support an active community of artists, talented painters went south to France to work directly for the duke and his court. The most famous of these are the Limburg brothers, Pol, Jehanequin, and Herman, who came from Nijmegen in Gelderland. They worked first at Dijon for Philip the Bold and John the Fearless, and later at the court of the duc de Berri, brother of the French king. There they produced one of the finest examples of miniature painting, the *Très Riches Heures du Duc de Berri*, a book of hours in which, for perhaps the first time, we see that attention to the details of landscape and to the tools and techniques of manual labor that were to characterize Flemish and Dutch painting for the next three centuries.

At his Brussels court Philip the Good encouraged three of the greatest artists of the early northern Renaissance: Jan van Eyck, Robert Campin, and Rogier van der Weyden. Born around 1390 at Maaseik in Limburg, Jan van Eyck worked first at The Hague for John of Bavaria, count of Holland, who named him head painter of the Binnenhof. After the count's death in 1424, van Eyck entered Philip's service, settling first at Lille and finally in Bruges, where he worked until his death in 1441. Philip must have valued him not only as a painter but as a courtier, for he sent van Eyck on diplomatic missions.

The immense altarpiece at St. Bavon Cathedral in Ghent, completed in 1432, is justly van Eyck's most famous work. Its size alone—more than eleven feet by fourteen feet—serves to distinguish it from the usually far smaller medieval altarpieces. But more significant—and much more moving—is van Eyck's success in rendering humanity and in placing his clearly felt and clearly executed forms in a landscape no less real and no less felt. The panels at extreme left and right portray Adam and Eve, about whose almost lifesize figures light and shade play delicately, modeling them and endowing them with a quiet human dignity. This man and woman do not represent Original Sin, but rather God in man. In the center of the top panels is Christ; to each side, John the Baptist and the Virgin—who are flanked, in turn, by angelic musicians. The lower set of panels portray earthly life. In the center, just below the Christ figure, is the Lamb, around whom are gathered figures from the Old Testament on the left and the New Testament on the right. The two smaller panels on the left depict the defenders of the faith—soldiers and righteous judges; on the right are pilgrims and hermits. The path these travelers have taken winds deeply into the background of the pic-

Robert Campin's superb Mérode Altarpiece depicts the Annunciation amid a scene of everyday clutter. Medieval symbolism, to be sure, abounds: in the lilies that recall the Virgin's chastity; in the basin and towel, a reference to her biblical epithet, "the vessel most clean"; and in the rather mysterious snuffed-out candle on the table beside her. But like Campin's contemporaries we are less distracted by the symbolic significance of these objects than by their appearance, which he depicts in all their brilliance.

ture, and the trees, fields, and castles they have passed are carefully and completely drawn. This real, outdoor world was increasingly important to the far-ranging merchants of the north, and more and more frequently this world will be the subject of the Flemish and Dutch masters, who were now serving a worldly people with worldly interests.

It is chiefly in the lower register of the altarpiece that we see van Eyck's real miracle: the illusion of depth he was able to create through the use of "atmospheric perspective"—hues subtly blended so that objects in the distance are less and less distinct and the farthest objects melt almost completely into the horizon. The subtle haze that envelops his landscape and the radiant colors of the objects and garments result from his mastery of oil, a new technique in painting first developed among the Flemish artists of the fourteenth century.

Robert Campin pioneered, along with van Eyck, the use of oil. It allowed a far greater range of tone than the customary tempera medium, which was more suited to the high-keyed and flat surfaces prized in medieval panel painting. Campin's Mérode Altarpiece, now at the Metropolitan Museum's Cloisters in New York, is another and somewhat earlier example of that world of depth and continuity van Eyck created in his altarpiece. Campin was not a court painter, which perhaps explains in part the extraordinarily detailed view of a simple domestic interior he was able to portray. More removed than van Eyck from the devotional and courtly traditions so prized by the Brussels nobility, Campin was able to indulge in that realistic depiction of the everyday that pleased the new middle class and would characterize later Dutch painting.

The Mérode Altarpiece of 1428 is an Annunciation scene, and the Virgin is portrayed at home in cluttered domestic surroundings. In the panel to her right is Joseph, the humble carpenter at work in his equally cluttered shop; this is one of his earliest appearances in devotional art. Scholars assign a symbolic significance to most of the objects with which Mary and Joseph are surrounded, and no doubt the etiquette of devotional painting at the time required that even the humblest scene be sanctified with theological connotation. But what moves and startles us are not the symbols—in any case now somewhat obscure—but the sense of reality, completeness, and humanity that Campin is able to convey. It is a rich work, and it was to bequeath an even richer heritage.

If Campin and van Eyck brought to devotional art the feeling of place, in- or out-of-doors, Rogier van der Weyden offered it drama—the anguish and pathos that were always a part of the Gothic spirit. In his *Lamentation of Christ*, which hangs in The Hague, the artist focuses on the Virgin, kneeling before the body of her dead son. Solicitously, protectively, St. John the Baptist places a cloak over her shoulders, while Joseph of Arimathaea and Nicodemus arrange a white sheet on the ground for Christ's body. In the background we see the walls of a town, a castle, a horseman, a dovecote, and trees—but we are not drawn into this background as we are in van Eyck's altarpiece. The almost unbearably sorrowful faces of the mourners, the tortured body of the Savior ex-

Pieter Bruegel's Children's Games *belies our idea of the Dutch as a sober people. His peasants, here pictured in a wealth of detail, revel in the robust, bawdy village life of the Low Countries in the sixteenth century. Bruegel delighted in the human figure, which he took pains to capture in dramatic and often telling movement. Abandoning the tradition of starting with the nude and then clothing it, Bruegel painted his figures as if body and dress were inseparable, thus ensuring that his subjects were the people he actually saw, living the harsh, boisterous life of the country he knew so well and painted so accurately.*

Erasmus's In Praise of Folie *exemplified the keen wit, moderation, and tolerance that he practiced all his life. His works were known throughout Europe, and although he criticized the Church and fought for reforms, he remained an ordained Catholic priest throughout his life. The marginal drawings found in this 1515 edition of Erasmus's masterwork, published in London, are by Hans Holbein the Younger.*

tended across the foreground, and the pitiously frail and bereaved face of the Virgin all reflect van der Weyden's concern for the human drama rather than the religious significance in this terrible event.

One particular painter stands apart from the traditions already so well established by the mid-fifteenth century in the Netherlands—Hieronymus Bosch. He was born in 's-Hertogenbosch, Brabant, around 1450 and died there in 1516. Even among his contemporaries, Bosch was a "primitive." While others were creating the feeling of depth in landscape, exhaustively drawing and modeling their figures, and painting recognizably human faces and familiar, dramatic passions, Bosch was creating a world of dreams. His figures, with their pale faces and distorted limbs, stand not *in* but *in front of* landscapes composed of sickly, meager branches and tree trunks—and they stand amid demons neither wholly beasts nor wholly men. His is a world where the supernaturally horrible comes alive, where the nightmares of the Gothic mind come true.

By the 1470s the influence of the northern provinces was making itself felt. This was true in politics and economics as it was in art. Philip the Good had died in 1467 and was succeeded by Charles the Bold, who tried, without much success, to centralize his power through military conquest, only to be killed at Nancy in 1477. His heir was Mary of Burgundy, called, appropriately enough, "the rich." Louis XI of France took the opportunity of her succession to seize Mary's French possessions. The Netherlands, for its part, offered to resist Louis if Mary would consent to local participation in running state affairs. She acceded to this demand in a document known as "The Great Priviledge." The Netherlands was a rich prize, and every prince in Europe looked longingly upon it. In keeping with his family's motto, *Pugnant alii, tu, felix Austria, nube* ("Let others wage war, you, lucky Austria, marry"), Maximilian of Austria won that prize by wedding Mary the Rich—and thus the Netherlands passed to the Habsburgs.

By this time Amsterdam was beginning to prevail in its competition with the Hanseatic League cities, and Holland's wealth was growing. "Hollanders," as they were known, were trading at almost every European port, and since these traders felt more attachment to their province than to the larger political entity of which it was a part, it was natural that the whole country would become known abroad as Holland.

In Gelderland, the Brethern of the Common Life had been founded by Geer Groote in 1382. This movement, open to laymen and clergy, was formed in reaction to the growing secularization of the church. Its members, forbidden to own personal possessions, earned their living by copying books and teaching. They advocated the simple, introspective, and peaceful life; the avoidance of bitter theological disputes; and the importance of the individual conscience in deciding moral questions. Thomas à Kempis produced his *Imitatio Christi*, the most widely read book of its time, within this community. Desiderius Erasmus, the famous Dutch humanist from Rotterdam, received his early education from the Brethern. His book *In Praise of Folly* ac-

cused the church of many of the sins the Reformation would later seek to correct. Through its teaching and the books produced by its members and students, the philosophy of this lay order spread throughout the north, thus paving the way for the Protestant movement of the sixteenth century.

By the beginning of the fifteenth century and continuing well into the sixteenth, the influence of Dutch composers, teachers, instrumentalists, and singers was felt throughout Europe. Indeed, in music it was the Age of the Netherlands. In Italian cities, residences, and cathedrals, in German courts both large and small, and in Habsburg Spain, Netherlanders were bringing the rich innovations of the Burgundian court composers to international renown. We see this in the early fourteenth-century handwritten manuscripts as well as in later printed compositions. Guillaume Dufay, who was born around 1400 and worked at the court, is credited with founding the Burgundian school, whose French members would soon take second place to musicians from the north like Johannes Ockeghem, whom Dufay trained, and Jacob Obrecht. Perhaps the greatest of these, Josquin Desprez, taught Erasmus; Martin Luther heard and praised his motets and chansons. By 1460 Desprez was in Milan and after 1485 he was singing in the papal choir. Nicolas Gombert, Desprez's greatest follower, served Charles V, and his secular works reflect the love of nature we see in the painted art of the Netherlands.

In the mid-1500s one painter emerged who, while departing from some of the traditions of the older generation, in many respects summed up the quintessentially Dutch achievement. Pieter Bruegel was born around 1525 in Brabant and worked first in Antwerp and then in Brussels, where he died in 1569. In the relatively few works that have been preserved—he was not much more sought after than Bosch—he captured that feeling for the landscape which first began to emerge a century before with van Eyck. Bosch believed in the direct observation of nature in all her forms: bleak and inhospitable, rich and bountiful. Although people always play a part in his narrative pictures, they are usually overwhelmed by a landscape at once detailed and broad. But when Bruegel did choose to observe humanity from closer range—peasants at a wedding feast, for example—he endowed them with a reality no painter since antiquity had accomplished.

By 1515 the Netherlands had a new ruler, Charles V of Spain, and it had become part of an empire as great as any in history. The son of Philip I and Joanna of Castile—and the grandson of Ferdinand V and Isabella of Castile, patrons of Christopher Columbus, and Emperor Maximilian I and Mary of Burgundy—Charles had inherited the Netherlands, Luxembourg, Artois, and Franche-Comté from his father. Aragon, Navarre, Granada, Naples, Sicily, Sardinia, the American colonies, and joint sovereignty with his unfortunate mother—nicknamed *la loca*, "the mad"—over Castile, came to him on the death of his grandfather Ferdinand. When his other grandfather, Maximilian, died, Charles gained the Habsburg lands and was designated emperor.

Charles struggled ceaselessly and successfully to keep his empire strong and cohesive. But by the age

of fifty-five the effort had cost him his health and had made him an old man. He decided to retire to Spain and leave his son Philip most of this empire.

On October 25, 1555, Charles summoned the estates of the Netherlands to the Great Hall of the palace at Brussels to witness his abdication. By nature simple in dress and manner, Charles nonetheless knew well the value of ceremony, and he ensured that this, the end of a reign almost as powerful as Charlemagne's, would be appreciated and remembered. At exactly three in the afternoon the emperor entered the Great Hall, which was decorated with the famous tapestries of Arras and with flowers and votive garlands. Leaning on the shoulder of William, the young prince of Orange, he walked slowly past benches filled by a brilliantly clad multitude toward a stage on which the principal lords were to sit. In his train were his son Philip II; Mary, dowager queen of Hungary; Archduke Maximilian; and the duke of Savoy. They, in turn, were followed by warriors, councilors, governors, and the Knights of the Golden Fleece. The assembly rose, the imperial entourage took its place on the dais, and Charles, Philip, and Mary took their seats on gilded chairs under a canopy decorated with the arms of Burgundy.

First Philibert de Bruxelles, a member of the privy council of the Netherlands, rose to read the deed of cession, which gave to Philip all the duchies, marquisates, earldoms, baronies, cities, towns, and castles of Burgundy—including, of course, the seventeen provinces of the Netherlands, the richest of his new possessions. Then Charles himself rose and,

again supported by William, spoke to the assembly, reviewing the events of his reign, begging both their allegiance to his son and their forgiveness for his own errors and sins. In the best tradition of medieval reportage, witnesses recount sobs from everywhere in the hall and tears in all eyes, not least in those of Charles, who, ashen and close to fainting, now regained his chair. Next Philip rose and dropped to his knees before his father, who blessed him; then, rising again, he apologized for speaking neither French nor Flemish and begged the assembly's attention to the Bishop of Arras, his interpreter. Orations and replies followed. Finally, in the same order in which they had entered, Charles, William, Philip, the queen of Hungary, and the whole court left the hall for the chapel.

Thomas Carlyle once remarked that "the history of the world is but the biography of great men." The statement is often disputed, but to everyone gathered at Brussels that autumn afternoon it must surely have seemed that a profound change was taking place. How great a change, they could not have imagined. For as Charles concluded his long reign, he also initiated the end of foreign domination over the Netherlands. Indeed, the very men who assisted this frail despot to perform his last regal act were the ones whose ideals and emotions would sunder the empire he had so strenuously maintained. Looking back now on the splendors of this ceremony and the ironies that laced its proceedings, one wonders if some unseen dramaturge did not, in fact, construct the full eighty years of turmoil and bloodshed that were to follow.

II

The Eighty Years' War

By July 1581, the members of the Estates-General of the United Netherlands had been conferring for well over two months—far longer than anyone had expected. They had originally convened in Amsterdam, then as now the commercial center of Holland. But as the deliberations dragged on and the summer heat of the great city grew oppressive, the delegates decided to retreat to The Hague—at the time nothing more than a small, aristocratic country town, but one that could claim historical precedent for hosting such a gathering. And this particular meeting of the Estates-General was certainly historic: the nobility and burghers of the Netherlands were gathered in solemn conclave in order to declare their independence from Spain; to name William, prince of Orange, as head of state; and, ultimately, to proclaim the Netherlands a united and free nation.

So it was that on July 26, 1581, The Hague, for a quarter century the quiet eye of a political hurricane, witnessed the close of the first act of what would prove to be an eighty-year drama. That storm had pitted Catholic against Protestant, proletarian and merchant against nobleman, feudal obligations against modern statecraft—and, as opponents, two of the grandest figures of modern European history: Philip, king of Spain, and William, prince of Orange. In a conflict so complex and protracted it would be foolhardy to look for explanations in a mere conflict of personalities, yet it is surely true that, had Philip not ruled in Spain and had William not assumed the role he did in the Netherlands, the great drama of independence might very well have taken an altogether different course.

The passions of history die hard, and even now, some four centuries after his death, it is difficult to judge Philip without bias. Catholic historians usually saw him as an idealist more sinned against than sinning despite the excesses of the Spanish Inquisition and despite his attempts to establish the Inquisition elsewhere in Europe. Protestant historians—that is, most of those writing in English—tended to portray him as the arch-villain of the Counter Reformation, a butcher of dissenters, and a blind fanatic whose attachment to the idea of a Catholic and feudal Europe cost him the Netherlands and would cost his heirs what was left of the Spanish empire. What is undoubtedly true is that Philip, managing the affairs of most of Europe from his remote and gloomy Escorial, could not see that the world his father had delivered to his keeping was rapidly changing and that accommodation to Protestant dissent and national yearnings as well as to an increasingly mercantile economy was not antithetical to his duties as king and emperor but, rather, essential to the preservation of his patrimony.

Philip was born to rule, but William, though no commoner, was born only to the life of a country squire. The son of William, count of Nassau-Dillenburg, he spent the first ten years of his life in the quiet German countryside, studying the pious precepts of the new Lutheran faith. The Nassau family was old and distinguished, but as a second son William had little hope of sharing in the lands and titles of his elder brother, Henry, whose inheritance lay in the Netherlands. Henry had married an heiress of the French family of Chalons, whose property

The dunes of Loosduinen appear on that municipality's simple crest.

included the small but independent principality of Orange in France. Their son, René, eventually came into the joint inheritance of the county of Nassau and the principality of Orange. In 1544, as he was preparing to leave for battle in France, René was forced by the emperor to name his young cousin William as his heir. William's father, the logical choice, was unacceptable to the emperor because of his Lutheranism. Young William was also Lutheran, of course, but he was also a child—and the emperor not unreasonably assumed that if anything happened to René it would be easy to persuade this child to accept the true faith.

Something did happen to René: He was killed at Saint Dizier. And so, at age eleven, young William suddenly and quite unexpectedly became William, count of Nassau and prince of Orange, heir to much of Brabant, Luxembourg, Flanders, Franche-Comté, Dauphiné, and the county of Charollais. He had become, in short, one of the wealthiest noblemen in Europe—and he had no choice but to leave Dillenburg for the imperial court at Brussels, there to accept the Catholic faith and learn the duties and bearing of a *grand seigneur*. He soon became a favorite of both the emperor and the court. To the English-speaking world, William is known as "the silent," which is a direct translation of the Latin epithet *taciturnus*, itself a mistranslation of the Dutch *schluwe*, meaning "sly." This tag was originally applied to William by his enemies, but as the emperor himself perceived and as Philip was to learn, the young prince was a master at the "sly" art of statecraft; he was "silent" only when it mattered.

By the middle of the sixteenth century, the Netherlands could well regard itself as "the first nation in Europe." Its population totaled some three million, and it had close to three hundred walled towns and cities, which housed the most advanced trading and manufacturing centers on the Continent. Its court at Brussels was refined and elegant; its nobility was among the oldest and richest in Europe; and its pride matched its lineage. In the struggle to rid itself of Philip's yoke, the Netherlands saw itself not as a poor nation oppressed by its wealthier motherland but as a vastly wealthy nation asserting against the upstart grandees of Iberia its ancient claims to sovereignty and its more immediate claims to control its own produce and purse.

During the reign of Charles V the Netherlands had been well content with its sovereign, who had grown up in Flanders, spoke its language, and employed its nobility at his court. Indeed, Charles was probably more foreign to his Spanish than to his Netherlandish subjects. But this was not the case with Philip, who had grown up in Spain and whose most trusted advisors came from the Spanish court. He could not speak Flemish or even French, the official court language, and he had no first-hand knowledge of conditions in the northern lands he inherited. Newly arrived in Brussels, he may not have understood, for instance, that the subsidies always granted the emperor by the Netherlands estates were becoming a burden since the Spanish treasury, drained and mismanaged, needed a constant and constantly increasing influx of northern money. Subsidies had been granted more or less

34

willingly to his father; but they would be only grudgingly and sparingly granted to him—a foreigner using native cash for foreign adventures. Nor could Philip have understood that, while a majority of his northern subjects were still Catholic, Calvinist and Anabaptist teachings were increasingly taking hold in cities where foreign merchants and thus foreign ideas mingled frequently and freely. And certainly he would not have understood that, in an increasingly mercantile society, ancient feudal bonds were weakening and that, as a result, he could no longer count, as his father had done, on the unquestioning loyalty of the nobility. It is doubtful that William understood these things any better, but his thoroughly northern, practical, Protestant upbringing prepared him to learn and, when pressed, to lead.

Philip inherited a situation that a master statesman would have found barely manageable—and one in which his success would depend on an ability to compromise and cajole. This dour, pious, and proud young man could do neither; he could only confirm the feudal and Catholic past. Indeed, it was the religious question that first signaled the inevitable conflict. Heresy had never been tolerated by the Brussels court, and heretics had been executed in the first year of Charles' reign. He had confirmed his opposition to the Reformation in the infamous 1580 Edict of Blood, which declared heresy, once an offense against the church only, an offense against the state as well. Following this, many more heretics died or fled. Upon his accession, Philip reaffirmed his father's edicts. But now more was at stake. Many of the merchants upon whom the prosperity of the

Netherlands depended were Protestant—Lutheran, Anabaptist, or Calvinist—and while most of the nobility were either hostile or indifferent to the new teachings, they were passionately interested in maintaining peace in their cities. Burning heretics or forcing them into exile was beginning to be bad for business and was, in any case, distasteful to a practical and never especially pious people. Resentment against the new king grew silently but swiftly; it found its tongue over the question of money.

In 1559 Philip declared his intention to return to Spain, and he asked the Estates-General for a nine-year subsidy. After some heretofore unheard-of grumbling, it was granted, but with an equally unheard-of condition: the withdrawal of Spanish troops from Dutch soil. Joined in this demand were William, now an important figure among the Netherlands nobility, and Egmont, the hero of Saint-Quentin and Gravelines and a *stadtholder* in Flanders and Artois. Philip reluctantly agreed, noting bitterly that William, his father's favorite, had betrayed him. Indeed, as he ceremoniously boarded his ship at Flushing for the trip to Spain, he is reported to have hissed in William's ear, *No los estados, ma vos, vos, vos* ("Not the estates, but you, you, you"). They were never to meet again, but their enmity bound them for a lifetime.

The government of the Netherlands at this time was made up of the king (or his regent); a council of state comprising the *stadtholders*, army leaders, and heads of departments; and the Estates-General. With good reason, Philip mistrusted the lot of them, and he advised Duchess Margaret of Brabant, his regent, to consult not the council of state but a smaller body, the *consulta*, whose chief member, the Bishop of Arras (later elevated as Cardinal Granvelle), would inadvertently trigger the first of the revolts. Granvelle believed, as did Philip, that every effort must be made to stamp out the growing heresies. To this end he pressed for a reorganization of the bishoprics, planned in Charles' time but put into effect only in 1561. This scheme aroused opposition of Catholic and Protestant alike: for the Catholic clergy and nobility, it struck at the ancient privilege of appointing their own nominees to wealthy sinecures; for the Protestants, it augured the imposition of a Spanish Inquisition in place of the pitiless but at least familiar Netherlands Inquisition that had been operating for years. Cardinal Granvelle was the focus of the anger, which by 1564 had reached such proportions that the Estates-General demanded his retirement. Margaret, fearing full-scale revolt, arranged his departure, but this improved the situation not at all. It may even be said to have aggravated it; the nobility and the masses now clearly recognized both their power and their enemy.

As Anabaptist and Calvinist doctrines spread, the ferocity of the Inquisition intensified, and moderate Catholics—a group that included most of the nobles and merchants—and Protestants alike were sickened by the imprisonments, executions, and exiles. Added to this was the growing resentment against church wealth—always present in medieval and Renaissance Europe, but now blessed by the iconoclastic teachings of John Calvin. Isolated acts of defiance multiplied: imprisoned heretics were set

free and illegal Calvinist meetings were widely attended. At these meetings the poorer classes were taught the ungodliness not only of the "graven images" and "idolatry" of the church, but now of her vast holdings as well. By 1566 the situation had grown desperate, at least in the eyes of the regent. The nobility was demanding the right to handle dissenters as they saw fit, and the mobs were becoming unruly. In August, Margaret summoned the Knights of the Fleece to Brussels to force an affirmation of their allegiance. But with these powerful and moderating men away from their posts, there was nothing to restrain a populace grown almost hysterical with hatred for the Spanish and the idolatrous church they upheld.

As soon as William left Antwerp for the gathering at Brussels, rioting began. The great cathedral at Antwerp was sacked by Calvinist mobs, and destruction of the other churches of Antwerp followed. Similar mob actions occurred in Ghent, Valenciennes, Tournai, Leiden, Amsterdam, Utrecht, and Delft—always unopposed by the local officials. In less than a week, it was clear to the regent that some compromise, however insincere and temporary, had to be reached. On August 24 she issued the Accord, which for the first time permitted open Protestant worship in the Netherlands. William recognized that this was merely Margaret's way of buying time until military help could arrive from Spain to quell the violence. He did help to pacify Antwerp, though, and his efforts, coupled with the issuance of the Accord, brought an uneasy peace.

Things could never be the same again, however;

for everyone involved the moment of decision had come. For the regent it was a choice between her sworn loyalty to Philip and the church and the necessity of compromise with the dissident nobility and the mob. She chose Philip, and many nobles made the same choice; they may have felt less duty than she felt to their king and their confession, but in the iconoclastic ravages of the mob they saw a dangerous movement toward social leveling and a clear threat to their property and privilege. William, Egmont, and the other nobles faced the same alternatives: between their vows of fealty to the king and their own yearning for an end to the imposition of an order they knew could not be peacefully maintained. In a Europe still largely medieval in its political philosophy, an open break with the king was unthinkable, but for William and many like him, a distinction had to be made now between Philip and his policies. They would remain, technically at least, loyal to their king, but they would question and, if need be, oppose with arms the present policies and the harsher measures they knew were to come.

And come they did, in the person of the duke of Alva, who was commissioned by Philip in May 1567 to raise an army and then depart for the Netherlands to restore order at any cost. By August 22 the duke was in Brussels, and Margaret, betrayed by the people she governed and mistrusted by the king she served, resigned. Her successor, Alva, was a soldier, not a statesman; and if Margaret, William, Egmont, and the rest questioned their duty and their consciences, Alva questioned nothing.

The terror had begun.

Alva quickly established the machinery of oppression and set it in motion. The chief vehicle was the Council of Troubles, known almost immediately and forever afterward as the Council of Blood. This tribunal was staffed with judges who could not vote—only Alva and two advisers had that right—and it indicted, tried, and condemned victims who had no hope of legal process. The council was headed by Juan de Vargas, who, Motley remarks, "executed Alva's bloody work with a merriment that would have shamed a demon." Mass arrests, confiscations, torture, and executions multiplied with each passing week, culminating in the execution of Egmont himself. True, he had once joined in a plea of leniency toward dissenters, but he died loyal still to Philip and Catholicism.

Fortunately, William had sensed what was coming and had fled to Germany. Around him grouped opponents of the terror. In April 1568 he issued his famous *Justification*, the first of many documents in which he would seek to make clear that his loyalty to Philip remained firm, and that only the king's policies, ascribed to evil or unwise councilors, forced him to act in defiance of the royal will. This defiance took military form, and by late spring of 1568 he had an army ready to attack on three fronts. Despite scattered victories, it was largely unsuccessful against Alva's better-trained regulars. Such victories as William did win, however, enraged Alva, who vowed to destroy this opposition utterly.

While William met only stalemate or defeat on the battlefront, Alva's policies in the Netherlands were quickly provoking active resistance at home. The persecution of heretics, real or suspected, proceeded. And to this insult Alva added an injury even the most loyal citizen could not endure: he proposed a system of taxes based on the Spanish model, including the infamous "tenth penny"—a 10 percent tax on sales. In Spain, still largely agricultural, this tax had been in effect for years. But in the industrialized Netherlands, the tax aroused furious opposition. It was debated for almost two years, and when in 1571 Alva finally enforced it, there was general refusal to pay, and the great exchange at Antwerp closed. Persecution of dissenters offended the moral sensibilities of those it did not actually harm, but the tax harmed everyone; it struck at the artery of commerce, and it was on commerce, after all, that Catholic and Protestant alike depended. Feeling against Spain grew increasingly intense and vindictive, and it became, in time, a *national* hatred.

Hatred of Spain was forging a national spirit, and as resistance grew and military clashes increased, the future physical shape of the Low Countries became clear as well. Alva's army and his court were based in the south, at Brussels. There heretics who had not been executed fled or went underground, and the nobility and merchants, whether out of conviction or convenience, remained loyal to Spain and Catholicism. In the north, however, Alva's government was less effective, and dissenters there organized into disciplined bands ready to act when help could come from William, still based in Germany, or from groups operating on the seas. These sea-borne raiders were known as the "Sea Beggars"—a name adopted by dissident petty noblemen years before,

A political-allegorical painting by an unknown
artist of the Flemish school shows Queen Elizabeth
I of England feeding the Dutch cow, on which
Philip II of Spain—her sometime suitor, sometime
enemy—is seated. William, Prince of Orange, is at
the queen's side; the duke of Parma, Philip's
representative in the Netherlands, is milking the
cow. At the left is the duke of Anjou, who hoped
to become sovereign of the Netherlands when, with
the Spanish army close to final defeat, William of
Orange sought someone whose lineage would
qualify him as king and whose political ties would
ensure strong foreign support for the Netherlands.
As this well-peopled canvas indicates, the issue of
Dutch independence involved all of Europe.

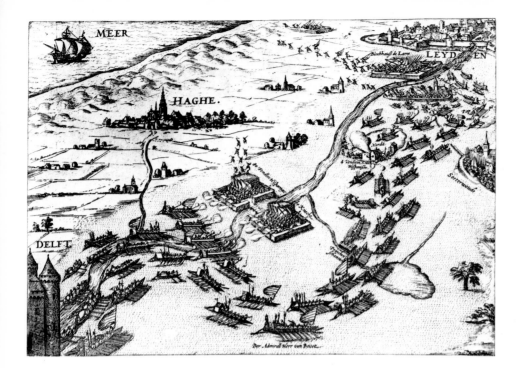

when, having driven the regent, Margaret, to tears with their disloyal demands, they heard one of her councilors remark, *Quoi, Madame! Peur de ces gueux!* ("What, Madame! Afraid of these beggars!"). Now these "beggars" had an organized fleet that flew the flag of Orange—technically, at least, still an independent principality ruled by William. In April 1572, England, up to now friendly to these opponents of her old enemy Spain, closed her ports to the Beggar fleets. Seeking a haven, they discovered the Dutch port of Brill temporarily undefended by the Spanish garrison. They took the town, which welcomed them, and proceeded south. By the end of July, the entire province of Holland, except Amsterdam, was in Beggar hands, and William had crossed the Rhine at Duisburg. Full-scale war ensued in the north, and it went decisively in favor of the rebels. In October 1573, the Spanish, led by Francisco de Valez, laid siege to Leiden. That campaign lasted a year, during which the city withstood both famine and plague. Help arrived only in September, when, having opened the dykes, the Beggar fleet finally brought relief. To commemorate the heroism of the populace and to mark this great turning point in the war, William established the University of Leiden, which remained open for four centuries until another invading army, this one German, closed it during World War II.

After their victory at Leiden the rebels could finally envision success. But William knew that his army, largely mercenary and therefore unreliable, and the national and religious fervor of the population could not alone conquer a force as strong as Philip's. They needed a unified front, and they needed allies. Protestant England and Huguenot factions in France sporadically supplied the latter, but it took the Spanish themselves to forge unity among the rebellious but wavering provinces. Spain, as usual, was bankrupt, and despite his governor's constant pleas for funds to pay the troops, Philip sent only encouragement and orders to fight. The Spanish troops were garrisoned without pay and without action—a dangerous situation for a mercenary army. Their hatred of the Calvinist Antichrist combined with their fury against their unforthcoming paymasters led to mutinies, and in October 1576 they attacked Maastricht with unbelievable savagery, sacking the town. All eyes then turned to Antwerp, still the wealthiest city in the Netherlands, if not in all Europe, and the seat of the largest Spanish garrison. On November 4 mutineers unleashed what soon became known as the Spanish Fury. Within a day some nine thousand of Antwerp's citizens were dead, killed outright by the Spanish troops or burned alive as almost a third of its wealthiest homes and businesses were put to the torch. As the initial tumult quieted, the inevitable rape and pillage followed. By nightfall, nothing could be heard in Antwerp but the peal of the great cathedral chimes.

Reports sent to Philip recorded another great Spanish victory, but in reality nothing had been gained and something invaluable had been lost: disunity, which as much as Spanish arms had served Philip's cause, was turned overnight into solidarity. Within a week many members of the Estates-General, still largely a Catholic body, and the Protestants

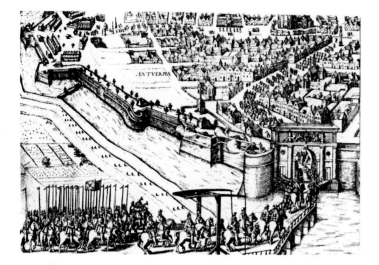
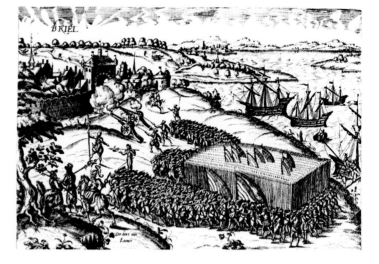

of Holland and Zeeland signed the Pacification of Ghent—an alliance of the provinces against Spain.

Alva had been replaced in 1573 by Don Luis de Requesens, who himself had been replaced just a day before the Spanish Fury by Philip's half-brother, Don Juan of Austria. By the time Don Luis was prepared to take up his duties in Brussels, hatred for the Spanish was so high that the Estates-General forced him to agree to the terms of the Union of Brussels before he could enter the capital. Don Juan reluctantly agreed and signed a document known as the Perpetual Edict. He dismantled the Spanish garrison and the troops were sent home.

William was now solidly in command in the Netherlands, and his military victories, combined with the new anti-Spanish feeling, made him a national hero. On September 18, 1577, he entered Antwerp, and five days later Brussels; in both cities he was greeted as a liberator. But the sentiment in William's favor was not shared by everyone, and the unity forged in reaction to the Spanish terror had no real basis. The majority of the Dutch population were almost certainly Catholic. In the north, where the Calvinists had been able to seize the machinery of state, Catholics were persecuted; but in the south Calvinism had never been able to take hold.

By 1579 yet another Spanish governor was in place. He was Alexander Farnese, duke of Parma and son of Philip's former regent, Margaret. His predecessors—Alva, Requesens, and Don Juan—had all fought unsuccessfully against the tide of Reformation and nationalism, then at its full; in retrospect, their failure was inevitable. Parma ar-

rived on the scene at a moment when the forces of reaction were gathering strength. He would not be able to reverse the tide entirely, but he would successfully prevent total Spanish defeat.

The first break occurred in January 1579, when the largely Catholic southern provinces of Artois and Hainault signed the Union of Arras, through which they took the first tentative steps toward reconciliation with the king, whose religion, after all, they shared. At the same time, five northern provinces—Holland, Zeeland, Freisland, Utrecht, and Gelderland—signed the Union of Utrecht, pledging mutual aid in the likely event of a royal counter-offensive against them. The signatories of both unions, Arras and Utrecht, still claimed to be part of the larger union formed by the Pacification of Ghent, and both groups still claimed loyalty to the king. It was clear, however, that a break in the nationalists' united front was forming. In the fall of 1579 Parma, with the king's blessing, signed the Treaty of Arras. On the surface, at least, this was a great victory for the rebels: all Spanish troops were to leave the country within six weeks, and the terms of the Pacification of Ghent were ratified by a royal plenipotentiary. But Parma had no real intention of honoring the terms of the treaty; indeed, while it was being discussed he successfully executed a surprise attack on Maastricht, frightening the rebels and giving hope to the forces still loyal to Spain. The future seemed to favor Spain now, but Philip's bitterness toward William led to a tragic blunder.

In the summer of 1580, Philip decided to move openly against William, certain that without this

Despite the ravages of the early sixteenth century—war, pillage, and their attendant epidemics and pestilence—by 1570 The Hague was well on its way to reasserting the prominence it had enjoyed when the counts of Holland and Bavaria made it their chief court. With the defeat of the Spanish in the north virtually assured, the Estates General made The Hague their official seat, and the stadtholder *Maurice took up residence here. He was followed by other members of the House of Nassau, themselves frequently related to European royalty, and by ambassadors accredited to the new nation. Young nobles attracted by the military prowess of the* stadtholder, *and men of learning drawn by Holland's spirit of toleration and liberty, also settled in The Hague. Many made their homes near the Binnenhof, visible at center right in this highly detailed 1570 map.*

ever more popular hero the revolt in the Netherlands would die away. He had always hoped that someone would remove this villain for him, and in this hope he had been encouraged by the still-bitter Granvelle. For years they had plotted secretly. Then, with Spain's fortunes looking brighter, Philip issued a "ban," declaring William "the chief disturber of the whole state of Christendom." William's subjects were freed from their allegiance to him and anyone was authorized to injure or kill him. William's assassin would be given twenty-five thousand écus, patents of nobility, and pardon for all past offenses. Philip had miscalculated: even the provinces most opposed to the prince of Orange were disgusted and outraged by the ban, and a new tide of feeling for William swept the Netherlands.

In response to Philip's proscription, William issued his *Apology* early in 1581. Heretofore he had scrupulously observed a technical loyalty to his sovereign, but now Philip had given him a chance to openly renounce his feudal bonds. William declared that since Philip had failed in his duties as king, his vassals owed him no further allegiance. And while the *Apology* was being printed and read all over Europe, the Estates-General met at The Hague to adopt their historic Act of Deposition of the Lord of the Low Countries, or the Abjuration.

The fight had begun a quarter of a century before, and it was hardly over yet. But an irrevocable step had been taken: the Estates had declared that the rights of kings were not divine but were sanctified only insofar as they were compatible with the rights of a nation and the rights of man. On July 25, 1581,

AGA·COMITIS·IN·HOLLANDI

1570

43

Three period engravings depict, from left to right, The Hague's Prince Maurice gate; Het Oude Hof, remodeled by Pieter Post and renamed Noordeinde Palace; and the entry into the Binnenhof, then as now the center of official life in The Hague and the Netherlands. By the end of the Eighty Years' War, The Hague was an important and stately town. To be sure, it was only a town—the nation's commerce and industry were centered elsewhere—but its wealth and gracious style of life rivaled those of the great capitals of Europe. Once independence from Spain had been secured, official missions to The Hague became frequent, and travelers were favorably impressed with both the cultured and aristocratic atmosphere of the town and its restrained but elegant architecture. The prosperity that followed the end of hostilities with Spain only served to increase the splendor and power of this ancient and beautiful village.

in The Hague, a new nation was born, and the words used to christen it would be echoed again and again over the next two centuries.

Parma's forces, meanwhile, were slowly capturing town after town in the south in preparation for a new offensive against the north. The south seemed to have lost the will to fight and welcomed ever more warmly an escape from Calvinist preaching into good Catholic order. William's influence in the south, never firm, was waning, and only in the north could he be certain of enthusiastic backing. He set up housekeeping in Delft, always his preferred home, and there, in a former convent renamed the Prinsenhof, he received embassies, petitioners, and well-wishers with his customary informality. One of these visitors was Balthazar Gérard, a Catholic fanatic whose hatred of William had been given purpose and direction by the king's ban. Masquerading as a devout Calvinist, he was able to gain an audience with William, who sympathized with him and sent him to aid his ally, the duke of Anjou, then residing in northern France. As Gérard reached the border, he heard of Anjou's death and volunteered to carry a detailed report back to the prince at Delft. There, on July 10, 1584, as William was retiring after dinner, Gérard stepped forward and shot him at point-blank range. William died almost immediately. Gérard, captured within minutes, was tortured and, a few days later, publicly executed and savagely dismembered. William was buried at the New Church in Delft on August 3, where a great black-and-white marble tomb was later erected to "William of Nassau, Father of the Fatherland."

If Philip had hoped to succeed by assassination where he had failed militarily and diplomatically, he was to be sorely disappointed. But if he secretly hoped simply to avenge some twenty years of treachery, then William's death must have been greeted at the Escorial with a joy few events since Philip's accession had warranted. For a while, at least, Parma seemed to be capitalizing on the sudden loss of Dutch leadership. By August 1585 Antwerp was again firmly in his hands, after a long, devastating siege, and he was moving eastward toward Cologne. Spanish policy in the Netherlands had long been coupled with designs on Protestant England, which, despite the vicissitudes of Elizabeth's statecraft, had been a constant threat to Spanish hegemony and Catholic unity and a support to the rebellious Dutch provinces. In 1588, with the southern Netherlands secure, Philip launched his Armada, whose attack on England was to be coordinated with Parma's seaborne fleet. Most of Philip's ships were lost before Parma could even launch his, and much of Parma's army was destroyed in the debacle. It become clear to him and to the Dutch that, whatever the outcome in the south, the north was now free. Elizabeth was now firmly in the Netherlands' camp, and in France a Protestant king, Henry IV, had ascended the throne.

In the early years of the war, the Spanish had occupied The Hague, but its fortunate citizens had escaped the pillage to which inhabitants of larger and wealthier towns were subjected because The Hague had no strategic importance. Its significance lay rather in its history, and so it was natural that it

should once again become a capital, this time of the United Provinces of the Netherlands. Although still eclipsed by the great commercial and industrial centers of the Low Countries, The Hague would henceforth be the site of the legislative and ceremonial rites of nationhood. Here peace, war, national policy, and both royal and republican succession would be ratified, and the ancient Binnenhof would again host rulers, their courts, and their councilors.

With its status regained, The Hague experienced a great deal of new construction during the first half of the seventeenth century as important political and military figures chose to live close to the center of power. Shortly after William's death, the Estates-General recognized his services to the nation by offering his widow, Louise, princess de Coligny, a manor close to the Binnenhof—the Huis van Brandwijk, built in 1512 by William Goudt, the rent master of North Holland. In 1591, the princess and her seven-year-old son, Frederik-Henry, occupied the house, which became known as Het Oude Hof.

At around this time the Assendelfts—a family of great wealth and power—established their manor in the Westeinde. The site is now the residence of the British ambassador—and a ghost. It appears that one of the Assendelft heirs, Gerrit, consented to the execution in the Gevangenpoort of his wife, Catherine, who was accused of counterfeiting coins in 1541. A former British ambassador to The Hague, Sir Peter Garran, wrote an article entitled "Die Haghe," detailing Catherine's long, complicated, and sad story, and her ghostly reappearance in the Westeinde residence.

After Louise's death, Frederik-Henry asked the painter and architect Peter Post to reconstruct Het Oude Hof in consultation with Jacob van Campen, Post's mentor and the Netherlands' greatest architect. Post, like Campen, a leading exponent of what has become known as Dutch Palladianism, devised a simple, classical design that made use of brick and stone decoration and a straightforward classical pilaster. The remodeled Het Oude Hof was renamed Noordeinde Palace. The richly decorated interior, with Indian and Turkish brocades covering the walls and Venetian mirrors hung over the fireplaces, was justly thought of as The Hague's most beautiful residence. Noordeinde served as the royal residence until the German occupation of Holland.

Post's second major commission in The Hague was offered him some years later, after Frederik-Henry had succeeded his half-brother, Prince Maurice. In 1645, Frederik-Henry selected land in the eastern edge of The Hague Woods, not far from the Binnenhof, his official residence, for a summer retreat. The original plan called for a simple two-story chamber, the Orange Hall, with large windows that would allow ample light for viewing the picture collection the prince had accumulated. Frederik-Henry died only two years after work began, however, and his wife, Amalia van Solms, asked van Campen to design the interior as a memorial to her husband. Although it would be expanded and redesigned many times over the next three centuries, the core of Huis ten Bosch, or House in the Woods, remains Orange Hall, which is still in much the same state as Post and van Campen conceived it.

46   *Since August of 1981, Huis ten Bosch has been the official residence of Queen Beatrix of the Netherlands. On this page, the interior of the Orange Hall, designed by van Campen. Some ten artists were responsible for the murals in* *this great hall, with the Flemish painter Jacob Jordaens contributing the large central panel. On the opposite page, above, the exterior of Huis ten Bosch; below, the dining room with its famous grisaille paintings by Jacob de Wit.*

After William's death, the Estates-General had appointed his seventeen-year-old son, Maurice, to head a newly formed council of state. Maurice was to prove himself a brilliant military strategist and, together with the master politician Oldenbarnevelt, he succeeded in finally organizing a standing army, one which was regularly paid and in which advancement was based more on training and success than on birth and bribery. Perhaps for the first time in Europe, there existed an army that was no threat to the people it defended. Maurice also reformed military planning, relying on trench warfare, long-range siege gunnery, and mines. Beginning in 1590 he began to enjoy an almost unbroken series of military victories. By 1592 Maurice was able to enter The Hague a national hero, there to receive expressions of gratitude at least as warm as those his father had enjoyed. In 1594 he captured Groningen and, like his father at Leiden, established a university there as thanksgiving for his victory. In 1596 a combined English-Dutch naval expedition surprised the Spanish at Cádiz and burned the royal fleet while it was riding at anchor in the harbor.

On September 12, 1598, Philip II died. The first act of the new king, Philip III, was to seize Dutch merchant ships in Spanish harbors and put to the Inquisition all the Dutch citizens on board. It was not uncommon at the time for warring nations to limit their hostilities to the field, and to go on trading peacefully; indeed, these two enemies could probably not have sustained their long and costly war had they not continued a brisk trade. Philip's action forced the Dutch to seek new markets, and they looked beyond Europe to the New World, Africa, and Asia. This actually expanded the war, for the Dutch either sought markets in Spain's American possessions or simply hounded and seized Spanish vessels loaded with American silver. It also vastly expanded Dutch mercantile ambitions: the Netherlands soon became a world power, trading and colonizing and threatening her much larger European competitors, Spain and England.

Except for occasional mutinies by the irregularly paid Spanish mercenary troops, the southern Netherlands was now relatively quiet, and the north was secure from attack. But the dream of a united Netherlands had not died among the northern patriots. Against Maurice's advice, Oldenbarnevelt and the Estates-General decided on a major offensive aimed at removing the Spanish from the south. The first objective was Nieuport, for which Dutch ships departed from Flushing on July 1, 1600. To Maurice's surprise, the mutinous Spanish mercenaries responded to the pleas of the Infanta and the new governor, Archduke Albert, and on July 2 they forced the Dutch to give battle—which, to Maurice's further surprise, the Dutch won, dispersing the Spanish army and even capturing the admiral of Aragon. In retaliation the Spanish laid siege to Ostend, the last southern possession held by the republic. The siege lasted 1,173 days. Ostend surrendered on September 20, 1604, but by that time Spanish resources were exhausted—it had cost some four million dollars and a hundred thousand lives to regain what was little more than a sandbank. Spain's defeat was now assured.

49

By this point both sides were tiring of the war, and for the next few years they fought only intermittently and often inconclusively. Then, on April 25, 1607, a Dutch fleet under Jacob van Heenskerk encountered a larger Spanish fleet under Juan d'Avela off Gibraltar. The Spanish fleet surrendered, and when the Dutch boarded the ships they found many of their countrymen working as slaves in the hold. In revenge, they slaughtered the Spanish sailors. By the end of the month Philip III was ready to sign a truce, and as an interim measure both sides agreed to an eight-month armistice. In December 1607 Spanish envoys met with their Dutch counterparts in the legislative chamber overlooking the Binnenhof and the Hofvijver at The Hague. After months of negotiations, the Dutch obtained every concession they sought. In gratitude for his military victories, the Estates granted Maurice and the entire House of Orange a large endowment; his family would rule off and on as the nation's *stadtholders*, and later as its sovereigns. A twelve-year truce with Spain began.

To our age, which has lost the taste for such things, the passionate theological controversies of earlier times seem fantastic and fantastically arcane. But the seventeenth century found questions of predestination, universal grace, and the efficacy of saints infintely absorbing. The best minds of the time were engaged in constructing and deconstructing elaborate doctrines that explained God and his earthly worship, and armies of inquisitors were employed to give to these matters the substance they might otherwise have seemed to lack. So when a professor at Leiden, Jacob Harmensen, argued, con-

trary to orthodox Calvinist doctrine, that predestination was conditional rather than absolute, that regeneration through the Holy Ghost and universal atonement were possible, and that a man could resist divine grace or relapse from it, battle lines were drawn and the Dutch ship of state, so recently and proudly launched, almost floundered.

In 1610 these shocking arguments were officially presented to the legislatures of West Friesland and Holland in a document called the Remonstrance. Its supporters, known either as Arminians—from Harmensen's Latin name—or Remonstrants, were supported by the states-rights faction led by Oldenbarnevelt. Orthodox Calvinism was defended by Maurice, the military, and the disenfranchised multitude. Oldenbarnevelt represented the burghers, whose power, in the absence of a sovereign, was formidable. As sovereigns or would-be sovereigns often did at that time, Maurice offered himself to the people as their protector against the lordly merchants and local nobility. He favored a liberal but absolute state church; Oldenbarnevelt, local autonomy in deciding religious questions.

By 1617 Maurice and Oldenbarnevelt had come into open conflict. In The Hague the Calvinists had been worshiping first at the home of Enoch Much and later at the small Gasthuis Church, which could not accommodate their numbers. Legally, they had a right to a church paid for by the town magistrates. In March, Maurice ordered that the Cloister Church, formerly a convent and more recently a cannon foundry, be converted to an orthodox Calvinist house of worship. It was still not ready by July, and

OVERLEAF: *In 1617 Prince Maurice and his retinue rode out toward the Kloosterkerk to signify their anger at delays in converting that church for Calvinist worship. The conflict between the* stadtholder *and an elder statesman named Oldenbarnevelt was brought to a head by this act, and within two years Oldenbarnevelt, who upheld both the provinces' rights against the central authority of the* stadtholder *and the Remonstrant religious faction against orthodox Calvinism, was defeated. He was sentenced to death and executed in the Binnenhof in 1619. This painting gives a fine view of the Hofvijver and the Binnenhof as it must have looked early in the seventeenth century, the Netherlands' first years of independence.*

the delay outraged the Calvinists. Early in that month the congregation defiantly occupied the unfinished building, and on July 25 Maurice and his whole household rode out from the Binnenhof, down the great avenue, past Oldenbarnevelt's house, to the Cloister Church. Oldenbarnevelt retaliated for this demonstration—more political than religious—by having the Estates issue the "Sharp Resolve," which rejected a national synod to end the controversy and called up the *waartgelders*, the state militia, to defend the state's rights.

On November 13, 1618, the synod was convened at Dordrecht, with the cards already well stacked against the Remonstrants. The following May the expected judgment against the Arminian heresy was proclaimed at the Great Church at Dordrecht, and two months later it was ratified by the Estates-General. Remonstrant worship was permitted only in private; more than two hundred Arminian ministers were deposed, with the surprisingly liberal provision that their salaries would continue to be paid, whether they chose retirement or exile. A year later, on May 13, 1619, sentence was passed on Oldenbarnevelt: despite universal pleas for clemency, he was executed in the great court of the Binnenhof on a platform erected in front of the ancient Hall of Knights, where the battle flags of Alva, Requesens, and Parma hung. Even at the time few were comfortable with this judicial murder of the man who, as much as Maurice and William themselves, was responsible for the nation's freedom. A tablet on the north wall of the Binnenhof marks the event.

In 1621 the truce with Spain ended and hostilities resumed. Spain now had a new king, Philip IV, and the Spanish governor who had ruled the obedient provinces for twenty-five years, Archduke Albert, was dead. Maurice attempted to seize Antwerp but failed. He did, however, raise the seige at Bergenop-Zoom and entered that city in triumph—just as a plot against him by Oldenbarnevelt's two sons was uncovered. This discovery so embarrassed the Remonstrants that thousands deserted the Arminian for the orthodox Calvinist faith, and the Remonstrants ceased to be a major political force in the republic. On April 25, 1625, Maurice died without heir and his inheritance passed to his brother, Prince Frederik-Henry—who also inherited the Netherlands' half-hearted, inconclusive war with Spain.

Frederik-Henry, the last of William's sons, died in 1647, a year before the Congress of Münster, convened to devise the peace, resolved the last remaining issues and declared the Eighty Years' War at an end. William's dream of a united Netherlands was not fulfilled, however, for the south, impoverished by a war fought mainly on its territory, remained Catholic and in Hapsburg hands. Antwerp, the site of sieges, mutinies, and fearful oppression, had lost almost half of its population as her bankers and merchants fled recurrent famine and Inquisitorial terror. The north, however, was now a free republic, prosperous and powerful. Here wealth and security would lead to a second flowering of Dutch culture, rivaling the former splendors of the Burgundian court, from whose heirs eighty years of conflict had now freed the Netherlands.

51

III

The Golden Age

After the truce of 1609, politically ambitious men rushed to settle in The Hague, there to distinguish themselves as much by their sumptuous style of living as by their services to the new nation. In Amsterdam, where the real money was being made, everything was business, and that city's solid merchants had little time and even less patience for the luxurious leisure favored by those with more aristocratic tastes. The Hague, on the other hand, existed for the nobility—or those who had the money to ape noble life successfully. It often seemed that there never had been anyone but aristocrats in The Hague, a town that had probably seemed just a bit slow and old-fashioned even by fourteenth-century standards.

Johann-Maurits, count of Nassau-Siegen, was both ambitious and wealthy, and he was related to *stadtholder* Frederik-Henry. Count Maurits was also a brilliant general, and in the course of his career he would serve the Great Elector of Brandenburg, who made him *stadtholder* of Cleves, Mark, and Ravensberg and conferred on him the title of prince. In 1633, Maurits requested permission from the government to settle near the Binnenhof in a wooded area called the Reygerbosch. The count commissioned Jacob van Campen to design his *hôtel* and Pieter Post to oversee the execution. While it was being built, Maurits left to take up his duties in Brazil, where in addition to serving his country he made a fortune exporting sugar to the motherland. In fact, those who knew his financial affairs called his mansion "the sugar house" and the count himself "the Brazilian."

By 1644 the house was completed. It is van Campen's finest piece of work and perhaps the Netherlands' handsomest building. Van Campen followed the style he was finding so successful in a house Post was designing for Constantin Huygens and that he himself would employ again a little later for the Amsterdam Town Hall: a classical structure adapted to suit Dutch materials and Dutch tastes. The plan of the house is thoroughly symmetrical, with giant Ionic pilasters raised on a low ground floor to support a stone pediment. The façade itself is brick, a particularly Dutch feature, as is the high, hipped roof sloping in a concave line from the eaves. Unfortunately, the monumental chimneys van Campen built have since been removed, and the windows, too, have been unwisely altered. As seventeenth-century mansions go, Maurits' house is rather modest in size, and its brick façade suggests solid Dutch comfort more than it does the opulence that characterizes classical buildings constructed elsewhere in Europe during the same period.

The original interiors of the count's mansion were another story altogether: dark Brazilian wood was used throughout for the staircases and floors, and the walls were richly decorated with exotic scenes of South American tribal life and pictures of tropical birds. After Maurits' death in 1679, the house reverted to its mortgagers and their heirs and was used chiefly as a guesthouse for foreign dignitaries, the last of whom was the duke of Marlborough. In 1704 a fire destroyed this interior, which was redone by Giovanni Pelligrini in a style no less sumptuous. It is largely Pelligrini's handiwork, fit for a doge,

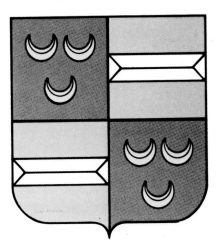

The municipal crest of Wassenaar,
The Hague's northernmost suburb.

that we see today. In 1820 the mansion was converted into a museum to house the Royal Cabinet of Pictures, one of the most impressive collections of seventeenth-century Dutch art in the world.

The Mauritshuis, as it is now called, inherited from the princes of Orange a collection of some one hundred thirty pictures, bought over the years by the royal family. Since then, the collection has grown to almost one thousand works, chiefly by seventeenth-century Flemish and Dutch masters. These were artists who followed the traditions established in the 1400s and 1500s by van Eyck, Campin, and Bruegel, but they were also artists working in a wholly different society, one whose every feature they were to record during a century of prodigious achievement. Their artistry is unquestioned, and their observations are unequaled in completeness and richness of detail. Probably no society before or since has demanded and received from its artists so accurate and so splendid a picture of how it looked, what it did, and where it did it.

In all of this, of course, there was a certain vanity. From the first portraits of "donors" in late medieval devotional works through the fourteenth, fifteenth, and sixteenth centuries, European noblemen had made a point of having themselves portrayed for posterity in garments and poses attesting to their greatness. The burghers of Holland wanted this same flattering memorial for themselves; and, by and large, portraitists like Rembrandt van Rijn and Frans Hals handsomely complied with their clients' wishes. But new interests and a new spirit emerged in the new century as well, and they had little to do

with rich commissions. The Calvinist church had no use for religious images; indeed, it destroyed some of the best in its early and violently iconoclastic period. It placed man in direct communion with his God, and as the church, its fathers, and saints ceased to mediate with the deity, men turned from contemplation of the holy-made-visible to the merely visible. A landscape, for example, no longer had to represent the road taken by the magi to Bethlehem; it could simply be the highway from Haarlem that Jacob van Ruisdael set out to record. Artists began, in short, to look at things as they were and to marvel at how beautiful—and, often, how exciting—they were. Johannes Vermeer discovered how a strong shaft of light could both illumine and throw into shadow the delicate lines of a girl's face or the rich napery at her table, while Abraham van Beyeren captured the play of light and color in the common clutter of food and dining utensils. Outdoors and indoors themselves became subject enough for artists. Worldliness and wonder and the crowded and exciting business of a commercial society brought a certain democratic vision, too. Now even servants were portrayed, as were innkeepers, their clients, and women of easy virtue.

Rembrandt van Rijn, born in 1606 at Leiden, is undoubtedly the Netherlands' greatest painter, and there is hardly a major collection in the world that does not have at least one canvas by this prolific master. His famous *Anatomy Lesson of Dr. Nicolaes Tulp*, at the Mauritshuis, is in many respects the quintessential seventeenth-century Dutch picture. When it was painted, around 1632, it was consid-

ered shocking, and even today it is probably not for the faint-hearted. Commissioned by the Amsterdam Surgeons' Guild, it shows the renowned Dr. Tulp in the process of dissecting the left arm of a cadaver. The body itself, clothed only about the loins, is stretched out on a table across the foreground. It is brightly lit and starkly white. The long tendons running to the phalanges of the fingers are exposed in the very center of the picture, and the doctor has grasped several of them with his forceps. Their central position in the painting, Dr. Tulp's pointing at them, and their red coloring—which contrasts sharply with the browns, blacks, and whites in the rest of the picture—draw attention to their shockingly real presence. Indeed, these exposed muscles seem almost alien to the body itself. The onlookers are grouped pyramidally at the left and center. Dr. Tulp is off center to the right, and in the righthand corner an anatomy book lies open on a lectern.

The stark realism of this painting is something we encounter for the first time in the seventeenth century. To be sure, earlier portrayals of the crucified Jesus or martyred saints were often quite painfully vivid, and we might speculate that Rembrandt is recalling such pictures by using a composition traditional to them: a naked and bloodied body stretched out across most of the painting, with onlookers grouped at either end. But in devotional art the painter's task was to suggest the imminent assumption of the body and spiritual transcendence of suffering. Here the suggestion is quite the opposite: we are not asked to worship earthly suffering but to seek its cure through the study of human anatomy.

There is, of course, a second subject here—the seven surgeons and Dr. Tulp, whose group portrait the Surgeons' Guild had, after all, commissioned. To render them, Rembrandt chooses not the strong white light that falls on the cadaver, but a warm, golden light. He dramatizes and individualizes the portraits by allowing light and shadow to play on their faces, here highlighting, here obscuring some part of their exquisitely drawn features. This technique, called chiaroscuro, was not Rembrandt's invention, but he spent a lifetime employing it in all sorts of pictures, exploring its effects ever more profoundly and dramatically.

The likenesses must have satisfied the sitters and the guild, for the guild commissioned a similar portrait from Rembrandt some years later. A century before, a wealthy donor would have chosen to have his portrait inserted into a devotional panorama or, alternately, to have a painter like Hans Memling portray him in rich robes against a suitably vague drapery background. But it was 1632 and times had changed: a group of men now commission a picture of themselves at work on a cadaver, and they are proud to be seen in so mundane a setting.

This was indeed the age of science, in the Netherlands and throughout Europe. As men turned from the contemplation of the next world to an examination of this one, remarkable advances were made in every field. The great university at Leiden, for example, was second only to that at Padua in the study of anatomy, and men like van Wesel and Pieter Paauw eagerly engaged in the sort of anatomical study Rembrandt portrayed so vividly.

Rembrandt van Rijn painted the self-portrait at upper left in 1669, the year of his death. Directly below is his study of the blind Homer, executed in 1663 for Don Antonio Ruffo. The Anatomy Lesson of Dr. Nicolaes Tulp, below, reveals that Rembrandt was already a remarkable portraitist by 1632, the year he received his commission from the Amsterdam Surgeons' Guild. But it is in the intensely profound vision of his old age that we see the true master, unequaled in his ability to reveal as well as depict. All three canvases are on display in the Mauritshuis.

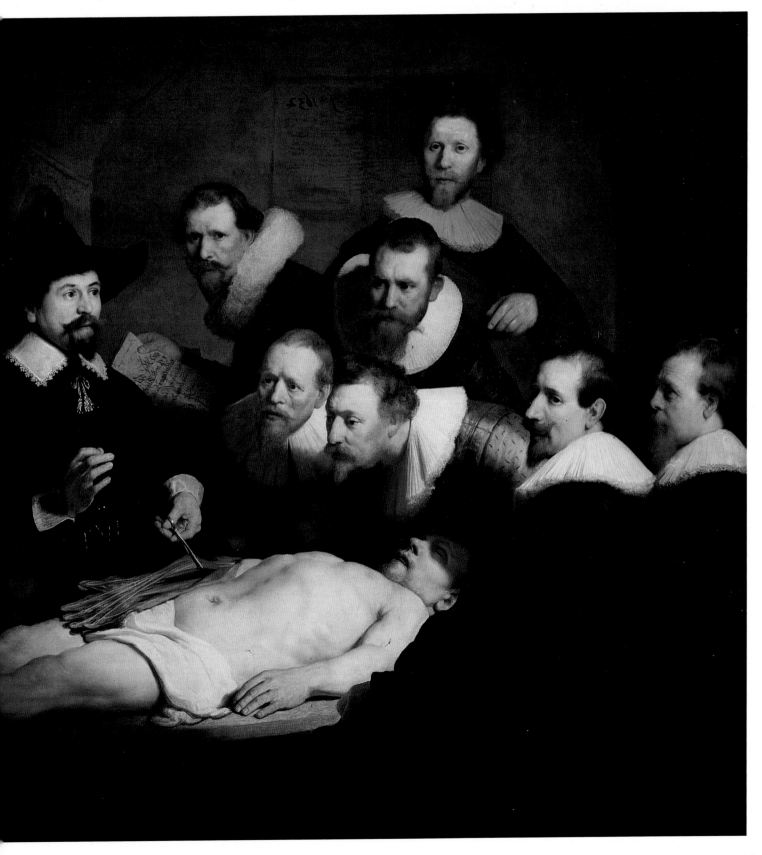

Dutch landscape painters of the seventeenth century sought to reproduce faithfully the look and feel of the Dutch countryside. In a low-lying northern land like Holland, the most striking and characteristic feature of the out-of-doors is neither the contours of the land nor its vegetation, but rather the vast and heavy sky. It overwhelms the flat countryside, and against its billowing mountains of clouds the land, buildings, and people seem miniaturized and frail—as indeed they do in Jan van Goyen's Sea at Haarlem. *Here van Goyen, one of the Netherlands' greatest landscape painters, captures that aspect of his sea-going country; fishermen, boats, and a windmill are all dwarfed by a sky that looms over three quarters of the canvas.*

Dutch scientists contributed to the study of physics, astronomy, and botany as well as medicine. Many of the remarkable discoveries attributed to her men of learning resulted from the development of the lens, probably Holland's single greatest gift to science in the seventeenth century. It was used by men like Lippershey, credited with inventing the telescope, and also by Antony van Leeuwenhoek, who developed the microscope. Christiaan Huygens, born in The Hague in 1629, was one of Europe's greatest scientists. Using Lippershey's new telescope, he not only explored the rings and satellites of Saturn but also developed a series of astronomic principles that rank him with Sir Isaac Newton.

Advances in optics were rapid and widespread, and it is not surprising that they had an important effect on contemporary artists. The *camera obscura*, a device for projecting the image of real objects, had been in use for centuries, but the recent development of a wide variety of fine lenses improved it greatly. It is likely that every artist in Holland had some familiarity with the *camera obscura*, and many are documented as having used it in their experiments with perspective.

The marvels science discovered in the real world were revealed only to the relative few who could either manage the new devices for microscopic and telescopic vision or who could read and understand others' findings; but the miracle of creation could be apprehended by the naked eye as well, and Dutch artists turned to the landscape to bring this revelation to everyone. One of the earliest masters of this new art was Jan van Goyen. For most of his life he worked in The Hague, where he held a respected place in the Painters' Guild. In 1651 he earned a commission to paint a panoramic view of the town for the burgomaster's room at the Stadhuis.

Before van Goyen's time van Eyck had used landscape as background for paintings with devotional themes, and later Bruegel had employed it as part of a narrative of mythic adventure or rustic life. But it was van Goyen who first turned to landscape as a subject in itself. In a brilliant series of canvases he was able to capture the look and feel of a country where the sky is always heavy with moisture and the land, stretching endlessly and almost without contour, seems to rise to meet it. A distant windmill, a shepherd, a farmhouse are painted as they must have looked, but they tell no story and have no special narrative or spiritual significance. It is the land itself van Goyen cared about, and he was able to picture it as every Dutchman saw it.

Jacob van Ruisdael was born in Haarlem in about 1628. By this time van Goyen's paintings were already famous, and it is likely that Ruisdael was as much influenced by van Goyen as by the paintings of his own uncle Salomon. In certain important respects, however, Jacob was to depart from the landscape art of the older generation. In his youth he had been fond of studying the effects of light and shade in the wooded dunes outside Haarlem, and this light-dark play would be his theme throughout his career. His pictures are, for the most part, geographically nonspecific—often dark and shadowy forest scenes that are largely imaginary. An eerie, almost Gothic mystery pervades many of his land-

scapes, where twisted branches and tree trunks overhang rushing brooks and winding paths. Using a far heavier impasto than either van Goyen or the elder Ruisdael, Jacob was able to give his pictures a richer, denser quality. Foliage, for example, is no longer part of a general tonal theme but has instead its own rich presence. As Jacob's style matured, the landscapes became heroic, the color more vivid, and the forms themselves larger. The subjects changed, too, as he turned to the sea and the wide plains, which, as in all Dutch landscapes, were placed beneath a broad and heavy sky. But it is for the ruined castles, overgrown cemeteries, and shadowed forests that we best remember Jacob Ruisdael, who found in the Dutch landscape a poetry that a century or two later we would call Romantic.

If poetry could be found in nature out of doors, the seventeenth century also discovered it indoors, in the branch of painting most peculiarly Dutch—the still-life picture. The simple objects of everyday life—books, candles, a drinking vessel, a vase—suddenly revealed a beauty of their own to eyes newly awakened to the visible world. Pieter Claesz, for example, found the same sort of poetry in light and shade falling across the objects scattered on a table that Ruisdael found in forest glades. In his *Still Life with Burning Candle*, books, a pair of reading glasses, a metal candle-snuffer, and an almost burnt-out candle are mirrored in a half-filled drinking glass in the center of the composition. The light of the candle creates stark shadows that enhance the diagonals of the objects on the table, which themselves contrast with the two horizontal planes of the table and the dark background. It is a remarkable composition, and it is all the more remarkable for having been created out of so little—light, shadow, and a few trivial objects.

Like Claesz, Willem Kalf used only what every good burgher might see about him daily to create his rich and complex studies of color and texture. In his untitled still-life at the Mauritshuis, an orange and a half-peeled lemon shine almost as if they were themselves sources of light, while a filled wineglass reflects their glow. Another goblet, upside down, and a silver plate and knife catch glints of light that make them shine like jewels scattered on the canvas. A rich red Persian rug is casually folded on the table and, like the glasses and silver, only partially reveals itself as the light picks out spots of its ornate design while throwing the rest of it into deep shadow. On seeing one of Kalf's pictures, Goethe observed that it revealed how much superior art is to nature when the creative eye captures and transforms it. "Were I allowed the choice between the golden vessels and the picture," the German novelist declared, "I should choose the picture."

Still-life pictures of flowers had a particular appeal to the Dutch, and this vogue may well have been inspired by the bizarre episode that has been called "tulipomania." This strange madness seized the otherwise sober merchants of Holland around 1637, when the desire to own exotically colored and shaped tulips—whose classification and cultivation had been studied at Leiden by Carolus Clusius—resulted in a frenzy of buying that saw the price of a single hybrid bulb rise to thousands of guilders.

Buying and selling were so brisk and the profits so large that bulbs were even traded like shares on the Amsterdam Exchange. The bubble eventually burst, and many a speculator was ruined; but fascination with botanical subjects led to a spate of pictures, as the well-to-do sought to own not only the perishable flower but its longer-lasting representation in oil.

Ambrosius Bosschaert was born in 1573 at Antwerp and died in 1621 at The Hague, where he may have painted his most brilliant floral arrangement, which is set in a window that looks out over a hazy, Eyckian sort of landscape. We know that Bosschaert's paintings fetched large prices—he is reported to have been paid one thousand guilders for a floral painting of a courtier at The Hague—and we also know that many other painters in this period received substantial sums for their work. Everyone, even peasants, bought pictures, and perhaps this extraordinary outpouring of talent during so short a time in so small a country was due largely to the new prosperity. Everyone who shared in it wanted to own something that would show what it was like to live in such a place at such a time.

Jan Steen studied at Utrecht and Haarlem before finishing his training under Jan van Goyen at The Hague, where he married his teacher's daughter in 1649. Certainly no painter captured so vividly, so completely, and so humorously the rich and boisterous life of seventeenth-century Holland as Steen. His *Theater of the World* depicts a panorama of human foolishness and playfulness in a scene often taken to represent the inn Steen himself ran in Delft. The trompe l'oeil curtain emphasizes his "theater"

theme, while in the rafters near the birdcage a small figure blowing bubbles is seated next to a death's head—a traditional metaphor for the transience of human life. Steen may be reminding us that life is short and all is vanity, but it seems fair to say that he knew how good it could be while it lasted.

An even bawdier depiction of tavern life was offered by Frans van Mieris in his *Inn Scene*. Here a woman of fine proportions offers wine—and, as her low-cut bodice and inviting smile tell us, something more—to a richly clad gentleman. Lest we miss the point, a pair of dogs in the background and bedding hanging over the landing make the nature of this encounter perfectly clear. Van Mieris' pictures, like those of Steen, were prized by seventeenth-century collectors, who eagerly accepted an art that was neither devotional nor heroic but simply real.

Not all life was lived in taverns, of course, and in other settings the real could be sublime. Johannes Vermeer has left a very small number of works— only thirty-five pictures have been credited to him— but they rank among the greatest achievements in art. His *Kitchen Maid* at Amsterdam's Rijksmuseum portrays a simple domestic scene, a maid pouring milk from a jug into a bowl on a crowded kitchen work table. The picture is at once forceful and delicate. Vermeer's precise modeling of the girl's large features and her placement at the center of the composition against a stark, illuminated background make her monumental; only her slightly tilted head, her look of concentration, and the way shadows gently darken part of her face and body serve to modulate her presence and keep her from overpow-

ering the composition. The paint is richly textured, heavily impastoed; the colors, mostly yellow and blue, are bright; the effect is quiet but intense—and intensely real. In the eighteenth century Sir Joshua Reynolds would describe it as one of the best Dutch pictures he had ever seen, and later Vincent van Gogh would think of its coloring when creating his own rich paintings.

The Kitchen Maid is an astonishingly beautiful, almost reverential rendering of nothing more than a simple household chore. Dutch painters produced hundreds of such scenes—called genre, or documentary, pictures—during the seventeenth century. Vermeer may stand apart from other contemporary genre painters in his mastery of color and composition, but numerous artists, among them Pieter de Hooch, Gerard ter Borch, and Caspar Netscher, splendidly re-created the look and feel of middle-class domestic life in this period. Netscher, who settled in The Hague in 1622, painted genre scenes in the manner of his teacher, ter Borch. Once in the capital, however, he increasingly engaged in portraiture, rendering small, delicate pictures of his aristocratic clients. His paintings reveal clearly the rich and comfortable life being led in the mansions and townhouses of The Hague at the height of the Netherlands' golden age.

The *Head of a Girl* at the Mauritshuis is peculiar among Vermeer's work in that it omits any setting. Starkly posed against a dark background, Vermeer's maiden looks directly out at us. Her parted lips, seemingly just about to speak, give her portrait an immediacy few painters have ever achieved. Her

headdress—a pale yellow turban with a pale blue band—is exotic, but everything else about her is ineffably innocent and timeless. Thoré-Bürger, who rediscovered Vermeer for the nineteenth century, called this girl *La Gioconda du nord*—the northern Mona Lisa.

It is both irresistible impulse and pure folly to use superlatives when speaking of Vermeer—or any master for that matter. But looking at his *Head of a Girl*, we feel we could stand forever in the Mauritshuis just staring at her. And then, close by, we come upon his *View of Delft*, and like many a viewer before, we are led to exclaim that, yes, here indeed is all that painting ever strived to be.

Toward the end of his life, Marcel Proust's Bergotte, in *Remembrance of Things Past*, is confined to his bed. A friend visits him and they chat about pictures. The friend mentions Vermeer's cityscape, and particularly that small golden wall toward the right of the composition. Bergotte cannot resist one final examination. Against his doctor's warnings, he goes off to view it and, having seen it again, dies. It is Proust's tribute to a painting already famous in his day and universally admired in ours. It is remarkable in so many ways. Working in a landscape tradition that preferred an almost monochromatic haze, Vermeer dared to use warm, bright, and decorative colors: a pale blue, heavily clouded sky hangs over the red rooftops of Delft, while the sun, from between the clouds, shines golden on the foreground shore and here and there on walls in the more distant city. Small dots of paint, called *pointillés*, brighten every color—even the homey browns of

the walls nearest the shore—without distorting either the forms or their colors. The distant golds contrasting with the nearer browns, and the whole reflected on the river, give a sense of depth and distance to a picture whose buildings are really quite solidly grouped left to right. Most of what Vermeer depicted is gone now, but early maps and engravings attest to his topographical accuracy. The picture itself attests to an unequaled hand and eye.

If the new middle-class patrons of art liked to see in painting reflections of the world around them—in accurately detailed land- and cityscapes, still-lifes, and genre scenes—their favorite subject by far was themselves. And when we think of Dutch art, it is always the great portraitists, Hals and Rembrandt, who first come to mind. Both men had long, productive, and lucrative careers; both gave to art techniques that would change it utterly; and both left to the world images as familiar as our own faces.

Frans Hals was born in Antwerp sometime between 1581 and 1585. His family was among the many thousands who came north to flee the religious persecutions in the Spanish Netherlands. They settled in Haarlem, where Hals worked all his life. It seems that almost everyone sat for him: the well-to-do and the poor, scholars and bawds, clergymen, soldiers, and children. He painted all of them with an incisive understanding of their personalities; and he endowed them all with an animating energy.

In Hals' 1635 *Portrait of a Man*, which hangs today in the Mauritshuis, we encounter a rakish sort of fellow whose large-brimmed hat and dark suit make him jump out from the gray-green background. He

Jan Steen was the greatest humorist of Dutch painting, and his lively, boisterous scenes reveal not only how life was led in the seventeenth century but how it was viewed—as a great feast, one at which peasant and burgher alike were privileged to sup. Steen's canvases are generally crowded with a wealth of finely rendered details, and even today in Holland the phrase "a Jan Steen household" is used to refer to very happy, if somewhat sloppy, home. In The Fishmarket at St. Jacob's Church *Steen is not content to choose one or two significant details; instead he gives us a panorama of Dutch town life: old and young, dogs and children, workers and loafers, all gathered before the great church at the center of The Hague and engaged in the getting and spending of a prosperous and lively society.*

seems to be staring with some amusement at something just beyond the picture's range. If we move closer, we can see just how Hals achieved this particularly energetic and lively portrait within a compositional structure that is itself fairly straightforward and traditional. By the middle of his career Hals was using a quick, sharp, and broken brushstroke few painters would be able to master again until the late nineteenth century. At close range, the surface seems wild and confused; but at a distance it resolves itself into an intricate and cohesive pattern of light and shade that imparts life to this marvelous—and marvelously good-looking—face. Light jumps about the man's features, catching the painted highlights and especially the spots where Hals has built up the paint into a heavy impasto. The flesh and the cloth seem to palpitate, but the subject is still firmly there, an animated but solid presence.

A Hals portrait of 1660 shows us that by this late point in his career—he died in 1666—he had completely mastered his characteristic brushwork, which is now more fluid and even quicker. Here we have a very different sitter, a serious, scholarly man whose large, dark eyes stare out from a face framed by wavy hair that melts into the background. If the eyes look out at us, we can also look in through them to a mind we wish could speak—so alive, so interesting, and so deep has Hals drawn this gentleman.

Born some twenty years after Hals, Rembrandt painted almost every subject—landscapes, biblical themes, historical events. But it is probably by his portraits that we know him best, and certainly they are among the greatest achievements of human cre-

ativity. Hals brought to portraiture understanding and energy, while Rembrandt brought to it majesty and depth. He created canvases in which there is a quality beyond composition and technique for which words and analysis will never be sufficient.

After a period of training in his native Leiden and later at Amsterdam, Rembrandt returned to his hometown, where he quickly established a considerable reputation. By 1629 the statesman Constantin Huygens was mentioning him as one of the brilliant youths of Leiden, and within a few years Huygens would secure him commissions from the prince of Orange. The undated but early self-portrait at the Mauritshuis already shows a firm command of the chiaroscuro that would become Rembrandt's most important and powerful technique: the young face of the artist, lit from the left, moves into shadow at the right, blending harmoniously with the gray-green background. This is among the earliest of nearly one hundred self-portraits Rembrandt would complete during a life in which he returned compulsively to himself as subject, almost as if he could not paint others or the world without an ever-deepening understanding of himself.

By 1632 Rembrandt had moved to Amsterdam, and there he began receiving the commissions that made him famous and wealthy almost immediately. Undoubtedly the commissioned portrait of Dr. Tulp, executed shortly after Rembrandt's arrival, established him as one of the leading painters in a city where everyone with means wanted a portrait. So sought-after was he in Amsterdam in the 1650s, it is said, that one had to beg as well as pay hand-

somely for a portrait by the young artist. In 1631, a year before the *Anatomy Lesson*, Rembrandt painted *The Presentation in the Temple*—one of his many biblical works. In its colossal columns and deep space we see the monumental style he developed during his first exposure to the High Baroque art already made fashionable by Flemish painter Peter-Paul Rubens.

The *Presentation* scene is based on a story in the Gospel of Luke: the aged Simeon, upon seeing the infant Jesus brought to the temple for ritual purification, lifts the child up and declares him "a light to lighten the Gentiles, and the glory of thy people Israel." Rembrandt places the principal figures not in the foreground, but about midway into the vast darkened space of the temple. A shaft of light from the left pierces the darkness and illumines the rich purple of the priest's robes and the faces of Mary, Joseph, and two of the onlookers. Simeon is lit by a stronger light that emanates from the infant himself. We view this tightly grouped assembly across a foreground marked by the parallel horizontals of the joints in the stone floor, and against a background of the parallel vertical lines of the giant columns. The vast space, the strong parallel lines that recede and carry us toward the deepening shadows, and the menacing darkness make the figures themselves seem particularly small, even though a bright light clearly shows us their faces. Rembrandt creates drama simply through the tensions of light, shadow, space, and line. In his handling of the scene, Simeon's metaphor seems to become the awesome reality of an infant who is indeed a light to lighten the sorrowing world.

In 1656 Rembrandt was forced into bankruptcy—probably more a result of his own unwise financial management than of a falling-off of commissions. In any case, an inventory of his possessions made for his creditors reveals an enormous and enormously varied collection of paintings and artifacts—arms, costumes, baskets, bowls, stuffed birds, minerals, and shells from the Near and Far East—attesting to Rembrandt's wide-ranging curiosity and his fascination with the exotic. Indeed, just as the world opened up to Dutch merchant seamen, we frequently see in Rembrandt's work and in the work of other painters exotic scenes and people. For the most part, they were painted as just that: strange and wonderful sights, marvelous to look at but difficult to believe in. Rembrandt, though, had no trouble believing and no trouble bringing to foreign subjects his infinite capacity to understand an individual spirit. For example, his *Two Negroes* at the Mauritshuis, painted in 1661, is as much a living portrait as those he made of himself or of Dutch subjects. It is a subtly colored picture of delicately modulated brownish tints. The head on the left, whose expression is quiet and melancholy, is cast in soft shadow, while the livelier man on the right is more brightly lit, especially about the eyes, on which we cannot help but focus. No doubt these people looked marvelously strange to Dutch eyes, but Rembrandt found in them distinct and deeply felt personalities, and captured them in his canvas.

Shortly after this picture was made, Rembrandt completed his incomparable portrait of the aged and blind Homer. It was commissioned by Don An-

70

Jan Vermeer, who is second only to Rembrandt himself in the noble pantheon of seventeenth-century Dutch painters, was as painstaking as his great contemporary was prolific. As a result, only a relatively small number of canvases can be attributed to Vermeer's hand, among them these two works from the renowned Mauritshuis collection. Head of a Girl, above, is a magisterial evocation of ineffable innocence, familiar to every schoolchild in The Hague and widely regarded as a supreme example of the portraitist's art. Marcel Proust, for his part, was so captivated by View of Delft, seen at left, that he included a description of Vermeer's masterpiece in his own masterpiece, the vast canvas entitled Remembrance of Things Past:

> At last he came to the Vermeer, which he remembered as more striking, more different from anything else he knew, but in which, thanks to the critic's article, he noticed for the first time some small figures in blue, that the sand was pink, and, finally, the precious substance of the tiny patch of yellow wall. His dizziness increased; he fixed his gaze, like a child upon a yellow butterfly that it wants to catch, on the precious little patch of wall.

The seventeenth century in the Netherlands was the Golden Age of science and literature as well as art. Caspar Netscher painted numerous portraits at The Hague, where he was in great demand because, like his teacher Ter Borch, he specialized in painting the rich garments of his sitters. Here his subject is Christiaan Huygens, son of the statesman and poet Constantin, and himself an important mathematician and physicist. Christiaan Huygens improved telescopic lenses and discovered the rings of Saturn. He also developed the wave theory of light. Netscher's portrait of him reveals an exemplar of the elegant, cultured, and inquisitive life led at The Hague during its Golden Age.

tonio Ruffo, a Sicilian nobleman living in Messina, who, some years earlier, had commissioned the famous *Aristotle with a Bust of Homer*, now in New York's Metropolitan Museum of Art. As in his *Aristotle*, Rembrandt uses a heavy impasto to create a shining, sparkling gold in the shawl and face, which forces these areas of the painting to stand out from the deep reddish brown of the rest of the picture. But while the golds of the *Aristotle* bespeak elegance, here the gold serves as light itself—the poet is not richly gowned but is himself incandescent. Rugged and forceful brushwork throughout the head and beard emphasizes the poet's aged features. The rest of his body and gown are deeper in shadow and more vaguely drawn, so that the head emerges like an essence from a deep and smoky background. There is all mind and all wisdom here, Rembrandt appears to say, and for that reason the blind eyes see more than any sighted ones. Rembrandt had been fascinated by old age since his own youth, and as he himself grew old, his portraits of the elderly took on more and more the qualities he always seemed to ascribe to age: experience, wisdom, and understanding of the most profound saint.

In the year of his death, 1669, Rembrandt painted his last self-portrait. Here again heavy brushwork pits and coarsens the face. But Homer, the immortal, glows gold; Rembrandt, a mere man, is white, even a little pasty. Homer's face is craggy; Rembrandt's own merely sags under a burden of years and loss, but the eyes seem to suggest that Rembrandt sensed his own immortality. They look out at us sharply and firmly—a painter's eyes.

By the middle of the seventeenth century, the Netherlands was undoubtedly the wealthiest nation in Europe, and what is especially remarkable for a place so small, she was also the most powerful nation. Her seamen and colonists were all over the globe: Dutch settlements were founded in the Caribbean, West Africa, India, and Japan. On the European continent her engineers, merchants, and bankers were conducting business in virtually every major city and court. And so to Amsterdam, Holland's great port, flowed goods and people from everywhere. Dutch painters reflected their nation's wealth in rich and crowded still-life and genre pictures, and in portraying exotic costumes and objects they reflected the cosmopolitan air of their cities.

Imperial Holland found its perfect reflection in the seascape, in which appeared the all-important merchant and naval vessels that were her lifeline. Among the most gifted of the many artists who specialized in the seascape was Willem van de Velde the younger, who, with his father, actually sailed out with the fleet to record naval battles during Holland's intermittent wars with Great Britain. Curiously enough, van de Velde was court painter to Charles II of England, and most of his paintings of naval engagements were made on board English ships in the service of the British crown. Van de Velde's eye for the details of ship construction and rigging is equaled only by his sensitivity to the shifting colors of sky and sea. His pictures of Dutch ships and naval triumphs provide a vivid record of the seaborne empire that gave to the Netherlands its golden age.

73

IV

The Mightiest Village in Europe

Despite a war that had lasted for eighty years, the Netherlands emerged in the middle of the seventeenth century as the wealthiest nation in Europe, and one of the most powerful. Holland had long been trading grain from Germany and Poland for salt from Portugal and Biscay and herring from the North Sea. This network, called "the mother trade," became more profitable than ever at midcentury when Europe, faced with a population explosion, found itself in desperate need of Dutch middlemen to ensure the provision of foodstuffs.

The long war with Spain, far from hindering Holland's economic growth, had actually encouraged it. Spain herself had been forced to trade her precious American silver for the food and raw materials available only through the Dutch. And Antwerp, once the great commercial center of the southern Netherlands, had been so ravaged by war, mutiny, and persecution that most of her merchants had fled north, bringing their wealth and their skills with them. Indeed, even after the peace, ships of the Dutch republic had blockaded the mouth of the river Scheldt, effectively cutting Antwerp off from the rest of the world. The war itself, especially in its last decades, had been fought chiefly in the south, which was already impoverished by the constant presence of hostile armies.

For these and other reasons Amsterdam now became the greatest European entrepôt, as shipments of food and raw industrial materials flowed into her warehouses, there to be refined or finished and then shipped out again to practically every city in England and on the Continent. The symbol of Dutch supremacy was the *fluit*, or "flyboat"—really a sea-going barge—which was cheap to build and operate and better able than other vessels of its time to store large cargoes and carry the equipment necessary for on-board refining or curing. The flyboat was seen in every port, on every sea. It sailed as far as the West Indies—where the Netherlands encroached upon the Portuguese and Spanish colonial empire—and the East Indies—where the Dutch East India Company had established itself in the Moluccas, Java, Malaya, Ceylon, India, Formosa, and Japan.

Dutch technological supremacy, most evident in shipbuilding, extended to all areas of navigation. Simon Stevin, who had taught the young Prince Maurice, introduced in his *Heaven Finding* a vastly improved method of navigation; Christiaan Huygens invented a pendulum chronometer that made it possible for mariners to determine their positions more accurately than ever before; and a school of cartography grew up in Holland to which most maps published in the sixteenth and early seventeenth centuries can be attributed. Gerard Kremer, known as Mercator, projected the world as it was really shaped, and Lucas Waghenaer published his *Mariner's Mirror*, a series of maps and navigational charts that sailors from every sea-going nation carried with them during the early 1700s. These scientific and technological advances combined with Holland's established trading experience to make her the merchant of Europe and a successful and ever-expanding colonizer throughout the rest of the world. Naturally enough, she was challenged in both arenas, commercial and colonial.

The crescents of Wassenaar also appear on Voorschoten's shield.

Spain and Portugal had been granted exclusive rights to colonize the New World by a papal bull of 1494, and they naturally resisted Dutch incursions in the West Indies. England, herself a growing sea power, looked anxiously on the Dutch hold over the rich North Sea fishing grounds. Iberian and English claims to own the seas were refuted by Holland's great scholar of international law, Hugo Grotius, who elaborated the doctrine of freedom of the seas and the laws governing international conflicts in his *Mare Liberum* ("On Freedom of the Seas"), *De Jure ac Pacis* ("On the Law of War and Peace"), and *De Jure Praedae* ("On the Law of Prize and Booty"). Grotius argued that the seas were not national territory but were open to everyone, and that non-Christian peoples or their leaders had the right to enter into binding agreements among themselves or with European powers. Thus, he concluded, Holland was free to sail in any waters and to establish trading posts anywhere in the world.

Grotius' doctrines eventually became part of international law—in theory if not in practice. But in seventeenth-century London, Madrid, Lisbon, and Paris, they were considered simply one more effrontery by a far too aggressive people. Already roundly defeated by the Dutch, the Spanish could do little to help themselves. The English and French, on the other hand, had suffered no such losses. They wanted a share of the world's trade, and they moved quickly against the new Dutch nation.

In 1651 the English Parliament passed the Navigation Act, which stipulated that goods being shipped to England or her colonies could be carried only on English vessels or on vessels belonging to the producing nation. This was a devastating blow to the Netherlands' economy, which depended on transshipment generally and on the English trade in particular. By the next year, England and Holland were at war. It soon became apparent that it was virtually impossible for the Dutch adequately to protect their long trade routes—all of which passed through the narrow seas between England and Holland. The alternative, shipping around the north of England, meant greater navigational hazards—and it further exposed the poorly armed or completely unarmed Dutch merchant vessels to English search and seizure. Within a year, the English had completely blockaded the Netherlands, and neither merchantmen—bringing precious specie to Amsterdam's bankers—nor fishing vessels—bringing even more valuable food to Holland's people—could enter Dutch ports. As food prices rose and shortages grew, the loose political structure of the new republic seemed about to collapse.

Following the death of William II in 1650, the Estates had decided not to appoint a new *stadtholder*. The House of Orange, which had won the first battle for power against the nobility and burghers under Maurice, would not be allowed to seize power again. The grand pensionary of the province of Holland, Johann de Witt, functioned as head of state. In England, Oliver Cromwell—named Lord Protector after the execution of Charles I—was in much the same position as de Witt. Both men were threatened by a popular and legitimate claimant, and, as it happened, these pretenders—the Stuarts

Het Catshuis in the Zorgvliet Park, now the prime minister's residence, was built in the early seventeenth century by Jacob Cats, a statesman, grand pensionary of Holland and West Friesland, and widely read poet. Like so many other buildings of this period in The Hague, Het Catshuis is characterized by its elegance and its simplicity. The seventeenth was a century that firmly believed in order and in moderation, and consequently even at the height of its imperial power and prosperity the Netherlands exercised a careful restraint that is clearly seen in the buildings constructed for the rulers and statesmen who ran that empire.

in England and the Oranges in Holland—were related De Witt and Cromwell agreed that peace was in their common interest, as neither side could afford the social strain of war. The ensuing truce, founded on the concept of a grand alliance of Protestant nations, was far more favorable to England, the probable victor of the war, than to the Dutch. The Navigation Act was retained by the terms of the treaty, and the Estates agreed never again to appoint a *stadtholder* from the House of Orange.

The peace of 1654 at least temporarily protected the positions of de Witt and Cromwell, but it did nothing to resolve the trade rivalry that had caused the war. During the next ten years, the Dutch vastly improved their capacity to fight on the sea by building real men-of-war to replace the armed merchantmen with which they had fought in 1652. They also united their naval command under a brilliant admiral, Michel de Ruyter. By 1665 merchants in both the Netherlands and Great Britain were again pressing for armed intervention to protect their interests, and the Dutch, at least, felt strong enough to pursue this course. In London, plague was crippling the city; the new king, Charles II, could not count on parliamentary support for a costly war; and a large peace faction pointed to other nations lining up on the side of the Netherlands as reason enough not to engage in hostilities.

In 1667 de Ruyter stupefied the English and amazed himself by sailing up the Thames, where he seized and destroyed the giant battleship *Royal Charles*. Rumors of Dutch landings at Sheerness, Devon, and other coastal towns swept England,

leading a harried Samuel Pepys to write, "By God, I think the devil shits Dutchmen." This time the Netherlands had a better hand at the peace talks and succeeded in having the most onerous provisions of the Navigation Act suspended. The Treaty of Breda, which concluded the peace, also granted Surinam in South America to the Netherlands in exchange for a small and indefensible settlement in North America called New Amsterdam, which the English renamed New York—in retrospect, not so shrewd a bargain.

By 1672 the Dutch and the English were again at war, but this time neither side had much heart for it. The English felt far more threatened by Catholic powers on the Continent than by the Protestant Dutch at sea; and, for their part, the Dutch oligarchs could see no profit in further burdening their already heavily taxed population.

The second war between England and the Netherlands, the one launched in 1667 by de Ruyter, had encouraged Louis XIV of France to attempt to seize the Spanish Netherlands. He was foiled in this ambition by an agreement between the Dutch republic, England, and Spain to resist the French. The renewal of hostilities between England and the Netherlands in 1672 gave Louis another chance. England and France secretly agreed to attack the Netherlands by sea and to coordinate this assault with a French army attack in the south and an invasion by troops of the bishops of Münster and Cologne in the west.

In spring of 1672 the three-pronged attack began, and by July the French were in Utrecht. In order to save the province of Holland the Estates ordered the flooding of the land between the two provinces.

Rombout Verhulst completed his busts of King William III and his wife, Mary Stuart, in 1683, and both are now in the collection of the Mauritshuis. William was born in The Hague in 1650 to William II, prince of Orange, and Mary, eldest daughter of King Charles I of England. At the time of his birth, the office of stadtholder *was suspended and Jan de Witt held power. In 1672, however, de Witt was overthrown and William was proclaimed* stadtholder. *Five years later he wed Mary, daughter of the future King James II of England. James's Catholicism worried the English, and when in 1688 James's wife bore him a son, William was invited by seven important noblemen to assume the English throne. He landed with an army of 15,000 men but met no opposition from James, who fled to France. Thus William III, prince of Orange-Nassau and* stadtholder *of the Netherlands, became king of England as well through the bloodless coup known to history as the Glorious Revolution.*

The French advance was checked, but only at tremendous cost in land, livestock, and, of course, lives. Hysteria seized the republic. The grand pensionary, de Witt, was forced to resign; he and his brother were imprisoned in The Hague's Gevangenpoort, from which they were dragged by angry mobs and lynched. The prince of Orange was asked to assume military and political control and to accept the title of *stadtholder*—despite the Estates' old vow never to so promote a prince of Orange again. The new *stadtholder*, William III, managed to prevent the Anglo-French landing and checked the advance of German troops in the west. After seizing the fortress at Bonn where French supplies in the Netherlands were stored, he forced the French to withdraw. The English, who had never much desired this war in the first place, also abandoned the fight, as did the bishops of Münster and Cologne. Spain joined the Netherlands in the battle still being waged against the French in the southern Netherlands, and in 1678 King Louis sued for peace with the republic.

The Estates had never been fond of the House of Orange, to which, it appeared, the title of *stadtholder* belonged whenever the decision was made to grant it. Not only did the princes of Orange threaten the sovereign power of the separate provinces and thus the personal power of the nobles and burghers, they also had a penchant for involvement in European politics that led inevitably to war. After a century of conflict, war was anathema to these burghers, who realized that the Netherlands could never afford to compete militarily with the other great European powers. When she tried, it led inevitably to taxa-

tion—and usually to defeat. For the next two and a half centuries the republic and, later, the kingdom of the Netherlands would struggle to maintain this policy of noninvolvement.

The prosperity and prestige of the seventeenth-century Netherlands had transformed Gascoigne's "pleasant village" into a far more stately and solid city, indeed a regal capital of an imperial nation. All Europe now referred to The Hague as "the most beautiful and mightiest village" on the Continent. It is often called "the largest village in the country" by twentieth-century Dutchmen, and there is no question that The Hague still retains a certain "village" quality. But during the late seventeenth and eighteenth centuries the statesmen and courtiers who settled in The Hague did everything they could to imitate life in the capitals of rival nations.

Statesmen settled in The Hague in the late 1600s, and because the Netherlands' prestige as a military power had grown considerably under Maurice and Frederik-Henry, young noblemen pursuing army careers also wanted to live near the renowned *stadtholders*. Artists knew they could secure rich commissions in this lavishly spending town, and merchants flocked to The Hague with their wares. And where the free spenders went, muggers, burglars, rapists, and murderers also went. The town magistrates had to warn merchants not to display their wares in the street; the hot-tempered young men of The Hague fought their duels in public; and in 1664 the town was scandalized by the abduction of a maiden by her rejected suitor. Tranquil village life had become a thing of the past for The Hague.

Near the Buitenhof and the Plein palatial residences were constructed, and streets like the Korte Voorhout, the Korte Vijverberg, and Tournooiveld also became fashionable building sites. On the outskirts of the town the poet Jacob Cats built his estate, Sorghvliet—now the prime minister's residence—and Constantin Huygens erected his smaller Hofwijck. The town itself was the scene of both patrician splendor and bawdy revelry. Court banquets, masquerades, and ballets were held in the new mansions, and every year The Hague Fair provided street festivities for nobleman, burgher, and commoner alike. Since the Estates of Holland met in The Hague but were forbidden by reasons of state and decorum from entertaining in public taverns, grand inns were constructed for the Estates alone. One of the present buildings of the Ministry of Foreign Affairs was once the inn for representatives of the city of Amsterdam, and the Ministry of War once housed Rotterdam's private tavern.

Although The Hague never developed as a commercial or industrial city, even during the great age of Dutch commerce, its cosmopolitan and aristocratic character did lead to the establishment there of two important industries: silversmithing and the production of porcelain. Silversmithing had actually been practiced in The Hague as early as the fifteenth century, but it was only after the war with Spain ceased to threaten The Hague and it became a seat of government that the production of silver plate became an important and prosperous industry.

The Haags Gemeentemuseum has assembled a large and impressive collection of local silver—some of the earliest pieces of which are dated about the end of the sixteenth century. The Hague's production continued until the end of the eighteenth century, when the guilds were abolished and factory-made silver replaced the delicate and graceful products of master smiths like Engelbert Joosten, Pieter van der Toorn, Cornelis de Haan, and François Marcus Simons. The first three of these men designed in the rococo style particularly favored in the mid-eighteenth century, a style that, in The Hague, developed along its own particular lines—its excellent and well-proportioned shapes never obscured by the elaborate ornamentation that rococo usually connotes.

The general prosperity of the Netherlands in the eighteenth century and the particularly cosmopolitan character of The Hague led to the production of large quantities of domestic silver, which the more formal and elaborate style of living being adopted by the burgher class helped promote. Prosperous businessmen who had been content with brass and pewter now sought the full panoply of formal dining: glassware and chinaware; silver utensils and candlesticks; silver breadbaskets, cruets, and saltcellars; and, to serve the newly discovered beverages, elaborate silver coffee and tea services.

By the last quarter of the eighteenth century The Hague also boasted its own porcelain works, started in 1777 by Anton Lyncker. Lyncker probably began his business by importing undecorated porcelain, but by 1777 he was making porcelain himself. The *stadtholder* William V bought shares in Lyncker's factory, as did many wealthy Haguenaars, and by 1779

the factory had outgrown its quarters on the Bagijnestraat and had moved to the Dunne Bierkade. In that year The Hague municipality ordered from Lyncker a large set of china to be used only by the magistrates of the town—a testament to the already recognized quality of Lyncker's product.

Three types of Hague porcelain from this period have been identified, and examples of all can be seen at the Gemeentemuseum: hard-paste porcelain manufactured, modeled, and decorated in The Hague; hard-paste porcelain imported from Germany but decorated in The Hague; and the soft-paste, or *pâte-tendre*, variety, which was modeled, fired, and partly decorated at Tournai and given final decorative touches in The Hague. The city emblem, a stork with an eel in its beak, is the identifying mark, but many pieces completely or partly manufactured in The Hague do not bear this seal. The decorative design of Hague porcelain made it appreciated throughout the world, both during the short time it was being produced—Lyncker's factory closed sometime before 1790—and throughout the next century, when it fetched high prices at auction. Landscapes, groups of birds, and soft-colored monograms and garlands of very small flowers characterize Hague porcelain, which, like Hague silver, can be found in public and private collections the world over—attesting to the particularly refined and cosmopolitan atmosphere in which both of these local industries flourished.

In 1649 construction was begun on The Hague's Nieuwe Kerk, designed by Pieter Noorwits and Bartholomeus van Bassen, the city's municipal architect. It is a singular and picturesque building, due largely to the amazing play of angles and roofs that results from its plan: two rectangles, each of whose short sides incorporates one polygonal apse and whose long sides incorporate two. Tall pilasters emphasize the geometric display, as do the six roofs of the apses, which compete with the church's main roof and simple wooden turret. The interior is, unfortunately, far less exciting, being rather bare, and the pulpit and baptismal screen are placed somewhere obscurely in the wall of one of the long sides.

Architects of this period found the opportunity for the freest display of their talents in the public and private commissions the Netherlands could well afford to bestow. During the seventeenth and eighteenth centuries, almost every politically powerful aristocratic family in the country built a home in The Hague. Arent van's-Gravesande was, along with Pieter Post and Philips Vingboons, a leading exponent of the Dutch classical style in which the Mauritshuis had been built. Examples of van's-Gravesande's work are scarce, however. His earliest documented building is St. Sebastiaansdoelen, which he began in 1636. Here everything that van Campen used so successfully in the Mauritshuis is repeated with equal elegance. Its façade looks toward the Hofvijver, in which are reflected three other important buildings of the period: the Mauritshuis, the Treveszaal, and the tower of the prime minister's office. This building was the headquarters of the society of St. Sebastiaan, one of two societies of archers entrusted since the fifteenth century with keeping public order in The Hague. The other soci-

Arent van's-Gravesande's 1636 St. Sebastiaansdoelen (left), which fronts on the Hofvijver, is, with the nearby Mauritshuis, one of the finest examples of the Dutch classical style. As a rule the Dutch adapted neo-classical architecture to their own restrained taste, but by the end of the seventeenth century they had begun to adopt the more ornate French styles for their public buildings. These were executed with a newfound taste for rich, opulent decoration, as can be seen in the Treveszaal (right), which Daniel Marot remodeled and redecorated in 1696 in the Louis XIV style. Marot was the chief proponent of this new style, and through his numerous public and private commissions he left The Hague a magnificent and durable legacy.

ety, St. Joris (or, more often, St. George), lost its military character toward the end of the sixteenth century, but the archers of St. Sebastiaan continued to act as civil guards, using firearms instead of bows. By the seventeenth century the membership had grown large enough to require a new building where they could meet and practice target-shooting—*doelen* means "targets." The society was disbanded during the French occupation and the building reverted to the municipality. It was used for some time as the local museum of history, a function now performed by the Haags Gemeentemuseum. St. George's guild is remembered today by the St. George's Tower in the Toornooiveld.

By 1700 the truly indigenous Dutch classicism began to give way to styles imported from Louis XIV's France, and it is to the Frenchman Daniel Marot and his sons that The Hague owes some of its most splendid eighteenth-century architecture. Marot, a Huguenot, fled north after the revocation of the Edict of Nantes in 1685 and almost immediately began to work for William III as an interior architect in both England and The Hague. His talents were universal: he designed furniture, porcelain, tiles, and fabrics; he planned gardens, monuments, and palaces; he even designed ballet sets and costumes; and he planned and supervised every interior detail of every building he built. In 1727 his designs were collected in the *Grand Marot*, a much-used encyclopedia of design styles and motifs.

Since 1588 the Estates-General had met in the Keizerhof, a series of apartments along the Hofvijver that had been built in medieval times and had once served as the residence of Emperor Charles V. In 1696 Marot was commissioned to make of these apartments one large assembly hall for the Estates and a smaller but equally impressive reception hall. Marot had the ceiling of the assembly chamber divided into squares whose overmantels were decorated with the symbolic figures of Prudence and Steadfastness. The reception hall, or Treveszaal—so named for the twelve-year *trèves*, or truce, of 1609, whose terms were negotiated in one of the apartments—is one of the best examples of the Louis XIV style outside France. It is an impressive room, measuring some 55 feet long and 25 feet wide, whose nine great windows look out over the Hofvijver. Beautifully carved white columns divide the walls, on which J. H. Brandon painted life-size portraits of the first five *stadtholders*. Above the cornices twelve caryatids sculpted in wood by Johan Bloommendael hold up Theodore van der Schuer's painted ceiling, which depicts in apotheosis the unity of the seven provinces, *Concordia res parvae crescunt*, "Union is Strength." This richly—one might almost say excessively—decorated chamber was where the republic's leaders received foreign ambassadors. Its opulence was itself an act of state.

As an architect of public buildings, Marot also designed the new wing of the Oude Raadhuis, or Old Town Hall, a building that now houses the Ministry of Foreign Affairs, the lateral wings of Huis ten Bosch, and the Portuguese-Jewish synagogue. The synagogue was begun in 1724 and completed in 1726, when the Great Bailiff of The Hague and other magistrates were present at its inauguration. It

In the seventeenth century The Hague produced a dozen painters of genius; in the eighteenth it produced one universal man—Daniel Marot. A Huguenot by birth but a Haguenaar by virtue of his longtime residence in the Dutch capital, Marot designed many of The Hague's most splendid mansions. He also designed the furniture, the fabrics, and the tiles used to decorate those houses—and the gardens and parks in which they stood. In 1727 his various designs were assembled in an encyclopedia known simply as the **Grand Marot**. It includes this small engraving of the vegetable market that was held each morning in front of the chapel of St. Nicolas Hospital.

is a small building, but its proportions are nonetheless striking. The nave, some 70 feet high and 45 feet long, has wooden balustrades at either side to accommodate women, who were not then permitted to worship with the men.

That this building could have been erected at all and that it was designed by so renowned a figure as Marot and placed in so elegant a district—at the Princessegracht and Jan Everstraat—testifies both to the toleration practiced by the Netherlands in the eighteenth century and to the power and influence the Portuguese-Jewish community must have wielded at the time. Jews, like Catholics, were permitted to build houses of worship in the eighteenth century, but those structures could not be visible from the street. This remarkable building is therefore hidden in a tree-lined garden behind a building that serves as the congregation offices.

The Portuguese-Jewish community in The Hague survived in large numbers until the German occupation in 1940, when most of its members were deported; very few returned from the death camps. The building itself was spared, as were most buildings designated as landmarks, and in 1972 contributions by the Ministry of Culture, The Hague municipality, and the provincial authority of Holland restored the building to its small congregation. On September 3, 1976, in the presence of Queen Juliana, the renovated building was inaugurated.

Shortly before the Portuguese-Jewish community applied for permission to build a synagogue, another "hidden" house of worship was completed in The Hague. The Old Catholic Church of Saints James and Augustine was not designed by Marot but certainly by someone deeply influenced by him. Records indicate that the design, inspired by the chapel at Versailles, was executed by Hendrick Kruijsselbergen. The stucco ceiling is Louis XIV in style; in its center is a representation of Christ ascending and surrounded by cherubs; columns with richly ornamented capitals support the vault. Above the altarpiece, designed by Mattheus Terwesten in 1734, is a tall retable that is itself crowned by the figure of Christ in judgment.

Even more impressive than his public structures are Marot's townhouses, some of which are frequently attributed to his sons but all of which bear his mark and were undoubtedly closely supervised by Marot himself. The exterior of the Hotel Schuylenburch, at number 8 Lange Vijverberg, was designed entirely by Marot and still reflects some of the restraint of the late seventeenth century. The interior—the work of several hands including Marot's—abandons all restraint, however, and is surely one of the finest and most spectacular eighteenth-century interiors to be found in the Netherlands. The house is actually two houses—or one and a half, to be precise—combined in 1715 for Cornelis van Schuylenburch, son of Willem van Schuylenburch, a confidant of the *stadtholder* William III. Plain channeled rustication balances the vertical lines of the façade, and raised strips that act as pilasters at either end echo the three projecting central bays. A dark blue and gold wrought-iron balcony hints at the increasingly free and elegant style that was replacing the more restrained and static Louis XIV style at the

time. Combed sandstone, beautifully carved and textured, blends easily with the new decorative exterior details.

Although some elements in the interior—either documented or simply obvious—are surely by Marot, the most striking aspect of the house, its plasterwork, is by Giovanni-Battista Luraghi. He had worked with Marot on the palace at Het Loo and become a citizen of The Hague in 1710. One can only describe his plasterwork at Hotel Schuylenburch as exuberant. Its wealth of ornamentation is far from Marot's baroque style, rather resembling Italianate and mannerist taste. The *piano nobile*, usually reserved in Dutch architecture only for palaces, is reached by a grand staircase of waxed oak with a blue-green and gold balustrade. The dark wood—painted over during the Napoleonic period when a tax was levied on untreated wood—beautifully sets off the brilliant white plasterwork of this two-story room, where swirling acanthus scrolls, winged sphinxes, and large shells contribute to a breathtaking display. Luraghi also created a plasterwork ceiling for the drawing room: a shallow trompe l'oeil dome in the center, allegorical bas-relief figures at each end, putti, and emblems of the four seasons.

Many artists are responsible for the mural and ceiling paintings of the Hotel Schuylenburch, most notably Jacob de Wit, whose Jupiter and Diana in the Green Room is surely the finest ceiling in the house and one of de Wit's best works. Philip van Dijck, Mattheus Terwesten, Abrahan Bisschop, Jan van Gool, Caspar Peter Verbruggen, and Giovanni Paolo Pannini are also represented in the house.

In 1888 the German foreign office bought the Hotel Schuylenburch for its embassy in The Hague. It was confiscated after the liberation in 1945 and returned to the Federal Republic of Germany in 1960. The building was completely—and, one must say, excellently—restored between 1964 and 1968 under the supervision of E. A. C. Canneman.

The Hotel van Wassenaar-Obdam is some twenty years later than the Hotel Schuylenburch, and here one can see Marot as the mature French ornamentalist; but it is the Hotel Huguetan, later used as the Royal Library, that shows Marot and the French decorative style at its best. It was built in 1734 for Adrienne Marguerite Huguetan, the widow of Hendrik Carel, count of Nassau-La Lecq. As in the Hotel Schuylenburch, the façade is sandstone, but here the ornamentation is far richer and livelier. The portal is topped by an arch in which Marot placed a large window—a new motif in buildings of this style. Above the cornice two baroque figures by the Antwerp sculptor Jan Pieter van Baurscheit—to whom, in fact, some scholars attribute the entire façade—hold the family coat-of-arms. Pieter de Swart added the somewhat heavier and less decorative wings about thirty years later.

De Swart replaced Marot as the principal architect of The Hague during the later half of the eighteenth century, and, like his predecessor, he built chiefly for well-to-do private clients. Many of the elegant homes along the Lange Vijverberg and the Voorhout are by de Swart. His finest surviving building, which now houses the Royal Theater, was originally the Nassau-Weilburg palace.

William the Silent had been content with a few apartments set aside for him on the Buitenhof. His successor, Maurice, erected a square tower at the corner of the Buitenhof and the Hofvijver to serve as his chief residence. Each successive *stadtholder* required larger and grander quarters, until by the middle of the eighteenth century the *stadtholder*'s quarters were regal indeed. William II built the princess royal's apartments, which now serve as the chambers of the Council of State, and in 1777 William V employed the German architect F. L. Gunkel to add a new wing to the complex.

Gerard de Lairesse was born in Liège, where he learned to admire French and Italian classical painting. When he moved to Amsterdam in 1665, however, he fell under the spell of Rembrandt's mature style for a short time and, in fact, had his portrait painted by the aging painter. De Lairesse later recanted this apparent lapse in taste and returned to modeling his own work after the strict precepts of seventeenth-century French classicism. The paintings de Lairesse made at The Hague—chiefly for William III—are telling examples of how well these principles served at the end of the seventeenth century. His most famous works, and probably his best, are the allegorical scenes of Roman history completed for the *stadtholder* at the Binnenhof, in the former Council Chamber of the Court of Holland.

By the end of the seventeenth century the energy and creativity that characterized Dutch art of the period seem to have virtually disappeared, and we really have no better explanation for its death than we do for its birth. Holland was still prosperous, although its economic foundations were now perhaps a bit shakier; she was still a world power, although far more isolationist than she had been; and she was still a land dominated by bourgeois life and bourgeois taste—despite the styles adopted by her aristocratic leaders. Whatever may have happened, we find in eighteenth-century easel painting some strong and some weak imitators of the painters of Leiden and Delft but little that is really new or brilliant.

In Cornelis Troost, who painted throughout the first half of the eighteenth century, we find not only the most interesting of the new generation of painters but also one who still reflects the themes characteristic of past masters. Troost painted many formal portraits, but he is best known for the sort of group portrait known as the "conversation piece" since it depicts its subjects in a social setting. He worked in oil and also in pastels, then a popular medium throughout Europe, and his pastel-and-gouache series from 1740 at the Mauritshuis is surely one of his best: five views of a group of men well in their cups. Troost's humorous portrayals earned him the sobriquet "the Dutch Hogarth," but he does not criticize and he seems to take as much joy in portraying pleasure as did such earlier painters of the good life as van Mieris and Steen. In his formal portraits, too, we see the older tradition of familiar settings and family life still very much alive. His subjects are seen surrounded by the things that define them as accurately as do their features, and they are engaged in the activities they must have most enjoyed, for they take such self-evident pleasure in doing them.

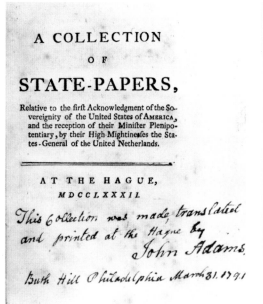

A COLLECTION
OF
STATE-PAPERS,

Relative to the firſt Acknowledgment of the So-
vereignity of the United States of AMERICA,
and the reception of their Miniſter Plenipotentiary, by their High Mightineſſes the Sta-
tes-General of the United Netherlands.

AT THE HAGUE,
MDCCLXXXII.

*This Collection was made, translated
and printed at the Hague by*
John Adams.

Bush Hill Philadelphia March 31. 1791

JOHN ADAMS, Schildknaap,
Minister Plenipotentiaris der
XIII Vereenigde Staaten van
Noord-Amerika, bij de Republijk
der VII Vereenigde Nederlanden.

On the far left, the documents ratifying Dutch recognition of the United States, which John Adams secured. Adams's portrait, drawn from life, appears at near left as engraved by an unknown Amsterdam engraver in 1782. At right is a view of the Fluwelen Burgwal from an 1830 engraving. Along this canal was situated the Hôtel des Etats-Unis, the first American legation building. Adams spent some two years in The Hague negotiating the loans and recognition vital to his nation's survival. Recognition was granted on April 19, 1782, and relations between the two nations have remained cordial and unbroken for the ensuing two hundred years.

After the death of William III the Dutch republic entered another period during which no *stadtholder* was appointed to give unity to the seven provinces. Foreign intrigues and wars had placed an enormous burden on the Dutch economy, and both the wealthy merchants and the lower classes were well content with a policy that would entail no new taxes. As the nation retreated from the theater of European politics, it also entered a period of slow but perceptible decline. The malaise evident in the Netherlands' cultural life was even more starkly apparent in economic affairs.

The volume of trade remained fairly stable throughout the eighteenth century, as did the population, but industry itself contracted. Meanwhile, England and France were developing far more efficient economies and were successfully acquiring colonies in North and South America, Africa, and Asia. High tariffs kept the Dutch from exploiting the English and French markets, and the fear of war prevented them from seeking outlets or new materials in the as-yet-uncolonized parts of Asia and the New World. The European population explosion that had so profited Dutch merchants a century before had eased by the end of the seventeenth century, and most European nations again found themselves agriculturally self-sufficient.

To the common people, the House of Orange had always appeared the savior—a bulwark against the Inquisition, foreign invaders, and their own oligarchs. As conditions worsened and as resentment grew against the wealthy burghers and local nobility who now wielded all the power in the provinces, the populace began to demand a new *stadtholder*. Then, in 1747, the War of the Austrian Succession broke out. The Netherlands, which supported Austria, was again invaded by the French, and the Estates were forced, as they had been in 1672, to fill the office left vacant since William III's death. They turned to the hereditary *stadtholder* of Friesland, who came from a collateral branch of the House of Orange (the main line having died out with William III, who had no male heir). The new *stadtholder*, William IV, insisted that with his appointment the office be declared hereditary and that he be given royal power. This he was granted, but he died only four years later and so never really had an opportunity to achieve what he most desired—to curb the power of the oligarchs. His son, William V, was only three years old when his father died, and the regency was assumed first by his mother and then by the duke of Brunswick, neither of whom pursued an aggressive domestic policy.

Events in North America now forced the Dutch again to confront their traditional rival, the English. Ever since New Amsterdam had been ceded to Great Britain in the Treaty of Breda, England had held a monopoly on trade with her own rapidly expanding colonies. When the Americans declared their independence from Great Britain in 1776, the Dutch saw a new opportunity to trade with North America, although political leaders in the Netherlands were sorely divided on the question of aid to the rebellious colonies. The prince of Orange and his backers were loyal to England, to whose royal house the Oranges were related. The Estates gener-

ally favored noninvolvement and neutrality—a realistic policy given the vastly superior English navy. But the Amsterdam bankers were anxious for the lucrative American trade and felt that if they did not aid the Americans now, England might grant independence to the colonies in return for their pledge to preserve the English trade monopoly. They therefore began negotiations in secret with representatives of the American Continental Congress regarding loans and a treaty of amity and commerce.

Dutch popular sympathy for the American cause was made clear when John Paul Jones sailed into the harbor at Texel in October 1779 on the *Serapis*, the English ship he had captured along with another, *The Comtesse de Scarborough*. He was greeted with wild enthusiasm, and despite urgings from the English ambassador at The Hague, the Estates did nothing either to arrest or deport him.

By the summer of 1780 the draft treaty had been examined by the American Congress, which dispatched Henry Laurens to the Netherlands to finalize the document, negotiate the loans, and obtain official recognition for the new nation. The British captured Laurens' ship, however, and discovered in a bag he had vainly cast into the sea the draft treaty and his letters of credence addressed to the Estates-General. This, along with the Dutch reception of John Paul Jones and the illegal Amsterdam–Antilles–American trade being conducted through the Dutch West Indies island of St. Eustatius, provoked England to declare war, claiming the Netherlands had violated its own professed neutrality. St. Eustatius was overrun and destroyed, and Dutch ships

and settlements throughout the East and West Indies were attacked. It was a costly war for the republic, and the prince of Orange, sensing the popular enthusiasm for the American cause and appreciating the even greater concern of Amsterdam's bankers, publicly disavowed his support for the English.

In 1780 John Adams arrived from Paris to conclude Laurens' work—while Laurens himself languished in the Tower of London. Adams argued in public and negotiated in private for two years, and by 1782 he was confident enough of the outcome to purchase a house near The Hague to serve as the official residence of the American minister. On April 19, 1782, the Estates-General accepted Adams' credentials as American envoy to the Netherlands and he was received by William V at Huis ten Bosch. Thus began the longest unbroken diplomatic relations between the States and a European power.

By October the treaty of amity and commerce, based on the notorious "Amsterdam draft," was signed at The Hague. In January 1783 the Continental Congress agreed to its terms as well as terms for loans amounting to some 12 million dollars. In June the Estates dispatched Pieter Johan van Berckel to the United States. Because conditions were unstable in Philadelphia—American troops were near mutiny—Congress was meeting in Princeton, New Jersey, at Nassau Hall, named for the late king of England and Netherlands *stadtholder* William III. It was there that van Berckel presented his credentials on October 31, 1783, as the first envoy of the United Provinces of the Netherlands to the United States of America.

V

Realists and Romantics

The latter half of the nineteenth century witnessed a phenomenon that has deeply affected the way people of our age view the plastic arts: the building of great national and municipal museums. To be sure, great painting and sculpture collections had been formed well before this time, usually by princely families, and these collections had frequently ended up as part of the national patrimony, either through confiscation—as in revolutionary France, for example—or by donation, as in the case with the Mauritshuis collection in The Hague. These collections were housed, quite naturally, in disused palaces, where they were displayed as a tribute to the national past, the royal donors, or the modern state. In cases where collections and the palaces to house them were unavailable—as, for example, in the United States—private donors and public money combined to form new collections and to build edifices deemed worthy of them. The great museums that arose during this period were palatial: a grandeur imitative of the Grecian, Gothic, or Renaissance past guided their design, and monumentality is evident in their execution. Thus Cuypers designed in the Dutch brick Renaissance style Amsterdam's Rijksmuseum between 1877 and 1885, and similar buildings arose in London, New York, and other great metropoles.

Most public buildings of the late nineteenth century are monumental—neoclassical and neo-Gothic tastes and the aesthetic of the Ecole des Beaux Arts all dictated grandeur. In the case of museums the result of all this monumental building was to set art, and especially the art of earlier and therefore hallowed ages, apart from daily experience and to encourage the idea that its viewing was an act of homage best conducted in awesome surroundings. As many spectators began to notice, however, these buildings not only awed but also exhausted their visitors—and made them feel that art was a princely pursuit inappropriate to those whose feet were unused to marble floors. As early as the last quarter of the nineteenth century, when museum building was at its peak, men like Albert Lichtwark, director of Hamburg's Kunsthalle, were beginning to criticize contemporary ideas of museum design and function and were asking for a more comfortable and accessible sort of building.

It was in this atmosphere that Dr. H. E. van Gelden, municipal archivist of The Hague, decided that the city should house in one building the old master paintings then hung at the Mauritshuis, objects and paintings of historical significance, modern paintings, and decorative objects. This was in 1906. At the time van Gelden's idea was a revolutionary one, and it took some time to mature. It was not until 1919 that the search for a site began and an architect was chosen to execute preliminary plans.

Hendrik Petrus Berlage, now considered the "father of modern Dutch architecture," was the likely choice. Born in Amsterdam and educated at the Polytechnic in Zurich, he had begun his career designing buildings in the largely imitative styles Cuypers had popularized. But by 1895, in his De Nederlander office building and Villa Henny in The Hague, Berlage had announced his break with the past. He disregarded symmetry and opened up his

The crest of Rijswijk, once farm land and now part of The Hague.

façades to show the interior of his buildings, and he reduced to a minimum applied exterior decoration. His most important building, the Amsterdam Stock Exchange, begun in 1897, had demonstrated that even while using period forms it was possible to be imaginative and expressive.

In 1920 Berlage, who was familiar with Lichtwark's theories of museum design, submitted his first plans. The building he offered was large and ambitious, and it was obviously guided by the new aesthetic that saw the plastic arts as simply one among many of humanity's expressive urges. The building was, in fact, not only a museum but a cultural center as well, with concert halls, meeting rooms, and galleries all coexisting in one structure. Berlage's plans were debated for four years—and finally shelved when no one could agree to the cost or the concept.

Planning was taken up again in 1927, and Berlage was asked to submit plans that would include only a museum of modern and decorative arts with expandable exhibition space, a print room, and an auditorium. By February 1928 his overall plan was approved. The definitive design was agreed to in December 1929, and contracts were signed. Construction began in 1931, but the building was completed only after Berlage's death in 1934. The Haags Gemeentemuseum, or Hague Municipal Museum, was opened to the public in May 1935.

The design, considerably altered from Berlage's original plans, is nearly square, with a central courtyard and separate wings for lecture halls and offices. With the scale of the building itself reduced, there was more space for parks, which surround the structure. The main entrance is reached by a covered, open-sided corridor between two pools. The exterior offers a striking display of planes but little decorative excitement. The interior, however, offers all the color and line absent from the exterior, and it demonstrates, as few other museums before or since, a perfect integration of monumentality and intimacy.

A rather dark and low entrance and vestibule give way to the high, light central hall, which links the administrative center to the museum. Its large space permits the display of objects and introduces visitors to the museum atmosphere. It is also designed for large receptions, and for that function Berlage employed tall columns, unencumbered side walls, and lighting from high on the ceiling—all of which give a sense of spaciousness and grandeur. There is actually far less space than one imagines there is, but Berlage was able to articulate the hall, staircase, and reception room—each at different heights and with different functions—into one unified design in which the play of primary colors prevents any sense of solemnity.

It is in Berlage's design of the galleries that one sees best the new concept of museum comfort and accessibility. Upstairs, corridors of rooms and galleries, each of different size, are arranged around three sides of the courtyard. At each corner a large staircase provides easy circulation. The low ceilings and absence of long perspectives maintain a human scale and also prevent "museum fatigue," an ailment endemic among tourists.

One of the most remarkable buildings erected in The Hague in this century is the Haags Gemeentemuseum, designed by Hendrik Petrus Berlage and opened in 1935. The play of lines and colors in the interior (near right) provides not only interesting perspectives but also a far less solemn ambiance than that encountered in more traditional nineteenth- and early twentieth-century museum buildings. The exterior (far right and below), although far less colorful, maintains the human scale that was obviously Berlage's chief design concern. The Gemeentemuseum serves as a repository of nineteenth- and twentieth-century Dutch art and as The Hague's historical museum. It also houses collections of porcelain, silver, and musical instruments.

The building was greeted at first by puzzled dismay. The plan, although really far simpler than that of most museums, with their warren of rooms and seemingly endless hallways, was unorthodox and, therefore, perplexing. The varied architectural forms and the bright colors were disturbing to visitors used to the stately elegance of most museums. It was not long, however, before most people—casual visitors and design critics alike—developed a fondness for this somewhat eccentric but appealing and comfortable structure, which has since been gifted with superb and varied collections of paintings, prints, objets d'art, furniture, musical instruments, and historical documentation.

It was natural that The Hague would feel the need for a new museum, since by the middle of the nineteenth century it had become one of Europe's most important artistic centers. The Pulchri Studio, founded in 1847; the Dutch Drawing Academy, founded in 1876; the established art academy that had been operating for years—all were magnets for artists in the Netherlands, who found in The Hague important teachers and sympathetic patrons. The Hague could not rival Paris, of course, but by the last quarter of the nineteenth century it had become the home of a school of painters who drew upon foreign sources like the Barbizon in France and the Norwich School in England—which themselves looked to the Dutch seventeenth century for inspiration—and, most importantly, upon their own native landscape tradition to create a new and wholly Dutch art. The Hague School artists responded to the new sensibility of the nineteenth century and

created an important body of work that heralded the modern age and paved the way for a Dutch contribution to the twentieth century at least as influential as the one made in the seventeenth.

There is perhaps nothing more characteristic of Dutch art of the Golden Age than its attention to the real details of landscape, interiors, and human faces. This is the heritage the Golden Age left to Dutch and foreign painters of ensuing centuries, and it is the tradition that every Dutch painter had to confront. Observation—and the "realism" that resulted from it, of course—meant something different in the seventeenth century than it would mean two hundred years later. In the seventeenth century painters were still working within a tradition in which the moral value of observed reality was crucial to the painter and to the spectator; both shared the same set of moral principles, after all, and both shared the symbolic references by which moral values could be communicated. When Jan Steen painted his *Theater of the World*, for example, it was as important for him to comment on the scene as it was for him to paint the details one might encounter in any Dutch tavern. His boy blowing bubbles in the corner of the picture—and the death's head nearby—allowed Steen's spectators to share his moral comment on the scene.

In 1860 Gerard Bilders formulated an aesthetic goal that has been taken to characterize the Hague School generally: "I'm looking for a tone we call 'colored gray,' that is, all colors, however strong, so united as to give the impression of a fragrant, warm gray." The fame of this statement, and its frequent

aptness in describing many Hague School pictures, led to the widespread criticism that these painters abandoned color for a hazy gray and subordinated form and detail to a misty vagueness. This criticism was wrong on three counts. First, of course, Bilders insisted his gray is a *colored* gray, and even in his works or those of others in which gray is the primary tone, color is not only present but vital. Second, the statement reveals something far more important than a color preference—or the preference for an absence of color. It reveals that the painters of the Hague School were seeking the color *impression* of nature—not the moral lesson it could reveal or be made to symbolize, and not the pastoral stories that could be told in its precincts.

In turning to the great subject of the seventeenth century, the landscape, the Hague School artists were seeking to re-create it with eyes sensitive to its optical effects. This was not precisely an objective or scientific pursuit, but it was surely influenced by the scientific and unmetaphysical outlook of the century. In France the Impressionists were seeking much the same thing. Unblessed by the iridescent light of the south, Hague School painters would produce far less luminous pictures, but they would nonetheless use light as their subject. Finally, in seeking to unite colors so as to give an "impression," Bilders makes clear that precision and multiplicity of detail—vital to the seventeenth century—will be subordinated to the requirements of a unified picture whose harmony will depend less on formally correct and symmetrical composition than on the effect of one single *color* impression.

Bilders himself was actually only slightly involved with the Hague School, and his writings influenced members of the school far more than did his canvases. The simplicity and calmness of his compositions, though, are indeed characteristic of the movement. In his overriding concern with the effects of tone and color, his work reflects the aim of both Dutch and French art of the midcentury.

Anton Mauve rather unfortunately became known as the painter of sheep, largely because his later work, produced to satisfy domestic and foreign demand, concentrated on this highly popular theme. A delicate and lyrical painter, he rendered his animals with a remarkable individuality. His nephew, Vincent van Gogh, remarked in his letters how struck he was by Mauve's ability to depict the suffering of animals—a paradigm, perhaps, for the suffering van Gogh himself so desperately wanted to portray, his own and that of the peasants he frequently depicted.

Jacob Maris, perhaps more than any other Hague School painter, typified the aesthetic aims formulated by Bilders. Maris himself was enormously popular, although his renown came late in his life. His subjects were the traditional stuff of Dutch landscape: townscapes, windmills, and beach scenes. His handling, as Bilders prescribed, aimed at creating a unified picture, with colors and forms harmonized by a predominant gray tonality, for which he frequently chose heavy, rainy skies.

Jacob's brother, Willem, also typified the foremost concern of the Hague School—the interpretation of light. Like Mauve, he frequently painted animals, although his preference was for ducks and

other small creatures. Unlike his brother, Willem painted in bright, full colors, with the sun shining as brilliantly as it does in French pictures of the same period. His landscapes are often idyllic, even lyric, and they are painted with a delicacy that accentuates their fragility and their transience. In his pictures we are always conscious that this splendid moment is only a moment—and, moreover, an inessential moment, painted for its beauty alone.

Matthijs Maris, the brother of Willem and Jacob, is the least like any other Hague School painter and is certainly unlike his two brothers. Painting in a fragile, delicate style, like Willem, he treated subjects that are almost always pure fantasy: fairy-tale subjects; remembered scenes of distant cities; and, later in his life, dream images in which cloudy grays all but obscure the forms. It is perhaps in this painter that we best see the new freedom of the nineteenth century, when painting was finally relieved of the task of representing anything or, at least, of representing things of a recognized significance. As Matthijs himself once wrote, "My paintings are the incomplete expression of my thoughts . . . they are a part of my soul and I alone understand them . . ." So hermetic a pursuit was something entirely new in art, and it led to an increasingly nonrepresentational sort of painting—until, by the turn of the century, recognizable form disappeared entirely.

Willem Roelofs was born in 1822 in Amsterdam, and at the age of eighteen he moved to The Hague to study under the landscape and animal painter Hendrikus van de Sande Bakhuzzen. Roelofs' landscapes are filled with innumerable, closely observed details—the hallmark of traditional Dutch art. But in rendering these scenes, he makes a bold and significant departure from the art of the past: his landscapes are almost always captured at a dramatic moment, one that simultaneously particularizes them in a way no seventeenth-century artist would have done and that renders them affecting, moving.

Jan Hendrik Weissenbruch, now considered by many one of the greatest of the Hague School painters, was born in that city in 1824 and remained there all his life. His special love was for that silvery sky so peculiar to Holland, which he painted with large, broad strokes, usually in beach scenes made at Scheveningen, Nieuwtroop, and Noorden. He captured, in a way other Hague School painters usually could not, the brighter blues that shine through a wet, gray sky; and in the way the light touches the sea or beach—or, in his town paintings, a piece of wall or pavement—he found even brighter colors, made luminous by the sun. Weissenbruch's compositions are far less dramatic than Roelofs'—indeed, he seems to borrow from Vermeer a simplicity of form and a quietude achieved by harmonizing every color—but like Roelofs and all his contemporaries, his special attention to the peculiarities of atmospheric conditions particularizes his pictures.

Weissenbruch's *Souvenir de Haarlem* is reminiscent of Vermeer in its stillness and the perfect harmony of its color. The streaky, silvery sky is the focus of attention. It looms above a low horizon line to which the waterway, itself reflecting the sky, and the cobbled roadway beside it point, as do the ships' masts. There are many details, but all of them are blended,

The literary impulse in Hague School painting, inherited from Dutch and foreign Romanticism, is typified by Jozef Israel's When We Grow Old, below. Israels is not telling an especially elaborate story here, nor is he necessarily preaching. Yet he is concerned as much with the portrayal of the harshness of peasant life and the sturdy character it bred as he is with the more painterly tasks of tone and composition. The pooling light that illuminates the old lady's hand and the carefully worked shadows that delineate her mean surroundings recall Rembrandt, to whom Israels was often compared by his contemporaries and from whom he clearly derived considerable inspiration.

OVERLEAF: *Jan Weissenbruch's view of the Prinsegracht is far different in both mood and technique than other paintings of the Hague School. Weissenbruch's clarity and precision remind us of the great architectural painters Saenredam and Houckgeest, and his clear and brilliantly blue sky creates an atmosphere in striking contrast to the heavy grays favored by his contemporaries. Although the mood is as quiet and cheerful as any street scene by Pieter de Hooch or Saenredam, the composition is far more dramatic: a triangle of sky above is echoed by the near triangle of the road below, and both meet at the stark, black, triangular sails situated dead center in the picture.*

partly by the translucent mist, and partly by their being dominated by so large and colorful a sky.

The simplicity of Weissenbruch's composition is echoed in the paintings of Paul Joseph Constantin Gabriel, the so-called "portraitist of the polder." Like both Weissenbruch and Roelofs, Gabriel approached painting objectively. The misty, rather bleak polder landscapes are painted precisely for their atmospheric and compositional value: there is nothing sentimental, nothing hazy or obscure in these sober, precise renderings. Some have compared his objectivity to Meindert Hobbema's, and surely there is much in Gabriel of the seventeenth-century exactness of detail and orderliness of composition. But there is an immediacy in Gabriel's work that makes him much more a painter of his time and his school, a concern that the landscape be captured in somewhat the same way a photographer might casually portray it, cropping the composition so that, whatever its internal symmetry, a part of it is left out, left for the spectator to complete.

Roelofs, Weissenbruch, and Gabriel inherited from the seventeenth century a dedication to the precise rendering of landscape. Their concerns were obviously somewhat different in that they turned from a style of painting that encouraged contemplation of the ideal and eternal through formal composition to a style that attempted to capture the momentary and encourage a sense of participation. Theirs was a precision in recording atmospheric effects rather than topographical details, and they employed a far wider range of color to achieve it. Still, we have no trouble seeing these painters as the

heirs of Ruisdael, Hobbema, and van Goyen. Other painters of the Hague School, however, broke more completely with their past, and their work, perhaps less interesting to us than the work of their contemporaries in the Netherlands and abroad, is surely closer to the new aesthetic.

Hendrik Willem Mesdag was born in Groningen in 1831, but he did not begin painting until 1866; up to then he was a successful member of his father's banking firm. In 1870 Mesdag won the Gold Medal at the Paris Salon for his *Brisants de la mer*, and he soon became one of the best-known painters of his generation and the spokesman for the Hague School, which he helped to organize and promote. In 1869 he settled in The Hague in order to be close to Scheveningen, where each day in a studio near the beach or on the beach itself he recorded the changing colors of the sky and water.

Like Weissenbruch, Johannes Bosboom was born and always lived in The Hague, and he, too, studied with Bart van Hove. His early work consists of church interiors and views of The Hague, Amsterdam, Nijmegen, Coblenz, and Rouen. Later he concentrated on the church interiors for which he is most famous.

The importance of such personal vision is probably nowhere more evident than in the paintings of Jozef Israels, who was the acknowledged leader of the Hague School and its most extravagantly praised member. He was born in Groningen in 1824 to a devout Jewish family.

In 1871 he moved to The Hague, where some six years later he painted *When We Grow Old*, a canvas that sums up not only Israels' own techniques but the midcentury sensibility as well. As in most of his pictures of peasants, the old lady here is shown not at work but rather lost in thought beside her fire. This contemplative stillness characterizes Israels' work and is, in fact, the chief characteristic of Dutch Romanticism generally.

Israels' contemporaries compared him to Rembrandt, and while it is impossible now to be that generous it is surely true that he shares with the seventeenth-century master a sympathetic depiction of humanity. He also shares the use of a faint, golden light, one that allowed Rembrandt, as it does Israels, the opportunity to model with shadow and to harmonize his subjects with their surroundings.

To the nineteenth century it was not only fitting to reveal oneself in art, it was, in fact, the very point of artistic creation. The painters of the Hague School were able to build upon the established tradition of Dutch painting and perform this self-revealing task even while making pictures that undeniably reflect the heritage of the Golden Age. Their work would be continued in an art that we call "expressionist," art in which a more radical break with the past was necessary to achieve self-expression, even at the cost of distorting the "reality" painters always claimed to reproduce.

Vincent van Gogh was a great admirer of the Hague School artists, especially Jozef Israels and Anton Mauve. He saw in Israels a man who, like himself, was sympathetic to and deeply moved by the life of the rural poor and who had succeeded in rendering their life and his vision of that life on

canvas. Van Gogh had wanted to become a clergyman, but when he found he did not have a scholar's interest in theology, he tried to minister to the practical needs of the miners in the Borinage in Belgium. They ridiculed him and forced him to leave. It was then that van Gogh decided to paint, hoping that through art he could contribute to helping the distressed. For a while he lived with Mauve in The Hague, where he made some of his first drawings.

As van Gogh's work matured—and his mental state, never very stable, worsened—his attention turned from peasant life to the countryside itself, which, at Arles in the south of France, he found ablaze with color. In a brilliant series of canvases, all painted in the years 1880 to 1890, he used bright, strong color and bold outline to reproduce his distraught state of mind through art. In the Gemeentemuseum's *Garden at Arles*, for example, we are struck as we rarely are in early painting primarily by the technique. That is, the frenzied brushwork is itself the subject—far more than the flowers and trees—and, consciously or otherwise, we are disturbed by the manner of the painting and thus led directly to the emotionally disturbed painter himself. Even the composition—a narrow path leading from the bottom edge of the picture off to the left edge and a wall at the right edge following the same diagonal—disorients the viewer. Here is an art that breaks irrevocably with its past: the landscape—once revered and reproduced to show the creator's presence; then painted to reveal its own optical wonders; then painted to communicate a vision—is now painted as a symbol for a state of mind. In van Gogh

nature is still clearly present—even if a bit vertiginous—but by the turn of the century, it will have disappeared from art almost entirely.

Piet Mondrian (or Mondriaan, as his family spelled it) was born in 1872 in Amersfoort, where his father was headmaster of a primary school. His family had lived in The Hague for generations; his grandfather had a wig and hairdressing salon on the Lange Poten, and his uncle Frits was a minor painter associated with the Hague School. His uncle gave Piet his first drawing lessons, and later, when he had to earn money to support himself as an artist, Piet copied on tiles well-known Hague School pictures. Thus this painter, whom we know today chiefly through his purely abstract grid pictures such as the famous *Broadway Boogie Woogie* in New York, began his career drawing in the traditional and by then accepted landscape style. Only later, when he was close to forty, did he find the style that was to have such a profound influence on twentieth-century art.

Through the bequest of S. B. Slijpen, a friend of the painter, the Haags Gemeentemuseum contains the largest collection of Mondrians in the world, and it is especially fortunate in having received many of Mondrian's early landscapes as well as his later abstractions. In the early pictures, such as *Summer's Night*, painted in 1907, we see the still-living tradition of Dutch landscape art, here heavily laden with the moody stillness that characterized its Romantic phase. This is achieved by the tonality—predominantly gray, green, and brown—but it is also due to its simplicity: there are no figures and almost no details, and the few elements in the composition—

Vincent van Gogh's Garden at Arles *was made in the south of France, where the painter found the brilliant, sunbathed landscape in which many of his best-known works were produced. Here colors gleam and compete in riotous profusions of flowers and trees that seems a world removed from the steel-gray skies and monochromatic polders of the north. The artist's own exuberant reaction to this landscape is clearly evident in this work, but obvious, too, is that frenzied brushwork and vertiginous composition that marks a mind that has found no peace. A brilliant painting, it is, at the same time, a deeply disturbing one.*

the trees and the buildings, land and water—are all blended and obscured by the prevailing haze. Indeed, what we are left with is really less a landscape than simply a structure: the horizontals of the land and water and the verticals of the trees. Even in pictures where bolder colors and longer, thicker brushstrokes give a more agitated feel to the work—in *Woods Near Oele* or *Red Trees*, for example—the composition remains amazingly simple, with color defining the form of the trees and serving as the only subject.

The painters of the Hague School and especially van Gogh had freed Dutch painting from its concentration on precision and detail largely by subordinating the "true" representation of a complex, multifaceted scene to concerns that reduced and simplified the subject. Thus by the time Mondrian painted his earliest pictures, there was little of the "real" world left to paint. He was left not the objects of nature or man but only the form of those objects as subject. By 1912 he began a series of pictures in which he frankly sought to depict the simple common denominator of all the visible world—its geometry. In two of these series, one based on an apple tree and the other on a cathedral, he abstracted recognizable forms until they became, in the tree series, only a set of curved lines, and, in the cathedral series, only a set of straight ones. These lines define the original object in its purest form, and the subject is unrecognizable without the original representational picture there as a guide.

By the 1920s Mondrian's pictures abandoned any reference at all to the visible world. In 1921 he painted his *Composition with Red, Yellow, and Blue*, an austere picture whose subject—if one may still use the term—is, in Mondrian's words, "the abstraction of form and color . . . the straight line and clearly defined primary color." Here articulation of the picture space is the artist's real concern. Heavy black lines and small blocks of color at the picture's edges fill and define the space. The eye is engaged not in the recognition of forms—as it had been in traditional figurative painting—but in the subtle play of lines that pull toward the perimeters and then fall just short of the edge; and in the play of colors, strong and primary or subtle variations of pale blue, which fill the spaces defined by the lines. It is a beauty of a peculiarly subtle and austere sort, one in which the particularities of the real world have been abandoned in favor of lines and colors that act like music, filling a space with only themselves as reference, recalling nothing of experience.

We cannot compare these pictures or the slightly more colorful and agitated pictures from the 1940s with anything in the nineteenth century. We may, however, see something of classical Dutch art in these canvases: the perfect order, clarity, and precision of seventeenth-century masters are renewed in an art that depends only on itself and that is painted to reveal nothing but the essential truth of its traditional materials: line and color.

Mondrian's observations on abstraction of form and color appeared in the first issue of *De Stijl*—"Style"—the magazine that Mondrian and Theodore van Doesburg founded in 1917. It sought to articulate for designers and architects as well as

106

At far left, above, Piet Mondrian's Windmill on the Gein, *painted in 1906/07; directly below,* Boerderij bij Duivendrech, *finished in 1916; next to it,* The Gray Tree, *done in 1912; and at near left,* Composition in Red, Yellow, and Blue, *1921. From the figurative painting of the lone windmill to the completely abstract* Composition, *Mondrian has made a great but not wholly surprising transition. The economy of the early painting and the carefully delineated horizontal spaces are echoed in the even starker picture of the farmhouse and trees and in the gray tree: both are primarily concerned with lines and space, the vertical panels created by the trees' reflections reach almost from the top to the bottom of the picture, while a clear horizontal formed by the shoreline bisects the picture in the middle. Likewise, the gray tree is far more a play of half- circles than an attempt to recreate a tree one might see in nature. By the 1920s, Mondrian abandoned nature even as his starting point, creating paintings in which line and color alone were the subjects.*

artists the new aesthetic principles of the twentieth century. The name *De Stijl* came to be applied to a wide range of buildings, furniture, decorative art, and, of course, paintings. Van Doesburg, Vilmos Huszar, Georges Vantongerloo, and Bart van der Leck are the painters most often associated with De Stijl. The architects Gerrit Thomas Rietveld, J. J. P. Oud, and Jan Wils also participated in the movement, producing austere, Cubist designs that employed the same primary colors favored by Mondrian and van Doesburg.

De Stijl had a profound and lasting influence on twentieth-century art; the simplicity of form and color it advocated became the chief characteristic of art and architecture throughout Europe and America. It would be wrong to insist too strongly on an unbroken tradition extending from the Golden Age of the seventeenth century through the twentieth. Obviously, painting and architecture in the Netherlands changed profoundly over three centuries, as did the society in which and for which they were produced. Yet it is also true that the clarity and order that so characterized the art of the Golden Age never entirely disappeared. Likewise, that "sober realism," as characteristic of Dutch art as it is of the Dutch themselves, guided seventeenth-century masters as it guided nineteenth- and twentieth-century painters, who never—even in their most romantic, expressionistic, or abstract works—denied that the essential truth of the real world was the stuff of which art is made.

VI

The House of Orange Ascendant

The American Revolution was the earliest success-ful expression of a general discontent with political structures and economic conditions that had pre-vailed throughout the eighteenth century. Dutch support for the American colonists, to be sure, had been encouraged by the economic interests of urban bankers, but the wide enthusiasm that the American Revolution sparked in the Netherlands was due both to the kinship the Dutch felt for a people oppressed by foreign masters—they had revolted against Spain for many of the same reasons the Americans were anxious to rid themselves of the English, after all—and to the popularity among the Dutch of the ideals of the Enlightenment that guided American revolu-tionary leaders. The Dutch population was largely disenfranchised—only the very wealthiest had a voice in choosing provincial leaders, who them-selves chose and supported the *stadtholder.* Econom-ic conditions, never good and rarely stable for the poorer classes, worsened when the English blockad-ed Dutch ports as retribution for the Netherlands' support of the Americans. The Enlightenment preached democracy—albeit a severely limited one—and offered, if not a detailed program of social and economic reform, at least a political system in which the real concerns of the disenfranchised class-es would theoretically be taken into account. The right to "life, liberty and the pursuit of happiness," won across the Atlantic, seemed a goal worth fight-ing for at home, and the American experience en-couraged the Dutch to dream of securing it.

Under the leadership of J. E. van der Cappelan, a movement known as the Patriots arose, dedicated to bringing a measure of democracy to Dutch society. Their chief goal was to secure, at least for the prop-ertied class, a voice in the government, which at the end of the eighteenth century lay in the hands of a small group of oligarchs, the *stadtholder,* and his court. The Patriots began to raise militias in the towns and cities, and their numbers grew so large that many oligarchs, fearing for their position, joined the movement or supported it indirectly by refusing to oppose it.

In The Hague the movement found wide support among the Estates of the province of Holland. Many of its representatives genuinely believed Enlighten-ment rhetoric; others supported it because it seemed politic to do so. The *stadtholder,* William V, felt uneasy in The Hague, where the republican movement was so vocal, and he retired to Nijmegen. His consort, Princess Wilhelmina of Prussia, refused to so compromise herself, however, and in 1786 she made some show of returning to The Hague. There she was stopped by the Patriot militia and restrained in a manner that seemed very much like arrest. William did nothing, but Wilhelmina's brother, Frederick of Prussia, sent an army to release her and enforce the position of the *stadtholder* against repub-lican claims—which threatened not only his sister and her weak-willed husband but every despotic regime in Europe. The Prussians were able to crush the Netherlands' revolt in all of its main centers; its leaders were either arrested or forced to flee south to France or across the Atlantic to America; and the *stadtholder* was again welcomed by the oligarchs who had all but deserted him some months before.

Coastal Scheveningen has long been home port to herring fishermen.

In 1789 the French king, Louis XVI, was deposed in a revolt whose causes and ideals resembled the Patriot insurgency in the Netherlands. The French Revolution, even more than its American counterpart, encouraged the hopes of republicans everywhere in Europe—and, of course, threatened every crowned head. Secure at home by 1793, the French moved to export the revolution. Reinforced by Patriot units recruited from among Dutch exiles, a French army attacked the Netherlands and was held back only by the river boundaries. Finally, during the winter of 1795, this composite army crossed the frozen rivers into Holland. The *stadtholder* bade farewell to the Estates in The Hague and set sail at Scheveningen for exile in Great Britain. The seven provinces greeted the French as liberators, and with the support of the revolutionary army they set up the Batavian Republic based on the French model.

The French entered the Netherlands as liberators but remained as conquerors. They claimed strongholds along the southern border and 100 million guilders as a return on their revolutionary investment, and the Dutch were forced to billet 25,000 French troops.

In 1804, to the dismay of republican and legitimists alike, Napoleon proclaimed himself emperor of France and set about to establish autocratic governments throughout French-dominated Europe. He immediately invested the Dutch envoy in Paris, R. J. Schimmelpenninck, with near-sovereign authority over the Netherlands. Schimmelpenninck was styled Grand Pensionary, a title disused since Oldenbarnevelt's time. During his brief, one-year tenure, he was able to enact some reforms that remained in effect for most of the century, primarily in education and taxation; but in 1806 Napoleon proclaimed his brother, Louis Napoleon, king of the Netherlands. With his wife, Hortense, the daughter of Napoleon's own wife, Josephine, the new king set up residence in The Hague, which had been the administrative center of the short-lived Batavian Republic and had gained by royal decree in December 1806 the status of city for the first time in its history. Louis Napoleon resided in the old *stadtholder's* quarters in the Binnenhof.

Within two years, however, the king decided to move his court first to Utrecht and then finally to Amsterdam, where the town hall, originally built by van Campen and now redesigned by Ziezenis, became his royal palace. The Hague, traditionally the residence of the *stadtholder* and the federal administrative center, suddenly found itself without its single largest employer, the government. A period of severe economic depression followed the removal of the royal court—a particular blow to Haguenaars already feeling the adverse economic consequences of Napoleon's Continental System, which forbade trade with England, Holland's chief market. The Hague suffered doubly. Many of its fine houses along the Vijverberg and Lange Voorhout were abandoned, and the growing number of paupers had to be fed in soup kitchens. Resentment against the "liberators" grew among the poor—who yearned, as always, for the House of Orange—and among the numerous merchants who had been brought to ruin by the Continental System.

In 1810 matters worsened. Napoleon, infuriated at the smuggling by which the Dutch evaded the proscription against overseas commerce and dissatisfied with his brother's ineffective policy against the contraband trade, dissolved the Kingdom of Holland and incorporated the Netherlands into the French empire. Now directly under French administration, the Netherlands was forced to submit to French law and French taxation, to give up its sons to the French army, and to suffer rigorous enforcement of the ruinous Continental System. With the rest of Europe, the Dutch organized resistance and awaited the collapse of the empire. As The Hague was the residence of the French prefect, the Baron de Stassart, who resided at the Hotel Huguetan, and Huis ten Bosch was the country palace of the French governor-general, the duc de Plaisance, the city soon became a center of resistance. The de Witte Society, a fashionable literary club for wealthy Haguenaars, was the meeting place for such men as Gijsberg Karel van Hogendorp and Leopold, count of Limburg-Stirum, who plotted the return of the House of Orange and the Netherlands' independence. The de Witte Society building still stands on the Plein in the center of The Hague—a turn-of-the-century Italian Renaissance structure that replaced the older white building from which the club, originally called the Nieuwe Literaire Sociëtat, took the name "de Witte" in order to confuse the French.

By the end of 1812 it was clear that the moment all Europe had been waiting for was at hand: Napoleon's invasion of Russia had proven a failure and most of the Grand Army had been lost. Van Hogen-

In the nineteenth century The Hague underwent a number of changes as, once again, it became the official seat of the Dutch government. New sectors were laid out beyond the city's original borders, and within the city itelf new houses were built and older ones demolished—all to make room for an influx of government employees and returning colonial officials. At far left is the house at Javastraat 26, on the so-called 1813 Plein, that has served since 1912 as one of The Hague's municipal offices. The original Plein at the city's center (near left) itself acquired the aspect of a governmental congeries when the ministries of war and foreign affairs took over buildings that had once housed the delegations from Amsterdam and Rotterdam to the Estates General. Somewhat later a new building was constructed on the edge of the Plein to house two additional ministries, those of justice and of the overseas territories.

dorp, Leopold van Limburg-Stirnum, and Van der Duyn van Maasdem formed a provisional government to ensure that when Napoleon met final defeat, a native government would be in place in the Netherlands to assume control. In mid-November 1813 this triumverate proclaimed independence, joined the international coalition against Napoleon, and invited the son of William V, who was residing in England, to accept the title of king. By the time the new sovereign arrived on November 30, a new constitution had been prepared, one that suppressed the powers of the provinces in favor of a centralized government under a powerful monarch and a weak parliament. The events of 1813 were later commemorated by a large monument in the so-called 1813 Plein.

The final form of the new government had to await the decisions of the European powers convened as the Congress of Vienna, which undertook the reorganization of Europe in the post-Napoleonic period. In order to establish a bulwark against renewed French aggression and thus ensure a measure of stability in Europe, the Congress decided to unify the southern and northern Netherlands. Events were shortly to prove that unification could be no more easily effected in the nineteenth century than in the seventeenth. Religious differences were still the chief obstacle: the south was unhappy with the provision for religious equality that the great powers had inserted in the constitution, and the north was equally unwilling to see a Catholic episcopate reestablished. The south balked at having to assume equal responsibility for the national debt, which was far larger in the north, and also objected to sending an equal number of representatives to the parliament, when its population totaled some 3.5 million against only 2 million in the north. Dutch was made the official language in the Flemish areas and bilingualism was instituted in the Walloon provinces. There were undoubtedly economic advantages to the union—Dutch shipping and Belgian industry would make a powerful economic partnership—but old religious antagonisms coupled with new political and linguistic squabbles overshadowed these considerations.

Prince William was officially named King William I in 1815, and his despotic manner did little to soothe the south's offended national pride. By 1830 resentment in the south was being openly expressed in riots that were fired, in part, by the success of the July Revolution in France. William sent an army under his son, a hero of Waterloo, to quell the riots, but offers of assistance to the Belgians from the British and French governments rendered the king's efforts useless. He was not a man given to negotiations or compromise, but by 1838 he was forced to recognize the southern secession. Embittered by the failure of his Belgian policy and attacked even at home for his autocratic methods, he abdicated in favor of his son, who became King William II in 1840.

Until Napoleonic times, The Hague had enjoyed the curious status of serving as the Netherlands' capital without ever having received a charter as a city. Louis Napoleon did finally name it "the place of our royal residence, the name and rank of third city of our kingdom, immediately after Amsterdam and Rotterdam." But he shortly abandoned The Hague for Amsterdam, and his government followed. When French authority began to crumble and van Hogendorp and his colleagues set up a provisional administration, they naturally chose The Hague, both because of its traditional role as capital and because it would have been unwise to establish an authority parallel to the nominal French administration in Amsterdam. When William I accepted the crown, however, he did so on the condition that he be proclaimed king in Amsterdam, since without the support of that city's population his position would have been untenable. Thus the 1814 constitution contained the provision that "the King, upon ascending the throne, shall as soon as possible be sworn in and inaugurated within the City of Amsterdam in a public joint session of the Estates-General." Since that time Dutch monarchs, wherever they chose to reside, have been proclaimed in Amsterdam's Nieuwe Kerk, and the old town hall in Amsterdam has served as a royal residence. But despite that stipulation parliament, most government offices, and the embassies of foreign governments to the Netherlands settled in The Hague, which became what it remains today: seat of the Dutch government, national administrative center, and royal residence.

After the Batavian Republic was proclaimed, the properties of the House of Orange in The Hague and elsewhere were seized by the new government. Upon the return of Prince William and his proclamation as the first monarch of the Orange-Nassau

line, the palaces of Noordeinde and Huis ten Bosch were restored to the House of Orange. They needed restoration, however, and the new king lived first with van Hogendorp in the Johan de Witthuis, designed by Pieter Post, in the Kneuterdijk, and then at the Hotel Huguetan in the Lange Voorhout. (Upon the king's departure in 1821, the hotel became the Royal Library.) The Wassenaar house on the Kneuterdijk was bought in 1819 to serve as the residence of the heir to the throne, Prince Frederick William, whose wife, Anna Paulowna, daughter of Tsar Paul of Russia, made it a center of court life. She had an Orthodox chapel built in the Kneuterdijk Palace, and the prince laid out gardens in the English style extending as far as the Javastraat and the Noordeinde. (When the Wassenaar house was later purchased by The Hague municipality, those gardens were destroyed.) It was at this time that the king, through the good offices of the duke of Wellington, secured the return of the pictures seized by the French during their occupation. After some haggling, the Louvre's guardians finally released many of the masterpieces now at the Mauritshuis, which became a state museum on July 10, 1820.

In 1821 King William took up residence in the now-restored Noordeinde Palace—still called Het Oude Hof—which remained the official royal residence in The Hague up until the German occupation in 1940. In 1845 the royal family purchased a small house on the Lange Voorhout—sometimes called the Palace of the Golden Balconies or the Palace Lange Voorhout and known to most Haguenaars as the former residence of Queen Regent Emma. It is now a "working palace" for Queen Beatrix. Huis ten Bosch served briefly as a picture gallery—The Hague's first—after the last *stadtholder* was deposed. In 1805 it became, briefly, the residence of the Grand Pensionary and then the country residence of the French governor-general. After the monarchy was proclaimed, Huis ten Bosch reverted to the royal family. There Queen Sophie, wife of King William III, lived abandoned by her consort, creating a sort of literary salon where she entertained, among others, John Lothrop Motley, the great historian of the Netherlands.

The Binnenhof no longer served as a royal residence but it did continue to serve as a government headquarters. The Ridderzaal, however, fell into disuse. In the last years of the republic, booksellers set up stalls in the hall, and drawings for the state lottery were held there. The French used it as a winter parade ground and military hospital. In the 1830s William II "restored" the hall in the Gothic style he had also employed in "restoring" Noordeinde. A tin roof and cast-iron pillars were added to the Ridderzaal and a Gothic façade to Noordeinde. Fortunately for both buildings, twentieth-century restorers have removed these unsightly and anachronistic additions. In 1904 the Ridderzaal roof was rebuilt in solid wood according to the thirteenth-century designs of Gerard van Leyden.

The first half of the nineteenth century saw a general stagnation in Dutch commercial life. The Continental System had profited the south by allowing industry to expand to meet the demands of the European market, which was forbidden to look

King Louis Bonaparte of Holland (right), who ruled the Netherlands for a brief period in the early nineteenth century, was the brother of the French emperor, to whom he bears a striking resemblance. King Louis's consort, Queen Hortense, the daughter of Napoleon's empress, Josephine, is seen below with the royal couple's children. At left, Louis and his entourage visit the beach at Scheveningen, a fishing village and seaport a few miles from The Hague. The Napoleonic period brought hard times to The Hague when King Louis moved his court—and consequently his courtiers and bureaucrats—to Amsterdam, but it was during this period that The Hague first received official municipal status. After the liberation of the Dutch nation from the French, the government again located itself principally in The Hague, although Amsterdam was proclaimed the capital. Thus the Netherlands enjoys the curious distinction of having, in effect, two capitals.

abroad for goods, but it only crippled the north, which was dependent on non-European markets. Attached as they were to foreign trade, the Dutch who had capital invested it abroad rather than in native industry and, consequently, the industrial revolution that was transforming other European nations did not really occur in the Netherlands until late in the century. While economic life stagnated, the numbers and conditions of the poor grew alarmingly until fully 10 percent of the population was dependent upon charity. The pressing need for social legislation to deal with unemployment and other problems went unmet, largely because parliament was still elected by the propertied classes, who saw no need for anything more than private charity.

Liberals recognized the need to extend the franchise, and they finally had their chance after William III's last male heir died in 1884. The new heir apparent, Princess Wilhelmina, was only four years old, and therefore the constitution had to be amended to prepare for a regency. In 1887 the constitution was finally changed and it contained a provision for further extending the franchise, which by 1894 included all male citizens who were able to support their families.

By the middle of the nineteenth century the Dutch again began to enjoy political stability and economic growth; and as the national government expanded to fulfill the demands of the modern industrial state, The Hague's population grew with it. In 1849 the population was 70,000; by the turn of the century it had increased to more than 200,000. Before 1850 the city's population was always contained within

115

By the end of the nineteenth century Scheveningen was a thriving, popular, and cosmopolitan seaside resort as well as the important fishing port it had always been. These three recent views of Scheveningen capture the tranquillity of its beach in the early morning—and the gaudier aspects of its famed Kurhaus by night. In the summer, thousands of tourists from all over Western Europe throng the broad, sandy beach and enjoy the amusements of its boardwalk arcades and cafes. In restored **fin-de-siècle** splendor, dining, dancing and gambling are offered in the Kurhaus, while fireworks light the night sky. Yet for all this one can still glimpse the Scheveningen fishermen and their wives, dressed in traditional black garb, practicing the trade that for centuries assured Holland its prosperity.

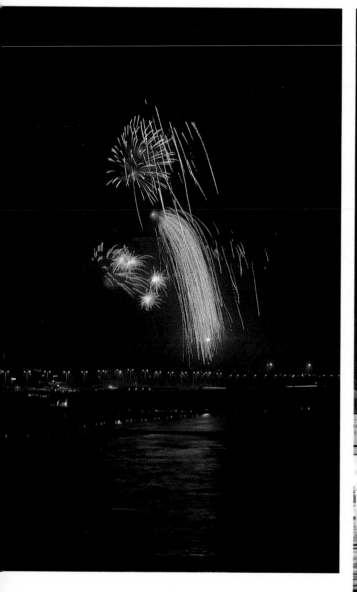

116

the boundaries formed by the grid of canals constructed in the seventeenth century. The most important government officials continued to live close to the Binnenhof.

Despite its population growth, The Hague still retained its quiet elegance, its quintessentially Dutch solidity and restraint. Factories were being built elsewhere in the country and skies were darkened with industrial smoke, but The Hague remained in many respects a village, and so it is no wonder that retired colonial officials chose to live where the Holland they dreamed of in the Indies lived on, virtually untouched by the rougher aspects of the new age. These officials settled in the newer districts such as the Nassau Plein or the 1813 Plein, or in suburbs like Sorghvliet and Scheveningen.

Scheveningen's growth in this period was especially rapid. Until the nineteenth century it had been little more than a fishing village, whose only notoriety occurred when Holland's *stadtholders* either departed from or arrived at its beaches as they headed for exile or returned triumphant from Great Britain. In the seventeenth century the nobility and their guests did occasionally visit Scheveningen, and in 1665 Constantin Huygens arranged for construction of the Scheveningen Road. It provided the first easy access to this village, which then had fewer than a thousand inhabitants.

In response to the nineteenth-century fashion among the upper classes for bathing and "taking the cure," Scheveningen began to grow into an elegant and cosmopolitan spa. In 1818 a local entrepreneur, Jacob Pronk, set up a wooden bathhouse on wheels

Perhaps nothing in The Hague so typifies its stately past and cosmopolitan present as the Hotel des Indes, the elegant hostelry that has hosted princes and starlets, statesmen and jurists since 1881. Careful restoration has now returned the hotel to much the look it had when Baron van Brienen first occupied it in 1859. The great central rotunda, open in the baron's day so that his guests could drive their carriages directly into the heart of the mansion, has been closed over with a skylight—and today guests take tea in this domed conservatory alongside officials and guests of the Dutch government and members of the International Court of Justice. Off to one side is the room in which the most famous ballerina of all time, Anna Pavlova, died while on a tour of Holland in 1931.

on Scheveningen beach, and within two years he replaced it with a brick structure. In 1824 the municipality took over operation of the bathhouse, expanding it, and by 1828 was calling it the Grand Hotel des Bains. In 1856 two wings were added to the hotel, which could now accommodate almost one hundred lodgers. Not only fashionable Haguenaars but travelers from all over Europe began to stop at Scheveningen. In 1883 the Grand Hotel des Bains was demolished and replaced by the Kurhaus, which opened in 1885 only to be gutted by fire a year later. Finally in 1887 a rebuilt Kurhaus opened—a lavish, eccentric building in the Moorish style then favored for buildings designed for pleasure. Additions were made frequently over the next quarter century. The Queen Wilhelmina Pier and Circus Building were constructed as part of Scheveningen's complex of amusements and lodgings.

By the 1970s it looked as if the Kurhaus would have to be demolished. Repairs made after the 1886 fire had not been careful, for one thing; and new floors had to be added to make the hotel profitable. The central hall, the Kurzaal, was declared a national monument, but the wings were torn down and replaced. The Kurzaal was then completely rebuilt after each of its details was recorded on microfilm, so that today only the wooden dome and ceiling paintings are original. It is estimated that Scheveningen hosts some 4 million visitors a year, and though its fin-de-siècle elegance may still be glimpsed in the Kurzaal, or Hall of Mirrors, and the Cor Ruys Hall, a distinctly democratic gaiety is now the predominant mood.

The entrepreneurial spirit that transformed Scheveningen in so short a time was also responsible for the most astonishing, though not the finest, work of art to be seen in The Hague—or anywhere else for that matter—the Mesdag Panorama, the world's largest painting. In 1880 a Belgian syndicate commissioned the Hague School painter Hendrik Willem Mesdag to paint a panoramic view of the beach resort, panoramas being a great fad in the late nineteenth century. Agreements were concluded on March 28, 1881, and within four months Mesdag and his wife, along with Theodore de Bock and G. H. Breitner, had completed a painting 394 feet in diameter, 46 feet high, and totaling some 18,000 square feet. The panorama was opened to the public on August 1, 1881, but the syndicate soon found that it could not make a profit from the work, and in 1885 Mesdag bought it back from them. In 1911, exhibition rooms were added to the building, still at Zeestraat 65 in The Hague.

In the panorama Mesdag shows his literal, almost photographically realist style in a sweeping canvas that depicts both the town and beach of Scheveningen as it looked in 1880—still more a fishing village than a resort, with boats and nets on the sand. The work is remarkable if only for its size and the precision and multiplicity of its details; set as it is on real dunes, the huge painting has an undeniable power.

The nineteenth century brought less dramatic changes to The Hague than to the surrounding villages, but the city could not remain untouched in the midst of the industrial revolution that was transforming much of the rest of the Netherlands. In

1843 rail lines were completed to Amsterdam and Rotterdam; linked thus to the country's two major commercial centers, The Hague began to attract some industry of its own. The Hollandse Spoor station was built, enabling tourists to reach the spas and visitors on state business to reach the city easily and quickly. A rapid growth in the number of workers engaged either in industry or service trades demanded more housing, and new and shoddy districts were created out of farmland surrounding the old city center.

The city center itself began to change in response to the rapid increase in traffic: canals like the Herengracht, Fluwelen Burgwal, Spui, and Prinsegracht were filled in as the railways replaced waterborne traffic and as carriages (and later, trams and cars) necessitated larger roads. Shopping had become a diversion for wealthy nineteenth-century ladies, and as in London and other metropoles, architects in The Hague felt the need to make the shopping trip easier and more genteel. In 1882 J. C. van Wijk and H. Wesstra, Jr., designed the Passage—an airy, light-filled pedestrian arcade of wrought-iron and glass. Additions were made to this popular design in 1929 and again in 1972.

Two structures in The Hague exemplify the architectural tastes and the style of life of the haute bourgeoisie in the last half of the nineteenth century. Javastraat 26, on the 1813 Plein, is an elegant building that has been used by The Hague municipality since 1912. Built in 1864, it is a perfect example of the Eclectic Style of the period, itself a reaction to the heavy neo-Gothic taste of the nine-

teenth century that characterized Prince Frederick-William's restoration of the Noordeinde and Ridderzaal—and that can still be appreciated in the Royal Riding Academy or the Williamskerk on the Nassaulaan. The 1813 Plein is situated in an area beyond the canal boundaries of the old city, and it was once part of the Schuddegest estate.

The 1813 Plein area was a little far from the center of things but still accessible and fashionable. Baron van Brienen's house, Clingendael, which stood on the outskirts of the town, was another matter. It was a long and disagreeable ride to van Brienen's, and this important adviser to King William III discovered that guests were reluctant to attend his parties in the suburban wilds. The baron intended to plant himself solidly in the heart of the city. Through his influence at court he was able to purchase three houses on the Lange Voorhout, where the nobility—titled or otherwise—lived.

By 1859 the baron was able to open one of the most luxurious mansions in The Hague—a house designed by A. Rodenburg with balconies resembling those of the nearby royal palace. Inside, sumptuous brocade, mirrors, and a fine collection of old master paintings lined the walls, and massive chandeliers hung from the ceilings. The baron died in 1873 and his sons sold the mansion to a M. Paulez, who already owned the Hotel Paulez on the Lange Voorhout. His son-in-law, Friedrich Wirtz, undertook to redesign the ground floor, then given over to stables and service quarters, and to add rooms on the floors above, where the baron himself had lived. By 1881 the former mansion was ready to be

occupied by paying guests, and it was opened as the Hotel des Indes—a name that captured both the French elegance so favored by the wealthy and the exotic eastern source of much of their money. Shortly thereafter the central courtyard on the main floor, into which carriages could still pass from a ramp on the street, was covered over with a high glass dome—and carriages and their attendant odors were confined to the street.

Des Indes was immediately established as The Hague's leading hotel, and it soon became one of Europe's most elegant and celebrated hosteleries. The cosmopolitan air of the turn-of-the-century Hague is perhaps nowhere more evident than in des Indes' grand lobby, where afternoon tea or cocktails may still be taken under the uncountable lights that trace the sumptuous lines of the mansion's interior well. As The Hague increasingly became an international meeting place, the Hotel des Indes played host to the famous: Theodore Roosevelt and Haile Selassie, Eleanor Roosevelt and Igor Stravinsky, Simone Weil, Lord Snowdon, David Oistrach, Danny Kaye, Charles Lindbergh, Dwight Eisenhower, the king of Rumania, and the queen of Denmark. Anna Pavlova died in her suite at des Indes, and Mata Hari, who lived around the corner at the Nieuwe Uitleg, entertained there. During the Nazi occupation it was forced to host the invaders, but it also managed to house—in the pigeon coops on the roof—six young Dutchmen who hid there to escape forced labor in Germany.

By the last quarter of the nineteenth century, The Hague was becoming a fashionable and cosmopoli-

tan town. The international set was drawn to it by diplomatic business; artists, by the civilized beauty and quiet of the town itself, coupled with its reputation for good studios and good patronage. Theater flourished in the palace William IV had built for his daughter on the Korte Voorhout—now the Koninklijke Schouwburg—while the literati gathered at de Witte or at Queen Sophie's salon in Huis ten Bosch. But for all that The Hague was not Paris or even Amsterdam but only a comfortable bourgeois town where good manners and good taste created a cultivated but restricted atmosphere. Nowhere is the style of those days better captured than in the novels of Louis Marie Anne Couperus, the son of a retired colonial, who was born in 1863 on the Mauritskade. He spent the first two years of his life in The Hague and then traveled to Java with his parents. After five years in the Indies he returned to The Hague, where he began to publish verses in the lush, oriental style then popular throughout Europe. He produced several historical novels and stories of life in the Dutch colonies, and he wrote of life in The Hague itself, especially in *Eline Vere* and *Old People and the Things That Pass.* The life he depicts is the life one can still sense in the cafés in the city center, in the lobby of des Indes, or when one strolls along the stately, tree-lined avenues near the Binnenhof—a world of solid wealth and solid respectability, of taste and leisure. It was, to be sure, a cultivated and cosmopolitan world, but one in which the rough edges of life were tucked away out of sight and where daring and adventure were dreamed of but not dared. The world, in short, of the eternal Dutch burgher.

The Hague's many faces and facets: a royal coachman on the Lange Voorhout, above; at right, a winter day on the Lange Vijverberg, a performance of the Netherlands Dance Theater, and the Van Roos en Doorn Laan; below, left to right, a home for the elderly, a statue of the philosopher Spinoza, who once resided in The Hague, tulip fields on the city's outskirts, and a shop on the bohemian Denneweg; at bottom, the Buitenhof tram stop, the Plaats, the gates of the Mauritshuis, an organ-grinder, a quiet local street.

VII

War and Renewal

In 1948, The Hague celebrated its seven hundredth anniversary. The date was chosen somewhat arbitrarily, of course, since there are no records to indicate its precise birth. But seven hundred years is just about how long the city's oldest buildings had been standing; and 1248 was, if nothing else, the year in which one of the founders of The Hague, Count William II, was crowned king of the Romans and returned in glory to 's-Gravenshage to do some more building. More likely, 1948 was chosen less as a birthday than as a thanksgiving day, for The Hague had just endured five years of appalling deprivation and slaughter at the hands of the Germans—and it was still, despite its ruined neighborhoods, bomb craters, destroyed woods, and brutalized population, a living, breathing city. And 1948 was also the golden jubilee year of the Netherlands' longest-reigning monarch, Queen Wilhelmina, and, by the queen's own decision, the year in which her daughter Juliana would succeed her. Altogether, then, an appropriate year in which to look back across the centuries and to plan, if not quite from scratch, a future—for itself and for the nation.

In 1890, at the age of ten, Princess Wilhelmina had succeeded her father, William III. Her mother, Queen Emma, acted as regent until Wilhelmina herself was old enough to take the constitutional oath in 1898. During her fifty-year reign, events and her own nature would make Queen Wilhelmina a symbol of the quest for peace and social justice on a continent increasingly hostile to both. For at least a century it had been the firm policy of the Netherlands to avoid entangling itself in foreign wars, and

until the country was actually invaded in 1940 the Netherlands successfully maintained its neutrality. Indeed, by the turn of the century the Dutch policy had become one of actively encouraging a peaceful solution to all international quarrels, and The Hague had become the center for these important—if ultimately fruitless—attempts to secure peace in Europe. Just a year after her inauguration the new queen hosted the First Hague Peace Conference at Huis ten Bosch. Organized at the initiative of Tsar Nicholas II of Russia, it was the first of many desperate attempts on the part of rapidly arming and hostile European powers to avert the calamity of war. At that first meeting it was decided to form a permanent court in which international disputes might be settled peacefully, and to erect a building in The Hague to house that court. The money to finance the building's construction was eventually solicited from Andrew Carnegie, the American millionaire. The queen's government bought two estates at the head of the Scheveningen Road—Buitenrust and Rustenburg—and donated them and the surrounding land to the Carnegie Foundation.

An international competition was held for the design of the building; the jury selected, from among 216 entries, the plans of the French architect L. M. Cordonnier for a French-style château with four Gothic towers that incorporated elements of traditional Dutch architecture. At the time many architects expressed dismay at what they saw as a banal, eclectic, and not very graceful design—which in any case had to be altered to meet a generous but nonetheless limited budget.

Voorburg was once a gateway to The Hague, as its crest attests.

The various states attending the conference were encouraged to contribute materials or objects characteristic of their national production to decorate the interior. The Hague municipality donated the grand staircase, designed after the stairs at the Paris Opera, and the Netherlands' government donated the seven stained-glass windows that can be seen from the staircase. The Permanent Court of Arbitration—really only a list of jurists nominated by the member states to serve in cases requiring arbitration—meets in the Japanese Room, so-called because of the embroidered tapestries, donated by the Japanese government, that hang on its walls. The library has one of the most complete collections of books on international law, comprising some 250,000 volumes. It also contains an extensive and rare collection of the writings of Hugo Grotius, the father of international law. The International Court of Justice meets on the main floor, under a seventy-foot-high oak-beamed ceiling. At a long green table sit the judges of the court, interpreters, stenographers, and attorneys. The grounds were designed by the British landscape architect T. H. Mawson.

On July 30, 1907, the Russian delegate to the Second Hague Peace Conference laid the building's cornerstone, and six years later, on August 28, 1913, in the presence of the queen, the royal family, and the Carnegies, the Vredespaleis, or Peace Palace, was formally opened. Less than a year later Europe was at war.

The belligerents in this war respected Dutch neutrality: the Germans avoided crossing the Netherlands in their drive through neutral Belgium, and the English likewise avoided using Dutch waterways to relieve Antwerp. But this did not mean that the Netherlands escaped the effects of World War I altogether. As had happened repeatedly in previous centuries, the advent of hostilities disrupted the country's vital sea trade, and it soon became rudely apparent that the Netherlands would have to find a way of ensuring itself a measure of agricultural self-sufficiency. Parliament decided to undertake the costly reclamation of part of the Zuyder Zee as a means of providing additional farmland.

Largely due to the presence of the court, The Hague became an important international meeting place in the first decades of the twentieth century. Both the continuing growth of the national government and the Netherlands' increasingly important role in world affairs helped to make The Hague a vital urban center. Building within the older parts of the city and in new suburban districts occurred throughout the first three decades of the new century, and modern architectural forms found their place in this ancient and conservative city. Throughout the newer, northwestern corner of The Hague and here and there in Scheveningen one can see the fanciful gables, murals, pinnacles, light-painted wooden loggias, balustrades, and narrow, elegant windows designed by exponents of the Nieuwe Kunst, or Art Nouveau. These eccentric but graceful forms mark the first real break with the Grecian and Gothic imitations of nineteenth-century builders.

On Denneweg 56, an old, narrow, and traditionally bohemian street not far from the Lange Voorhout, is perhaps the best example of the Nieuwe

In the years before World War I, European leaders tried desperately to avert the hostilities some saw as inevitable, and in this hope the Peace Palace was opened in 1913. Besides the International Court of Justice, which meets in the chamber at far right, and the Permanent Court of Arbitration—both now part of the United Nations—the imposing Peace Palace also houses an important library of international law. Its halls and gardens, all gifts from the Dutch government and other member nations, are among The Hague's chief tourist attractions and, more importantly, symbols of the world's quest for peace and justice.

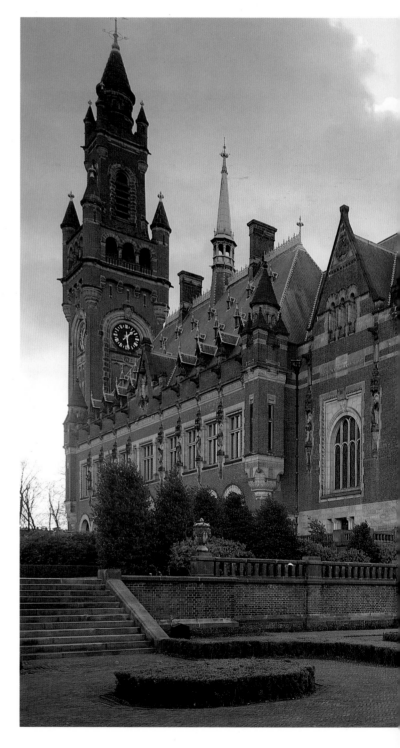

Kunst. The building was designed by J. W. Bosboom as an elegant showroom for the Beekman enterprises in 1898. Its glass façade is decorated with ornate combinations of flames and flowers in wrought-iron. Three stories high, it is intersected by two slim vertical columns. Inside, a series of bays is separated by slender, cast-iron columns and a wide, interlaced staircase. The municipality acquired this property in 1978, and it has been declared a landmark building.

Advocates of the Nieuwe Kunst opposed the imitative and heavy neoclassical and neo-Gothic styles of the nineteenth century with a new and graceful sense of architectural—or, at least, decorative—form. Later movements, known by various names—the Amsterdam School, De Stijl, and Functionalism—abandoned both the old dependence on imitation and the largely decorative aspects of the Nieuwe Kunst to seek instead architectural styles that embraced the "modern world." One of the best examples of the newer architecture of the interwar period is Berlage's Gemeentemuseum, but his office building for De Nederlanden and the Bijenkorf department store at Grotemarkt likewise show the expressive and powerful lines of modern Dutch architecture. Equally important is Jacobus Oud's Shell Oil building, in which the curiously fanciful element that is always present in good Dutch architecture finds expression in a strong, coherent building.

The number of buildings in the pioneering styles of the twentieth century testify to the importance of The Hague as an urban center. Amsterdam and Rotterdam remained the Netherlands' major metro-

poles; both were important ports, and both were national and international centers of commerce and finance. But The Hague was the seat of government, and as in all modern states, government is the one institution whose growth never slackens. The Hague was also the seat of the International Court, and thus a major international meeting place. Multinational firms such as Esso and Shell chose The Hague as the appropriate site for their headquarters, and workers in these large concerns swelled the population, which by 1939 had reached half a million. The automobile continued to have its effect on city planning in this period, as more canals were filled in to provide larger roadways.

By 1939 war in Europe seemed unavoidable. Many of Adolf Hitler's territorial demands in Eastern Europe had been agreed to by Great Britain and France, but it was obvious to all that further expansion would not be tolerated. The Rome–Berlin entente, later joined by Japan, and Germany's surprising Nonaggression Pact with the Soviet Union gave Germany sufficient support to risk war with the Allies—which came with his invasion of Poland in the fall of 1939. But the declared war was only that: at first, neither side moved against the other. Finally, in the spring of 1940, Hitler invaded neutral Norway and Denmark, and the Netherlands prepared for war.

On May 10, German troops crossed the Dutch frontier and German paratroops were dropped farther west, behind Dutch defensive lines. The Dutch organized behind the Water Line, a flooded area between the provinces of North and South Holland,

At the same time Piet Mondrian was pioneering abstract painting, a new school of figurative artists was working in Holland. Among the most important was Carel Willink, whose Wilma *was painted in 1932. Although the details are all clearly recognizable—the setting could easily be a residential neighborhood in The Hague—the vivid colors and eerie lighting impart an almost surreal quality to this portrait. Wilma's defiant pose harshly dominates the scene, one in which no other human figures or signs of life are discernable. The 1930s were desperate, frightening years all over the world, and many painters in Holland and abroad turned to paintings that revealed the lurking nightmares that seem to fill Willink's disturbing painting.*

historically their only topographical advantage. The Dutch army was in no position to withstand the far larger and better-equipped Germans, however, and in the face of an imminent air attack on The Hague, Queen Wilhelmina and her government fled—at the urging of the Allies—to England. The heroic defense of Rotterdam allowed the Dutch under Colonel Moorman to break the German ring around The Hague long enough for the government to depart. In revenge against the Dutch for having refused to capitulate immediately, the Germans attacked and destroyed most of Rotterdam by air. Rather than risk the same fate for other Dutch cities, General Winkelmann, commander-in-chief of the Dutch forces, surrendered on May 14. Meanwhile, the queen and her ministers set up a government-in-exile in London, from which Dutch ambassadors, the Dutch colonial administrators, and eventually the resistance in the Netherlands itself would be directed.

Despite the virtual destruction of Rotterdam, the Germans declared their intention to govern the Netherlands as part of the Reich, owing to Nazi racial theories that viewed the Dutch as "Aryans." A civilian, the Austrian Artur Seyss-Inquart, was appointed Reichskommissar for the Netherlands; he resided at Clingendael. The Hague's burgomeister, S. J. R. De Moncy, was deported to Germany.

Initially the occupation seemed reasonably benign. The civil service remained intact, and the Germans did not immediately appoint Dutch National Socialists to any important positions. Parliament and political parties were, however, abolished. In preparing for war the Dutch government had set aside large stores of food, so there was no immediate need for rationing; and exports to Germany—mandated by the occupying authority—actually helped ease unemployment and raise agricultural prices for a time.

The seeming benevolence of the occupation was belied by German measures against the Jews—their first target in every occupied country. The first anti-Jewish decrees were issued in the fall of 1940, and following a series of clashes in Amsterdam's Jewish quarter between German and Dutch Nazis and Jews, the city's Jews were forced to register. Some four hundred were seized and deported to the Mauthausen concentration camp in Germany. Spontaneously, on February 25, workers in Amsterdam called a general strike to protest the deportations. The strike was brutally suppressed, the Dutch were heavily fined, and martial law was imposed. Resistance would continue throughout the war, but the Germans succeeded in suppressing any further large-scale actions until the last year of the occupation.

German measures against the Jews grew increasingly harsh after February 1941. A year later forced-labor camps were set up in the Netherlands itself, and in April 1942 Jews were required to wear the identifying Jewish star. Deportations began in July and continued through the following year, although Jews in special "protected" categories—those in essential professions—were spared until 1944. Before the war some 140,000 Jews resided in the Netherlands; 110,000 were Dutch and the rest refugees, chiefly from Germany and Austria.

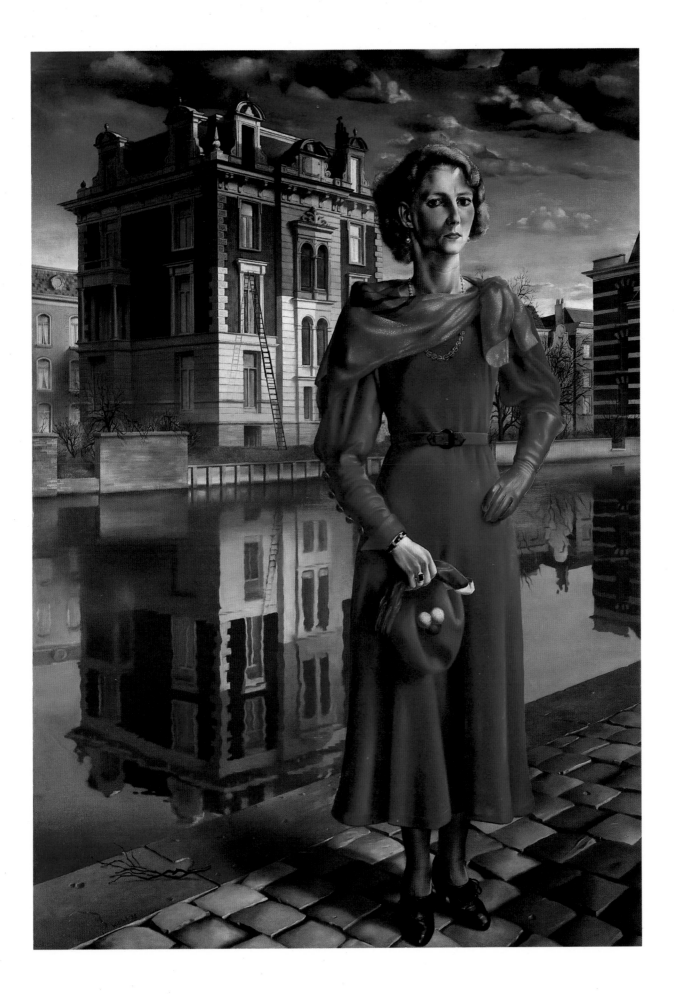

Amsterdam and The Hague were the principal centers of Jewish life. In both cities the communities were large and organized, although centuries of toleration had led Jews to regard themselves as Dutch, to assimilate, and to intermarry. During the war they were frequently helped by the Dutch resistance and by ordinary, otherwise uninvolved individuals—the story of Anne Frank and her family is only the most famous of many instances of heroism. But despite such acts, by the end of the war 75 percent of Dutch Jewry had died in Auschwitz, Sobibor, and other death camps. In The Hague alone the prewar Jewish population of 17,000 was reduced to 1,700 by 1945.

Jews, of course, were not the only victims of the occupation, which grew increasingly brutal as Germany suffered reversals in the war and as the Dutch resistance struck out at the invaders. Universities throughout the Netherlands were closed and students were forced to go into hiding or face forced labor in Germany. Resistance fighters were summarily arrested and either executed on the spot or deported to concentration camps. In The Hague, the Scheveningen prison became a notorious detention center, its hapless internees often shot and buried in the nearby dunes.

The Hague was spared Rotterdam's fate, but it suffered extensive damage when the Germans deliberately destroyed coastal neighborhoods in order to build the Atlantic Wall, a series of fortifications designed to repel the anticipated Allied landing in Holland. V-2 rockets were launched from mobile launching pads in and around The Hague, and a retaliatory Allied bombing of suspected V-2 sites in the Hague Woods on March 3, 1945, was mistakenly directed at the Bezuidenhout district and the nearby Princessgracht and Nieuwe Uitleg. Some four thousand homes and offices were destroyed, more than five hundred people were killed, and another four hundred were wounded; 20,000 were left homeless.

In September 1944, the Dutch government-in-exile ordered a rail strike in the Netherlands to impede German efforts to halt the Allied advance. Dutch workers responded by completely paralyzing the country. In reprisal, the Germans cut off the nation's already meager food supplies, and the Dutch endured the "Winter of Starvation," during which thousands did indeed starve to death while thousands more were rounded up for slave labor in Germany. During this dreadful winter, Haguenaars were forced to scour local farms for food and to destroy the Hague Woods for fuel. Adults and children alike went barefoot.

By this time the Allies had reached the Rhine delta, liberating the southern part of the Netherlands. An air attack at Arnheim failed, however, and Allied armies were unable to move north. Nonetheless, Queen Wilhelmina was able to return to the Netherlands for the first time in four years. In the spring the Allies succeeded in liberating the eastern provinces, and in May, as Germany surrendered, detachments of the Canadian army reached The Hague. On May 6 Burgomeister De Monchy and one of the queen's councilors, Jonkheer Bosch, Ridder van Rosenthal, announced Germany's surrender and the end of the occupation. A month later Queen Wilhelmina herself returned to The Hague.

Dutch neutrality, carefully preserved for a century, was suddenly violated early in World War II by the German invasion of May, 1940; within five days Dutch resistance gave way and the country was occupied. As a front line against the anticipated Allied invasion by sea, German gun emplacements were built along Holland's coast, as shown in the photograph at left, seized from captured German soldiers toward the end of the war. The Netherlands was not spared its share of the unspeakable brutality that typified the Nazis' treatment of civilian populations that fell under their control, as the miraculously preserved diary of Anne Frank so poignantly attests. The photograph at right shows Nazis rounding up Jews in Amsterdam in 1941 prior to sending them to death camps in the east, where three quarters of Holland's Jews— among them Anne Frank herself—were to die.

It was a much changed city. War, hunger, and deportation had reduced its population by almost 50,000. The Hague Woods had been devastated by military exercises and the need for fuel. Whole districts had been destroyed by demolition or air strikes. The Noordeinde Palace—around which Haguenaars had placed white carnations during the occupation to signal their defiance—needed restoration after five years of use by the Germans, and Huis ten Bosch—which had been miraculously spared demolition and bombing—was also in disrepair. The queen chose to live in a rented house on Parklaan until both official residences could be restored.

The government had operated from London during the occupation, and when the southern portion of the country was liberated in 1944, it had swiftly reasserted direct authority. It assumed control over the entire nation after the German surrender, and a year later, in May 1946, general elections were held. Within a month parliament was again in session.

Most cities in Europe have commemorated those who died in the battles and deportations of World War II, but probably none has done so in a manner as unusual or appropriate as The Hague. In 1950 Mrs. Boon-van der Starp proposed that a miniature city be built, the proceeds of which would go to the Netherlands Student Sanitorium. The money to finance this project was provided by the Maduro family of Curaçao as a memorial to their son, George, who died at the Dachau concentration camp in 1945 after serving in the Netherlands' army. The municipality provided 18,000 square meters of land and other institutions provided additional sums. In 1952

the city of Madurodam, designed by S. J. Bouma, opened. On a scale of 1:25, it is a reconstruction of well-known Dutch buildings and Dutch architectural styles. Adults tower over the miniature Vredespaleis, Ridderzaal, and Heilige Geesthofje, but children lose themselves in a city more nearly scaled to their height and dedicated at once to their amusement and to the memory of a time when, to their parents, the future seemed very much in doubt.

As the government resumed normal functioning and the Netherlands once again assumed its active role in international affairs, The Hague took up the task of restoring its state properties, rebuilding its demolished districts, and creating new ones for the influx of new residents. The Binnenhof again became the center of the national government, and the Vredespaleis again housed the International Court, now under the aegis of the United Nations. International businesses, which had begun to settle in The Hague during the 1920s and 1930s, continued to find the city a congenial site for their headquarters; KLM, the Dutch national airline, built its head office on the Raamweg in 1945.

By the late 1950s The Hague was hosting not only international conferences at the International Court but also a large number of other congresses and, increasingly, musical and theatrical performances for which its older halls had become inadequate. Berlage's original plan for making the Gemeentemuseum a civic cultural center in the 1930s had not been carried out then due to what was deemed the project's excessive cost, but his plan was realized, in somewhat altered fashion, in the 1960s by the archi-

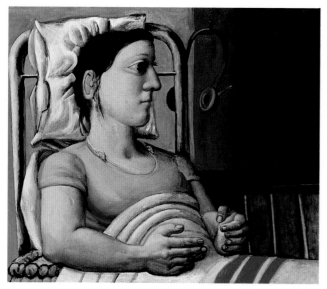

tect J. J. P. Oud, who had designed the Shell building before the war. Oud was close to seventy when he received the commission to design a congress center for The Hague, and although he completed his plans, it was his sons who carried out the actual building in the four years following Oud's death in 1963. The stark, almost Cubist lines of Oud's earlier work are gone from his last building—and gone, too, is the playfulness that characterized his decoration of the Shell building. Instead we have a severely "modern" building whose straight, efficient lines are softened only by sky-blue tiles and yellow bricks and by a long mosaic by Karel Appel in primary reds and blues. The great hall of the Nederlands Congresgebouw, or Netherlands Congress Center, is three stories high and seats two thousand. Here concerts—notably by the Residentie Orkest of The Hague—as well as theater and ballet performances are held. The basement can accommodate up to four thousand people and is used for banquets and expositions. A triangular tower seventeen stories high dominates the entire building, which is located near the Gemeentemuseum in the area largely destroyed by the Germans during the occupation.

The need for a hall as large as that provided by the Congresgebouw gives some indication of how much the nature of The Hague has changed in the postwar period. Certainly before the turn of the century—and less certainly up until the Second World War—The Hague retained that elegant but restricted atmosphere Couperus portrayed in *Eline Vere*—a world where the lucky few, members of the wealthy classes, enjoyed the "privilege" of culture

132

The realist tradition of Dutch art remains strong even today, as is evident in these contemporary paintings from the Haags Gemeentemuseum's collection. Despite the distortions of traditional perspective and modeling that the abstract, surrealist, expressionist, and pop movements have introduced into the figurative tradition, artists like Co Westerick, whose Sick Woman is seen at top left on the opposite page; Aat Verhoog creator of Hitler in Valencia, center; Walter Nobbe represented by Woman without Hat, this page, right; and Pat Andrea, whose Summer Evening Softball is reproduced below, still seek to represent the human form in modes that manage, in a disquieting century, to retain a sense of both the absurd and the playful.

largely denied to everyone else. The 750 seats in the Koninklijke Schouwburg, for example, were more than sufficient to seat all the Haguenaars who wished to attend the theater between the wars. The upheavals of the twentieth century changed all that, and the years following the country's liberation saw the audience for theater, dance, and music expand far beyond the capacity of The Hague's traditional auditoriums.

The Koninklijke Schouwburg, which has operated as a theater since 1804, when a performance of Voltaire's historical drama *Semiramis* inaugurated the hall, is the home of the Haagse Comedie, the Hague Theater Company, a government-supported repertory company. Founded in 1947 by Paul Steenbergen and the late Cees Laseur, it gives some two hundred performances a year of classic and contemporary pieces by Dutch and foreign writers. In 1968 the Haags Ontmoetings Theatre, HOT for short, opened as an offshoot of the Haagse Comedie. It presents experimental theater in an old church overlooking a canal in the city center. More than 4.5 million gilders—roughly two million dollars—are spent each year by the municipality to support these two groups.

In the last two decades The Hague has become the nucleus of the Randstadt Holland, the crescent of Dutch cities cradled in the Rhine delta that includes Amsterdam, Rotterdam, Leiden, and Haarlem. It forms the third largest urban complex in Western Europe, after only Paris and London. The Hague's population, about 475,000 in 1976, has been decreasing in recent years as space becomes

more scarce and rents increase, but the overall population has shifted only to the suburbs or to the other nearby cities in the Randstadt, all easily accessible to the center of The Hague by railway, tram, bus or automobile.

The Hague built its first railway station for the lines connecting it to Rotterdam and Amsterdam, the Hollandse Spoor, in 1843, and the city replaced that structure some fifty years later with a building still in use today. In 1870 a station intended to link The Hague with international rail lines, the Staatspoor, was opened in the Bezuidenhout district. Allied bombing during the war spared this station, but postwar reconstruction plans for the city center called for replacing the old Staatspoor with a new building, Den Haag Centraal, The Hague Central Station. Designed by K. van der Gaast, the station opened in 1973, with construction continuing until 1976. It is the center for the city's tram and bus lines as well as the station linking The Hague to other Dutch and European cities.

Next to Den Haag Centraal is the Babylonkomplex, opened in 1978 and designed by the architects Lucas and Niemeyer. It contains a hotel, theater, offices, and a commercial center. The exterior of this complex, like the Congresgebouw and, to some extent, Den Haag Centraal as well, exhibits the architectural principles first enunciated before the war by De Stijl and the Bauhaus: clean, functional design in which the raw materials of the modern age, chiefly glass, steel, and concrete, are exposed without flights of architectural or ornamental fancy.

Behind Den Haag Centraal and Babylon rises the new building designed to house the state archives. Faced in shining aluminum, this structure catches the reflections of clouds and sky as well as the images of surrounding buildings. The curved design, by Sjoerd Schamhart, provides a gentle contrast to the squarer lines of other buildings erected to replace the buildings of the Bezuidenhout district that were devastated in World War II.

The American Embassy is built on the site of the old Paulez Hotel on the Lange Voorhout, which was destroyed in the same air raid that leveled the nearby Bezuidenhout. This massive concrete structure, designed by Marcel Breuer, has little or no decoration to detract from its texture and color. Needless to say, the railway station and shopping complex, the state archives building, and the American Embassy all aroused—and arouse still—the passions of those who wish The Hague to be what, until the war, it had largely remained—elegant, old, and quiet. Breuer's building does successfully meld with the older buildings nearby, largely by blending its concrete with the neighboring stone façades and by keeping to the same height as the other buildings along the street. But the building, like others in the old Bezuidenhout district, does announce for good or ill the fact that The Hague has indeed entered the modern world.

The clash between the old Hague and the new has so far taken place largely in areas that were, in any case, in need of rebuilding. But today the pressing need for more space to house the Netherlands' legislature requires adding to the Binnenhof itself. Until the 1920s the Binnenhof and the Buitenhof were

Soaring modern forms have begun, in recent years, to dominate The Hague's skyline. On the left, the aluminum-faced building designed by Sjoerd Schamhart that houses the Royal Library rises behind The Hague's central railway station and the Babylon cultural and commercial complex. On the right, the Netherlands Congress Center, designed by J.J.P. Oud along the simple and functional lines favored by the so-called International Style. The Congress Center, located in the outskirts of the city, is home to The Hague's municipal orchestra and also serves as a site for national and international meetings as well as performances of visiting theatrical and dance troupes.

one unit. Berlage's plan for the renovation of the city center called for filling in the Hofvijver, which then reached to the Gevangenpoorte. A row of houses was indeed demolished along the Hofvijver, and by 1928 the Hofweg had been built, cutting off the Gevangenpoorte from the Binnenhof. New plans envisage building an addition to the Binnenhof complex on the corner facing the Spui and Lange Poten, the area between the Binnenhof, Het Plein, the Lange Poten, and the Hofweg; and the state has already acquired the Hotel Central, the PTT—the oldest telephone exchange in The Hague—and several other buildings to make way for the new legislative quarters. The Binnenhof is not, to be sure, a single structure of a single period, but rather a mélange of buildings each added as need or whim dictated. That they bear some resemblance to each other is surely more accident than design, and the new plans have been pondered for some time to ensure that the contrast will be no starker than the contrasts that now account for the Binnenhof's attraction. The addition will doubtless be a shock to some—and one more cause to remark that Europe's prettiest and mightiest village has become a city.

On April 30, 1980, Queen Juliana, who had succeeded her mother, Queen Wilhelmina, in 1948, abdicated in favor of her eldest daughter, Princess Beatrix. The new queen was inaugurated on the same day, according to custom, in Amsterdam's Nieuwe Kerk. Queen Beatrix was born at Soestdijk Palace in Baarn on January 31, 1938, but within two years she, along with the rest of the royal family, left the Netherlands for the duration of the war. She spent those five years with her parents in Canada and returned in August 1945 after the liberation.

Upon her accession to the throne, Queen Beatrix announced her intention of residing officially in The Hague at Huis ten Bosch, which between 1950 and 1956 had been fully restored and modernized. Although the palace has always been a state residence, first for the *stadholders* and then for the kings and queens of the Netherlands, this is the first time it has served as the principal residence of a reigning monarch. Queen Wilhelmina resided chiefly at Noordeinde until the war, and Queen Juliana resided at the Palace on the Dam in Amsterdam or at Soestdijk, where she continues to reside as Princess Juliana, the queen mother.

On August 15, 1981, Queen Beatrix; her consort, Prince Claus; and her children, the princes Willem-Alexander, heir to the throne, Johan-Friso, and Constantijn, took up residence at Huis ten Bosch. Although the palace itself is in a restricted area of The Hague Woods and rarely seen by Haguenaars or tourists, the flag signaling the royal presence may be glimpsed almost daily at the Palace Lange Voorhout, where the queen conducts state business and receives visitors in audience. Noordeinde, undergoing extensive restoration, will soon house visiting heads of state and other guests of the queen and the government. And so, in this last quarter of the twentieth century, as the modern world intrudes upon The Hague with its glass and steel, its traffic and noise, the city has been compensated by regaining its ancient role as the home of the Netherlands' sovereign.

THE NETHERLANDS IN LITERATURE

Ambrosius Bosschaert's **Vase with Flowers,** *painted in about 1620, shows the painstaking attention to detail that was so characteristic of Bosschaert and other seventeenth-century Dutch painters of flowers.*

Frederik Oudschans Dentz's A History of the English Church in The Hague *is an act of piety, not literature. Oudschans Dentz, a Dutch-born member of the congregation of the Church of England's outpost in The Hague, wrote this brief treatise for church elders in Great Britain, his effort as sincere as his ambitions were modest. He never imagined that this written report to his superiors would have a wide audience; that it does says something about the quality of Oudschans Dentz's scholarship—and more about his church, which has played an interesting role in The Hague's history since 1585.*

The connection between Great Britain and the Netherlands goes back many centuries; as early as 1285 the Dutch Government conferred certain immunities upon such subjects of King Edward I as chose to settle in the Low Countries, in return for the privilege of fishing on the English Coast. The United Provinces soon became the great Emporium for trade and merchants from all nations flocked there in quest of gain. . . .

In mercantile pursuits Britain took an important share; merchants and traders settled in the Netherlands and all the important English Irish and Scottish families had their own Chaplains with them. The Dutch Government gave them every assistance in providing for themselves and their families the advantages of a fixed Ministry. Hence the origin of many of the English Churches in Holland. In the Isle of Walcheren alone, three British congregations flourished, Vere being the staple port for the Kingdom of Scotland. The British also settled in Amsterdam, Rotterdam, Dordrecht, Delft and The Hague. In addition to the influence of commerce came the military campaigns; at the end of the 16th century Queen Elizabeth sent 6000 troops under the command of the Earl of Leicester to assist the United Provinces against the tyranny of Philip II of Spain. England also advanced large sums of money and as security for the repayment of these loans the towns of Flushing, Brielle and the fortress of Rammekens were given up to her and were held in pledge from 1585–1616. The Scottish Brigade, raised in 1595 served valiantly under the Princes of Orange. This large army of English and Scottish soldiers stationed in different parts of the Netherlands always had its full complement of Chaplains and in the course of time these clergymen formed themselves into an ecclesiastical body. They were spoken of as the Synod of the British clergy in the United Provinces. British Churches existed in not less than twenty-one towns, viz.: Amsterdam, Arnhem, Bergen-op-Zoom, Bois-le-Duc, Breda, the Brielle, Bruges, Brussels, Delft, Dordrecht, Gorinchem, Haarlem, The Hague, Heusden, Leyden, Middelburg, Ostend, Rotterdam, Utrecht, Vere and Zwolle.

We hear of an English Church at The Hague for the first time in the year 1585, when the English Ambassador was temporarily granted the use of the former Roman Catholic Chapel of the Sacrament Hospital, in Noordeinde, close to the Plaats. This privilege was accorded in order that the Chaplain to the Embassy might hold religious services for the Earl of Leicester's soldiers (Dec. 1585–Dec. 1587); in 1595 it was extended to include the entire English community.

This building, to be known henceforth as the English Church, had been in existence for about 150 years. The Sacrament Guild House was founded in 1440 on the East side of the Oude Molstraat, for the purpose of taking in old and crippled members of the Sacrament Guild. This Guild was a Church Institution with its own Committee of Management

The Nieuwe Kerk

consisting of a deacon and four members. About ten years later a chapel which was noted for the beauty and elegance of its architecture and decoration, was built behind the Hospital, for the use of the patients. . . .

From 1595 till November 1822 the English Government continued to take an interest in the Church, contributing annually, a portion of the chaplain's stipend; in the latter years of the Church's existence this grant was £30 sterling. . . .

When the differences in the Reformed Church became so sharp that a decisive and violent break took place, the Contra-Remonstranten received permission from the States of Holland to make use of the English Chapel. Through the influence of the Remonstrant fraction, the Orthodox clergyman was removed from his office and religious services were forbidden for those who continued to adhere to that sect. This strict Gomaristic Section held services at Ryswyk, but when this proved too inconvenient they obtained permission to use the English Chapel where their first service was held on Jan. 22nd, 1617. They were not, however, allowed to form a separate Church Council.

The large congregation speedily outgrew the building and moreover they desired the restoration of their religious rights; they accordingly took possession of the Klooster Kerk on July 9th, 1617. This building had previously been used as an arsenal and munition foundry. After this the partial connection with the English Church came to an end.

In April 1621 Frederick V of Bohemia, having been driven from the palatinate after a reign of one winter, (hence his nickname "Winter King") took refuge in Holland. He had married Elizabeth "Queen of Hearts" the daughter of James I of England; from this House of Brunswick-Hanover the present King of England is descended.

Among the followers of Elizabeth and Frederick were two clergymen, Ludovicus Amararius, and Theobald Mauritius, who preached for the Queen in English. After some years they received permission to hold services and to teach in the English Chapel, on condition that the collection money was given to the Elders and Deacons of the existing Church.

In this way a common interest was soon established between the Germans and the English. The deliberations in July 1626, when they obtained this permission, led to an agreement being signed on Dec. 25th, 1626 which lasted for many years. In this agreement it is clearly stated that the thirty years possession of the building which the English Church had enjoyed, created no rights of sole ownership, and it should always remain at the disposal of the municipal authorities.

In this respect the English subjects in the Netherlands were not so fortunate as the Netherlanders living in England, for on July 24th, 1550 Edward VI granted them the right to found a Dutch Church in London, and they were given in perpetuity part of the cloister of the Augustine Friars, which had been dissolved. To the present day this has remained their undisputed property. The first service was held there on September 21st, 1550. . . .

The first resident Chaplain was John Wing, who had already taken services in the English Church in 1595. He came from Flushing and was installed by John Forbes, English Chaplain at Delft, on May 11th, 1627. . . .

Thomas Melbourne was appointed Reader and Frans Corbitt Verger. The unbroken history of the Church can be traced from this time. There were ten Chaplains before the time that the Church was suspended in 1822 and since that time there have been seven incumbents. . . .

For many years, the Queen of Bohemia supported the Church as far as was in her power (it must not be forgotten that the Court of Bohemia suffered from a chronic lack of funds), but in 1658 she withdrew all her interest in the affairs of the community for the following reason:

When George Downing came to The Hague in that year as ambassador of Protector Cromwell, he learned that both clergymen were still accustomed to pray for King Charles II and his family. He was highly indignant and so influenced the Council of State, that in July of that year both preachers were forbidden to pray for Charles Stuart, as the Prince of Wales was then called. The Rev. George Beaumont obeyed immediately, but the other, a Scot, refused, preferring to lose his position.

When the Queen of Bohemia heard that there would no longer be prayers for her family, she declared that she would never again enter the Church; she had the curtains, the bibles and the cushions taken away from her seat and absented herself. Later on she allowed the preacher to understand that she would come to Church if he would refrain from alluding to politics, but this had no result, for the Rev. G. Beaumont carried his obedience so far that, though not actually offering prayers for Cromwell, he did not hesitate to make known that England was becoming most prosperous under his rule. As a result Downing used his influence with Thurloe, Cromwell's secretary, to secure for the English Church an annuity of £150, which was not however paid out after the restoration of Charles II.

The Queen of Bohemia attended Church no more, and left in 1660 for London where she died on Feb. 22nd, 1662. Before her departure however, she sent a sum of Fl. 250 to the Church Council to be used for the poor among the congregation. . . .

When William the Stadholder married Mary Stuart of England, a number of ladies and gentlemen came to live at The Hague and the Church received much support, especially of a financial nature. Princess Mary was a member of the congregation and a great benefactor. In 1680 the Princess of Orange commanded the clergyman to request the Burgomaster of The Hague to have separate seats built for her and her suite, and in such a way, that by her eventual attendance no disturbance to the public should ensue. . . .

When Princess Mary and her husband Prince William ascended the throne of England, the Queen manifested her partiality to this Church by procuring for it from the Exchequer an annuity of thirty pounds sterling for the maintenance of public worship. When the first grant was made it was stated that the sum was to be given in perpetuity to the English Consistory at The Hague so long as it was served by a Presbyterian Minister. . . .

The expenses for the Holy Communion in the Walloon Church were paid by the King Stadholder, and the Consistory of the English Church decided to ask the Rev. P. M. Bowie to approach the King with a view to obtaining the same favor. Mr. Bowie accordingly consulted the Intendant of the palace Mr. des Marets. The request was acceded to and the English

Church was granted the value of four loaves and twenty bottles of wine.

Queen Mary died on Jan. 7th, 1695, and the Church Council were afraid that her decease might prove a loss to them in many ways. Besides the moral support that she had given to the Church, she had rendered financial aid and the lack of this would have been severely felt. Accordingly, Mr. Bowie wrote concerning this to his friend Dr. Stanley of St. Paul's Cathedral. He received the agreeable news that "His Majesty King William has been graciously pleased not only to continue the late Queen's pensions to a great many other persons, but also that to our Church."

FREDERIK OUDSCHANS DENTZ
A History of the English Church in The Hague, 1929

ON SERVICE IN THE HAGUE

Letter drop, Smids Water

"It would amuse you . . ." Mary Isabella Waddington de Bunsen *declares at the outset of her memoir of diplomatic life in The Hague, circa 1870—and amuse us it does. It also captivates, fascinates, touches, and reveals, for Mme. de Bunsen shares the gift of so many diplomats' wives of the era, a talent for recording life in strange places in language and images familiar to those who stayed behind. Born of English parents in Normandy, Mary Waddington married a Prussian consular officer and followed him to various European posts. Their years in The Hague were especially eventful, for they arrived shortly before the Franco-Prussian War of 1870 and stayed long enough to witness the wedding of the Prince of Wied to Princess Marie of the Netherlands.*

It would amuse you, I think, to see how perfectly we are at home and settled here already, although we only arrived this day week. So far, we are quite charmed with the Hague, and find its quiet and comfort a haven of rest after the turmoil of Berlin. As we were sent off very suddenly, our last days there were all bustle and confusion. . . .

Count Bethusy sent me a lovely bouquet of white camellias and violets, and as B. had another big one, we must have looked almost like a wedding-party at the station. I was infinitely more sorry to leave Berlin than I should have thought possible some time ago, but we met with much kindness there, and have made some real friends, I believe. When we arrived at the Hague our Chief's carriage and servant were waiting at the station, rooms had been taken for us at the hotel, and before we had been there half an hour, Count Perponcher came to ask us to dine quietly with them that day. Since then all has gone on beautifully; the Perponchers seem to be ideal Chiefs, quite overpowering us with kindness. The children, too, are charming, and a great resource for B. Elizabeth is a beautiful child of ten, and there are two ducks of little boys. . . .

C. has gone out with his Chief, who is indefatigable in taking him his round of diplomatic visits, all in person and on foot, so that C. comes back pretty well tired, and his head in a whirl with all the Dutch names, which are generally long and complicated. The Countess and I have already been our rounds, leaving cards in abundance and finding few people at home. *We* go in her carriage. C. was presented yesterday to the King (King William VI. of the Netherlands), who appears to be somewhat in Vittorio's style, brief and abrupt. The interview was short and sweet, and the whole affair was over so soon, that when C. came back I thought there must have been some hitch, and that it had been countermanded. We are both to be presented to the Queen tomorrow, Sunday evening, at nine o'clock. Meantime I must tell you that we have succeeded in finding an apartment, which is a great relief, as we were told the custom here is to take a house for three years and furnish it, which seemed a very great trouble. The houses in Holland are small and independent, like in England, or rather, as the Dutch would claim, the English houses are copied from theirs. In general there are no flats, but we have discovered one in a large old-fashioned house which seems as though it were made for us. There is a polished black wood staircase and a very large and lofty drawing-room with a bow-window. The walls are not papered, but hung with huge oil paintings in panels, as is often the case in old Dutch houses. These represent views of Rome, and I think the sight of them made us take the apartment at once, but it really suits us perfectly. The house is in the Korte Vorhout, just opposite the palace of Prince Frederick of the Netherlands, uncle of the King, and at the entrance of the "Bosch" (wood), a kind of public park. Count Perponcher wants to go with his family to his *château* in Silesia, and our fate will evidently be to spend the summer here. Everybody says it is quite pleasant, hardly ever too hot, and with Scheveningen and sea-bathing within twenty minutes' drive. There is much to be seen in Holland which is all new to us, and the Hague, or "S'Gravenhage," which is its real name, is a clean, quaint, picturesque place. It is very amusing to study Dutch in the advertisements from the shops, &c., and we can understand it to read fairly well, as there are many English and German words, but when spoken, the pronunciation is so different, so harsh and guttural, that one is quite at sea. An injunction at a house door made us laugh heartily: "Drie mal bellen!" It meant, of course, "ring three times," but as *bellen* is to *bark* in German, it looked so funny. I am much amused at being addressed as "Mevrow," which is "Madame." We hope to get into our new home tomorrow, and I am quite looking forward to it, after three months of hotel life in Berlin. . . .

Our presentation to the Queen was a serious business. We were ordered in the evening, in full dress, and it lasted an hour and a half, *sitting*, I am thankful to say, in rather a prim circle, the two Perponchers and ourselves. The Hofdame (Lady-in-waiting) sat in the distance nodding occasionally. The Queen wears her hair in ringlets, like the portraits of Mme. dé Sevigné, and must have been very pretty. She is exceedingly clever and well-informed, but conversation carried on so long and under such circumstances is always an effort. Poor Perponcher declared afterwards that though it was a "grosse Anszeichung" (great distinction) H.M.'s keeping us so long, he felt quite exhausted.

The people here seem very pleasant and kind; the little Hofdamen come to see me on foot in short dresses. Some of them are clever and speak English perfectly, others are of a serious turn of mind and discuss last Sunday's sermon. . . .

The Perponchers went off yesterday in very good spirits. They have been five years at the Hague, and are glad, I imagine, to get away for a time; we miss them very much.

We went to Scheveningen, as it was fine, but *le fond de l'air* is still keen. We sat on the shore in the funny, comfortable basket-chairs with great hoods to them, which protect from both wind and sun. We paid a visit to the Jacobsons, who have a villa there. They are friends of the Queen's; he is an art *connoisseur*, and has the best private gallery at the Hague. Afterwards we dined at the Etablissement des Bains, at an immense *table d'hôte*, very well got up. In the evening we sat on the terrace and heard the band. The scene is pretty, with all the people about and the sun setting right opposite in the sea. . . .

It is perfectly astonishing how dull life feels here. I think it must depend to a certain degree on the additional weight of atmosphere above our heads, from the country being under the level of the sea. All our colleagues say they feel it as soon as they cross the frontier. In general I do not require much outside help to pass my time, but though I have a certain amount of visits and people are quite kind, the days seem endless, and one feels habitually bored. C. has been writing a report on the sugar question, which has been very grievous to him, but as Perponcher is expected back daily, even the little occupation C. has at present is likely to cease. He moans over this prospect very much, and it really is difficult, for one cannot read all day. In some respects I am better off, for I have B.'s lessons to look after, and the cook, who always talks a lot of Dutch; and then I copy in the picture gallery occasionally, when it is not too dark all day to see, and then there is work and other feminine resources, although I have the dismal dumps often enough too. Happily we do not generally have fits of despondency at the same time, so that we can manage to laugh at each other in turn, which is a help. Enough of that, however; we must get on as we best can!

M. Jacobson paid us a long visit the other day and went into ecstasies over my drawings. He appears to be an elderly and *Dutch* admirer of mine, and it was rather pleasant to be told that I was "artiste jusqu'au bout des ongles" by the first art amateur at the Hague. . . .

The diplomatic mind here is much exercised as to the *fêtes* of November 17th, and as to how far we shall be expected to join in them. A monument is to be unveiled on that day, to commemorate the deliverance of the country from French occupation and the return of the House of Orange in 1815. One does not exactly see why the Corps diplomatique should join in a national demonstration against France. But it is said on the other hand that the populace here is apt to be tyrannical on such occasions, and quite capable of actively resenting anything that might look like want of sympathy with their feelings. Most of the *Chefs de Mission*, amongst whom the French Minister, of course, have taken leave of absence and got themselves out of the way. C. wrote to Perponcher about it, but he only advised asking for directions from Berlin or consulting the other colleagues, both of which C. might have done by his own unassisted light. . . .

Last week the inauguration of the monument caused unusual excitement in the town. C. went to the ceremony in full uniform, and B. and I had the pleasure of decking him out in all his decorations. The *fête* seemed to have been curious and amusing; there was a great procession, all sorts of corporations, with banners and bouquets, passing before the royal stand. Their bows were peculiar and republican; many in the *cortège* smoked the whole time, and did not even take their cigars out of their mouths as they passed the Queen. Later in the day B. and I went to the Legation to see the procession, which it was said would pass the Vyverberg. We had orange bows on, for you could not venture into the streets

The Plein

otherwise, without running the risk of being insulted, or even being *painted* orange, as happened to some people. The Legation looked very well with three tremendous banners almost down to the ground waving before it, one of them Nord-Deutsche Bund, one Prussian white and black, and the third orange. We waited in vain, for the procession took another way and never came by the Vyverberg at all. . . .

The great event here at present is the arrival of the Prince of Wied, who it is generally supposed is destined to be the future husband of Princess Marie, daughter of Prince Frederick of the Netherlands and his wife, Princess Louise of Prussia. Our Legation is of course much interested in the marriage, as the Princess is a niece of our King, and we ourselves are particularly so, from knowing the Prince personally, as well as his sister, Princess Elizabeth of Wied, who has just been married to Prince Karol of Roumania. C., who is *chargé d'affaires* at present, went to see the Prince at once, to put himself "à sa disposition."

I had just written this when the servant, a German, opened the door and announced, with much apparent satisfaction, "Seine Durchlaucht der Fürst Wied" (His Serene Highness the Prince of Wied). He paid us a very nice visit, talking and laughing quite pleasantly. He said his sister had told him a great deal about her visit to Florence. Pastor Quandt's sermon at the German church this morning seemed to have struck him very much, which is not astonishing, as he is quite a remarkable preacher. The Prince could not stay long, as he was under orders to go to the Huis de Paauw (House of the Peacock) in the country, the residence of his bride-elect.

Gemeentemuseum, displays

We are living in a state of perpetual small excitement about the Wied affairs. It is rather an awkward position for C., as his Chief may arrive at any moment and he does not wish to put himself forward for the few days he may still be *chargé d'affaires*. We went, however, to the Huis de Paauw, Prince Frederick's country palace, in pouring rain, hoping to see the Princess Marie. The beginning was not auspicious. Mdlle. van Doorn van Westcapelle, the Princess's lady, was out, and of course we could not ask directly for H.R.H. We saw, however, one of the Princess Frederick's ladies, Mdlle. van Suchtelen van der Haare, and by the time we had finished our call Mdlle. van Doorn had returned and took us at once to the Princess Marie's drawing-room. H.R.H. received us very cordially, as usual, and when I asked if we might be allowed to congratulate her, pressed my hand warmly. She said she knew her *fiancé* had been to see us, and that we were acquainted with his family. She showed us some lovely portraits of the Princess of Roumania taken as *Braut* (betrothed), with and without Prince Karol, and kept us nearly an hour talking, in great spirits all the time. The Prince of Wied has been at the Loo to be presented to the King, and now one would think the marriage will be publicly announced, for till the present time it has been, as the Princess Marie said herself, "le secret de la comédie." Then arise many questions. Shall we have to go and congratulate officially, and will there be any festivities? Of course, if there are any I must put aside my black, so that for two days past I have been busy looking over dresses, &c.

I might have spared myself all thought and trouble about dresses. An invitation to dinner for to-day at the Huis de Paauw has come, but for C. *alone*. At first I was rather disappointed, but now laziness is prevailing, and I feel glad to be spared the trouble of a *grande toilette* and the long cold drive. C. will come in for all the honors, I hope, as the formal *Verlobung* (betrothal) is to take place. The Queen is to be there and all the grandees, but he will be the only diplomat. . . .

C.'s grand dinner went off very well, though stiffly. There was *cercle* before dinner for the Queen. Then the doors opened and the Prince of Wied and Princess Marie appeared, and went round receiving the congratulations of all present. Prince Frederick presented all the "Hof-Chargen" (court dignitaries) to his future son-in-law, but when he came to C. he said: "Herr von Bunsen brauch ich dir nicht vorzustellen" (There is no need to present M. de Bunsen to thee). The Queen was very gracious to C., and so were all the "Hohe Herrschaften." All the ladies who were there belonged to the Court in their own right (husbands did not bring their wives), so that my not being asked was explained. The dinner was very sumptuous and the Prince of Orange proposed the health of the *fiancés*. After dinner *cercle* again, and then it was over.

Count Bibra, who composes the whole suite of the Prince of Wied, came to bid goodbye yesterday, bringing a polite message from the Prince, who was afraid he would not be able to come himself. Bibra seemed much pleased at all having gone off well and his Prince being really *fiancé* to the face of the world at last. There had been so many delays that people were getting suspicious about it. . . .

After three chapters of Stanley I feel it necessary to make a change, so sit down to write—not that I feel in a mood for correspondence—rather the contrary, for I have been unusually sleepy and lazy, even for here, for several days past. The Perponchers have returned, which is a real pleasure. Baroness v. D. is very kind, and spends an evening with us about once a week. I go to see her on the days when she is in waiting, as after driving out with the Queen she generally is at liberty till dinner-time, although she must not leave the palace. It is not very easy to get to her, for the town palace has only one entrance, and you have to inquire for the person you want of a grand porter, who sits in a sort of hooded Scheveningen chair. If one is on foot, one is apt to feel rather insignificant. Moreover, the other evening just as I got in there was a call, "Der Prins van Oranien" (Prince of Orange, born at the Hague, 1840) (Dutch), and I had just time to get out of his way as he came in on foot, in a shooting jacket and Tyrolean hat, going up the grand staircase two or three steps at a time, to see his mother, I suppose. Even when the porter is safely passed, one's troubles are not over. He consigns you to a grand and generally cross-looking servant, who takes you up the grand staircase and through the first *salon* of the Queen's apartment to a corridor which leads to H.M. private rooms. It is only there that one gets to a private back staircase and to less exalted regions. Baroness van D. has two very nice rooms in the second storey, and there we have pleasant chats. The other day, after sitting with her for some time, I called on Baroness de B., the beauty of the Hague, who is most strikingly handsome. She gave me a cup of tea at four in the afternoon, which is a new fashion people are adopting here now, and a very pleasant one. The next day I had a good many visits, Mme. Baudin (France) among the number, very elegant in a velvet jacket and tunic trimmed with fur over a black satin skirt, and her hair half down her back. Also Mme. Schimmel-Penninck, who came to ask

Gemeentemuseum, lobby

B. to go and play with her children, at which I was much pleased, for they are extremely nice. . . .

I must give you an account of our Christmas-tree—a *fir-tree* for the first time, as we always had *laurel* in Italy, and I must confess to melancholy remembrances of the bright glistening leaves that used to light up so well. Perponcher, however, who came in to ask us to *their* Christmas-tree, would not sympathise at all. In his eyes laurel was only a *pis aller* when one could not get the real thing. We had 'a good many people—eight little children from Java, whom I had invited as they live in this house, and about a dozen individuals whom I had never set eyes on, brought promiscuously by our *propriétaire*, rather to my indignation. However, it all went off well, and after the presents were distributed, the children all had *Glühwein* (hot spiced wine) and what are called here *letters*. These are letters cut out in pastry on a large scale, and filled with some sort of almond stuff inside which is very good. B. had a cooking stove amongst her presents which really cooks! We tried it yesterday, and when the water began to boil I was almost as much excited as she was. She was much flattered: "Ce n'est pas souvent mamna que Beatrice a des joujoux qui t'amusent aussi."

After our own tree we went to the German church, where there was a big one for the schoolchildren, combined with a service. This was not very successful, as there were crowds of Dutch people trying to get in all the time, and much noise and pushing about. As soon as the service was over we went off to the Perponcher tree—our third that day! There we found all the children in the Chief's study, waiting in feverish excitement while the Count and Countess were mysteriously occupied upstairs. Presently Perponcher appeared, and asked us to come up for a first look, telling the children, "Sie sollen da bleiben und sie kriegen gar nichts" (You must stay there, and you will get nothing at all), whereat they laughed incredulously. The sight upstairs was one of the prettiest I ever saw: the inner drawing-room was brilliantly lighted, and in the midst stood the tree, most tastefully adorned—the first really German one I had ever seen. On each side of the room was a row of tables, spread with white cloths, and covered with a most tempting array of presents. As soon as we had seen it all the children were called up, and entered what must have seemed to them quite a fairyland of bliss. The tables were then appropriated, and the exclamations of pleasure on all sides were delightful to hear. There was a little table for B., one for Herr von Scheven, the head of the Chancellerie. All the servants had cakes and appropriate things; no one was forgotten. The poor Countess was in a great state of mind; she had hidden away the presents for her husband so well that it was some time before she could find them. As for herself, she told me the Count always gave her a handsome dress. She had so many uses for her money she hated spending it on dress, "et une belle robe tous les ans aide vraiment beaucoup; elle me servira pour toutes les soirées de cet hiver." It was pretty to see the children flying to their mother with their thanks after the first enraptured survey, "Mama, ich habe *Alles* was ich gewunscht habe" (I have all my wishes). They hung round her neck and kissed her hands. It was a very pretty family scene.

When arranging our Christmas dinner I found that turkeys are dreadfully expensive here—7 gulden, about 11 to 15 frs.—so I carried the

The Mauritshuis

146

matter to C., who decided in favor of the turkey, provided we had somebody to share it with us. So we asked Scheven and the Baroness D. It seems that according to etiquette here the Queen, who can do with one maid of honor all day long, must have two to dine with her, and the D. had undertaken to be the second one on Christmas Day, so we had Scheven alone.

We really suffer quite terribly from the cold; it keeps us awake at night. Auguste (the maid) calls it "eine feine Kälte" (a delicate cold), which seems to creep in, despite of fire in the room and any amount of covering and precaution.

C. and I sat out the Old Year very quietly together. We opened the window to hear the chimes of the Groote Kerk (big church) strike twelve, then we had a quiet glass of punch and went to bed. We have had cold, bright weather lately, with a good deal of snow, and there have been sledges, some of them very pretty, going about with much tinkling of bells and with their occupants well wrapped up in furs. Mme. Baudin asked us to pass the New Year's evening with them *en petit comité*. This turned out to mean pretty much the whole usual set, and at first I felt quite confused by the lights and the noise of voices, after my long seclusion in mourning. On the whole, I was rather glad not to have another solitary evening, for, as Baudin said, "C'est un de ces jours où l'on se compte." Monday was the Court ball, and I was at last presented to the King. We were just a little late, and I saw Mme. de Perponcher looking out anxiously for me to come and take up my place behind her.

We had still long to wait before the Queen came in, looking very well, with magnificent diamonds. She went down the row and the King came afterwards. Mme. de Perponcher named me, whereupon he gave me a look, muttered something, and went on. Nevertheless, the Countess seemed quite relieved "que cela c'était si bien passé." Then their Majesties proceeded to the ballroom and dancing began. I did not know many people, but Baudin, who seems to have got a quiet friendship for me, gave me his arm and took me about, showing me people and things. Precisely at midnight the music ceased, and we all went off.

"Une chose en amène une autre." The next evening we had to go to Mme. Rocst van Limburg's reception (Foreign Affairs), where I had not yet appeared. She is an American, no longer young, but very agreeable and well dressed. Most people went off to Mme. Baudin's, who receives on the same evening, but we did the thing in style and stayed on. Mme. Rocst got quite confidential, and made me turn all round to show my dress, which she pronounced a great success, black and woollen though it is. It is the first the woman Countess R. recommended me in Paris has sent, and besides being stylish is very practical, *à deux corsages*, and with a "pouf," which can be let down and forms a train at night. At present it has to do for all occasions, but I hope to get the next ones soon.

The next day C. dined at Knorring's (Russia), who has just returned from Paris, bringing us kind messages from our old friend and colleague at Turin, Count Stackelberg. The dinner, it seems, was "tout ce qu'il y a de plus fin," served on silver and old china, and the conversation most interesting. All the guests, about six, were discussing the most interesting debates they had heard. Knorring asked C. (who was *bescheiden*, as all the others were *Chefs de Mission*), and he answered the debate about the cession of Nice between Cavour and Garibaldi; this made rather a sensation, and certainly during his time in Italy C. has come across much that was interesting and exciting. . . .

It is high time we should be thinking of our plans and of getting away from here, for we are all getting frightfully lazy! We have very little to do, and even that little we find a burden. C. lies about all day, under pretext of a cold, reading deep theological books. He refuses to pay visits, even quite urgent ones, won't go to the Chancellerie, gets up late, munches bonbons, and in short does everything most opposed to all his former habits. Till now he used to write letters at the Chancellerie, but as the Government has again made a fuss about postage and we are obliged to pay for our letters, it is no use writing superfluous ones. This sort of stagnant life feels odd and decidedly dull, after what we have been used to.

Saturday we were reckoning on a quiet evening when we received an invitation "pour le thé de la Reine," for the same evening. Preparations there were scarcely any for me to make, for, as Auguste remarked, the choice of a dress was not difficult, there being only the one I told you of, as no new ones have arrived yet. We had to be there at nine and found the Queen alone. She was sitting near the fire, not as usual on the sofa, entrenched behind a table. It was rather stiff at first, as such things always are, but C. talked remarkably well, and the Queen, getting animated, told many anecdotes, and as she knows everybody and is so clever, the conversation was most interesting. Indeed, I found the *dame d'honneur*, Mme. de Papst, who made her appearance later, rather in the way, as she would talk to me in whispers when I would much rather have listened to what was going on. Tea was handed round, and at ten a small table was brought in ready laid for four people and placed in a corner of the room. The Queen got up, and saying she hoped we liked oysters, led the way to it. Fortunately we *do* like them, for there was nothing else, but they were very good; we had some punch to drink and it was altogether rather jolly—the Queen on a sofa, I in an armchair on her right, C. to her left, and Mme. de Papst opposite H.M. Our carriage had been ordered at half-past ten, for according to Dutch custom the servants when you arrive anywhere tell you at what hour you are to go away. We sat on, however, chatting at the supper-table, till the Queen, who had been laughing very much at some of C.'s stories, got up suddenly, said it was midnight, gave me her hand, and departed. It was not quite midnight, but over half-past eleven, so we can hope that H.M. did not bore herself too much. This *thé de la Reine* is a peculiar institution, but as her Majesty talks better than most of her subjects and is very good company, it is rather enjoyable than otherwise.

I am afraid it is so long since I wrote that I might give you quite a long list of solemn dinners and parties. Then there was a *thé dansant* at Court. At the *cercle* I was screened from any rays of royalty by being ensconced behind Mme. de Perponcher's rather ample figure, but the Queen came up very kindly afterwards, asking how I was "depuis l'autre soir." The King also spoke to me, and I got on very well. A Belgian secretary, who evidently had experience of such functions, took me in to supper, and managed to get in just as the first batch of grandees was coming out. As we came in M. de Knorring (Russia) rushed up, "Permettez, madame,

Romanesque chapel

que je vous offre une chaise," and he instantly established himself beside me, the Bavarian on the other side, leaving the astonished Belgian to his own devices. He made a very good supper notwithstanding, but has not forgotten the incident yet, and never meets me without alluding to it. "Il faut avouer que M. de Knorring s'est emparé de vous, madame, l'autre soir d'une façon," &c.

MARY ISABELLA WADDINGTON DE BUNSEN
In Three Legations, 1894

VAN GOGH'S VISION

Vincent van Gogh was not born in The Hague, but he did receive his first commissions there—an opportunity he characterized as "almost miraculous" in a letter he wrote to his brother, Theo, from The Hague in July of 1882. In this letter and others that followed, the young artist poured out his feelings about women, about painting, about color, about nature. All these feelings find their way into the letters excerpted below; the last opens with a description of the beach at Scheveningen that is at once accurate and evocative.

Theo, it is almost miraculous!!!

First comes your registered letter, secondly C. M. asks me to make him 12 small pen drawings, views of The Hague, a propos of some that were ready. (The Paddemoes, the Geest, the Vleersteeg, were finished.) At 2.50 guilders a piece, price fixed by me, with the promise that if they suit him, he will take 12 more at his own price, which will be higher than mine. In the third place I have just met Mauve, happily delivered of his large picture, and he promised to come and see me soon. So, "ça va, ça marche, ça ira encore!"

Yours,
Vincent

The Hague, July 31, 1882

Dear Theo,

Just a line to welcome you in anticipation of your arrival. Also to let you know of the receipt of your letter and the enclosed, for which I send my heartiest thanks. It was very welcome, for I am hard at work and need a few more things.

As far as I understand it, we of course agree perfectly about black in nature. Absolute black does not really exist. But like white, it is present in almost every colour, and forms the endless variety of greys—different in tone and strength. So that in nature one really sees nothing else but those tones or shades.

There are but three fundamental colors—red, yellow and blue; "composites" are orange, green and purple.

By adding black and some white one gets the endless varieties of greys—*red*-grey, *yellow*-grey, *blue*-grey, *green*-grey, *orange*-grey, *violet*-grey. To say, for instance, how many green-greys there are is impossible, there are endless varieties

But the whole chemistry of colours is not more complicated than those few simple rules. And to have a clear notion of this is worth more than seventy different colours of paint—since with those three principal colours and black and white, one can make more than seventy tones and

149

varieties. The colourist is he who seeing a colour in nature knows at once how to analyse it, and can say for instance: that green-grey is yellow with black and blue, etc.

In other words, someone who knows how to find the greys of nature on his palette. In order to make notes from nature, or to make little sketches, a strongly developed feeling for outline is absolutely necessary as well as for strengthening the composition subsequently.

But I believe one does not acquire this without effort, rather in the first place by observation, and then especially by strenuous work and research, and particular study of anatomy and perspective is also needed. Beside me is hanging a landscape study by Roelofs, a pen sketch—but I cannot tell you how expressive that simple outline is, everything is in it.

Another still more striking example is the large woodcut of "The Shepherdess" by Millet, which you showed me last year and which I have remembered ever since. And then, for instance, the pen and ink sketches by Ostade and Peasant Breughel.

When I see such results I feel more strongly the great importance of the outline. And you know for instance from "Sorrow" that I take a great deal of trouble to make progress in that respect.

But you will see when you come to the studio that besides the seeking for the outline I have, just like everyone else, a feeling for the power of colour. And that I do not object to making water-colours; but the foundation of them is the drawing, and then from the drawing many other branches beside the water-colour sprout forth, while will develop in me in time as in everybody who loves his work.

I have attacked that old whopper of a pollard willow, and I think it is the best of the water-colours: a gloomy landscape—that dead tree near a stagnant pool covered with reeds, in the distance a car shed of the Rhine Railroad, where the tracks cross each other; dingy black buildings, then green meadows, a cinder path, and a sky with shifting clouds, grey with a single bright white border, and the depth of blue where the clouds for an instant are parted. In short, I wanted to make it as the signal man in his smock and with his little red flag must see and feel it when he thinks: "it is gloomy weather today."

I have worked with great pleasure these last days, though now and then I still feel the effects of my illness.

Of the drawings which I show you now I think only this: I hope they will prove to you that I am not remaining stationary in my work, but progress in a direction that is reasonable. As to the money value of my work, I do not pretend to anything else than that it would greatly astonish me if my work were not just as salable in time as that of others. Whether that will happen *now* or *later* I cannot of course tell, but I think the surest way, which *cannot* fail, is to work from nature faithfully and energetically. Feeling and love for nature sooner or later find a response from people who are interested in art. It is the painter's duty to be entirely absorbed by nature and to use all his intelligence to express sentiment in his work, so that it becomes intelligible to other people. To work for the market is in my opinion not exactly the right way, but on the contrary involves deceiving the amateurs. And true painters have not done so, rather the sympathy they received sooner or later came because of their sincerity. That is all I know about it, and I do not think I need

Ridderzaal

Mantle, Ridderzaal

know more. Of course it is a different thing to try to find people who like your work, and who will love it—that of course is permitted. But it must not become a speculation, that would perhaps turn out wrong and would certainly cause one to lose time that ought to be spent on the work itself.

Of course you will find in my water-colours things that are not correct, but that will improve with time.

But know it well, I am far from clinging to a system or being bound by one. Such a thing exists more in the imagination of Tersteeg, for instance, than in reality. As to Tersteeg, you understand that my opinion of him is quite personal, and that I do not want to thrust upon *you* this opinion that I am forced to have. So long as he thinks about me and says about me the things you know, I cannot regard him as a friend, nor as being of any use to me; quite the opposite. And I am afraid that his opinion of me is too deeply rooted ever to be changed, the more so since, as you say yourself, he will never take the trouble to reconsider some things and to change. When I see how several painters here, whom I know, have problems with their water-colours and paintings, so that they cannot bring them off, I often think: friend, the fault lies in your drawing. I do not regret for one single moment that I did not go on at first with water-colour and oil painting. I am sure I shall make up for that if only I work hard, so that my hand does not falter in drawing and in the perspective; but when I see young painters compose and draw *from memory*—and then haphazardly smear on whatever they like, *also from memory*—then study it at a distance, and put on a very mysterious, gloomy face in the endeavour to find out what in heaven's name it may look like, and finally make something of it, always *from memory*—it sometimes disgusts me, and makes me think it all very tedious and dull.

The whole thing makes me sick!

But those gentlemen go on asking me, not without a certain patronizing air, "if I am not painting as yet?"

Now I too often on occasion sit and improvise, so to speak, at random on a piece of paper, but I do not attach any more value to this than to a rag or a cabbage leaf.

And I hope you will understand that when I continue to stick to drawing I do so for two reasons, most of all because I want to get a firm hand for drawing, and secondly because painting and water-colouring cause a great many expenses which bring no immediate recompense, and those expenses double and redouble ten times when one works on a drawing which is not correct enough.

And if I got in debt or surrounded myself with canvases and papers all daubed with paint without being sure of my drawing, then my studio would soon become a sort of hell, as I have seen some studios look. As it is I always enter it with pleasure and work there with animation. But I do not believe that you suspect me of *unwillingness.* It only seems to me that the painters here argue in the following way. They say: you must do this or that; if one does not do it, or not exactly so, or if one says something in reply, there follows a: "so you know better than I?" So that immediately, sometimes in less than five minutes, one is in fierce altercation, and in such a position that neither party can go forward or back. The least hateful result of this is that one of the parties has the presence of mind to keep silent, and in some way or other makes a quick exit through some opening. And one is almost inclined to say: confound it, the painters are almost like a family, namely, a fatal combination of persons with contrary interests, each of whom is opposed to the rest, and two or more are of the same opinion only when it is a question of combining together to obstruct another member. This definition of the word family, my dear brother, is, I hope, not always true, especially not when it concerns painters or our own family. With all my heart I wish peace may reign in our own family, and I remain with a handshake,

Yours,
Vincent

Parliament Buildings, Binnenhof

[The Hague, early September 1882]
Sunday morning

Dear Theo,

I have just received your very welcome letter, and as I want to take some rest to-day I answer it at once. Many thanks for it and for the enclosure, and for the things you tell me.

And for your description of that scene with the workmen at Montmartre, which I found very interesting, as you describe the colours too, so that I can see it: many thanks for it. I am glad you are reading the book about Gavarni. I thought it very interesting, and it made me love him twice as much.

Paris and its surroundings may be beautiful, but here we have nothing to complain of either.

This week I painted something which I think would give you the impression of Scheveningen as we saw it when we walked there together: a large study of sand, sea and sky—a big sky of delicate grey and warm white, with one little spot of soft blue gleaming through—the sand and the sea, light—so that the whole becomes blond, but animated by the typically strong and bright-coloured figures and fishing smacks, which are full of tone. The subject of the sketch is a fishing smack with its anchor being raised. The horses are ready to be hitched to it and then to draw the boat into the water. I enclose a little sketch of it. It was a hard job. I wish I had painted it on a panel or on canvas. I tried to introduce more colour into it, namely depth and firmness of colour. How curious it is that you and I often seem to have the same thoughts. Yesterday evening, for instance, I came home from the wood with a study, and for the whole week, and especially then, I had been deeply absorbed in that question of depth of colour. And I would have liked to have talked it over with you, especially as regards the study I made, and, look here, in your letter of this morning you accidentally speak about being struck on Montmartre by the strong vivid colours, which even so remained harmonious.

I do not know if it was exactly the same thing that struck us both, but I well know that you also would have certainly felt what struck me so particularly, and probably you too would have seen it in the same way. I begin by sending you a little sketch of the subject and will tell you what it was about.

The wood is becoming quite autumnal—there are effects of colour which I rarely find painted in Dutch pictures.

Yesterday towards evening I was busy painting a rather sloping ground

Treveszaal

in the wood, covered with mouldered and dry beech leaves. That ground was light and dark reddish brown, made more so by the shadows of trees which threw more or less dark streaks over it, sometimes half blotted out. The question was, and I found it very difficult, to get the depth of colour, the enormous force and solidity of that ground—and while painting it I perceived only for the first time how much light there still was in that dusk—to keep that light, and to keep at the same time the glow and depth of that rich color.

For you cannot imagine any carpet so splendid as that deep brownish-red, in the glow of an autumn evening sun, tempered by the trees.

From that ground young beech trees spring up which catch light on one side and are sparkling green there, and the shadowy side of those stems are a warm deep black-green.

Behind those saplings, behind the brownish-red soil, is a sky very delicate, bluish grey, warm, hardly blue, all aglow—and against it is a hazy border of green and a network of little stems and yellowish leaves. A few figures of wood gatherers are wandering around like dark masses of mysterious shadows. The white cap of a woman, who is bending to reach a dry branch, stand out all of a sudden against the deep red-brown of the ground. A skirt catches the light—a shadow falls—a dark silhouette of a man appears above the underbrush. A white bonnet, a cap, a shoulder, the bust of a woman moulds itself against the sky. Those figures, they are large and full of poetry—in the twilight of that deep shadowy tone they appear as enormous clay figurines being shaped in a studio.

I describe nature to you; how far I rendered the effect in my sketch, I do not know myself; but this I know, that I was struck by the harmony of green, red, black, yellow, blue, brown, grey. It was very de Groux-like, an effect for instance like that sketch of "The Conscript's Departure" formerly in the Ducal Palace.

To paint it was a hard job. I used for the ground one large tube and a half of white—yet that ground is very dark—further red, yellow, brown ochre, black, sienna, bistre, and the result is a reddish-brown, but one that varies from bistre to deep wine-red, and even a pale blond ruddiness. Then there is still the moss on the ground, and a border of fresh grass, which catches light and sparkles brightly, and is very difficult to get. There you have at last a sketch which I maintain has some significance and which expresses something, no matter what may be said about it.

While painting it I said to myself: I must not go away before there is something of an autumn evening air about it, something mysterious, something serious.

But as this effect does not stay, I needed to paint quickly—the figures were painted in at once with a few strong strokes with a firm brush. It struck me how firmly those little stems were rooted in the ground. I began on them with a brush, but because the base was already so clotted, a brush-stroke was lost in it—so I squeezed the roots and trunks in from the tube, and modelled it a little with the brush.

Yes—now they stand there rising from the ground, strongly rooted in it. In a certain way I am glad I have not *learned* painting, because then I might have *learned* to pass by such effects as this. Now I say, no, this is just what I want, if it is impossible, it is impossible; I will try it, though I do know how it should be done. How I paint it *I do not know myself*. I sit down with a white board before the spot that strikes me, I look at what is before me, I say to myself that that white board must become something; I come back dissatisfied—I put it away, and when I have rested a little, I go to look at it with a kind of fear. Then I am still dissatisfied, because I still have too clearly in my mind that splendid subject, to be satisfied with what I made of it. But after all I find in my work an echo of what struck me. I see that nature has told me something, has spoken to me, and that I have put it down in shorthand. In my shorthand there may be words that cannot be deciphered, there may be mistakes or gaps, but there is something in it of what wood or shore or figure has told me, and it is not a tame or conventional language, proceeding less from nature itself than from a studied manner or a system.

Ceiling detail, Eerste Kamer

Enclosed another little sketch from the dunes. Small bushes are standing there, the leaves of which are white on one side and dark green on the other and constantly rustle and glitter. Dark trees to the rear.

You see I am absorbed with all my strength in painting: I am absorbed in colour—until now I have restrained myself, and I am not sorry for it. If I had not drawn so much, I would not be able to catch the impression of and get hold of a figure that looks like an unfinished clay figurine. But now I feel myself on the high sea—the painting must be continued with all the strength I can give to it.

Ceiling detail, Treveszaal

When I paint on panel or canvas the expenses increase again. Everything is so expensive, the paint is also expensive, and is so soon gone. Well, those are difficulties all painters have. We must see what can be done. I know for sure that I have an instinct for colour, and that it will come to me more and more, that painting is in my very bone and marrow. Doubly and twice doubly I appreciate your helping me so faithfully and in such measure. I think so often of you. I want my work to become firm, serious, manly, and that you too will get satisfaction from it as soon as possible.

One thing I want to call your attention to, as being of importance. Might it be possible to get colours, panels, brushes, etc., *wholesale*? Now I have to pay the retail price. Are you connected with Paillard or anyone like that? If so, I think it would be very much cheaper to buy wholesale—white, ochre, sienna, for instance, and we could then arrange about the money. It would of course be much cheaper. Think it over. Good painting does not depend upon using much colour, but in order to paint a ground emphatically, or to keep a sky clear, one must sometimes not spare the tube.

Sometimes the subject requires delicate painting, sometimes the material, the nature of the things themselves requires thick painting. Mauve, who in comparison with J. Maris, and still more in comparison with Millet or Jules Depré, paints very soberly, has in the corners of his studio cigar boxes full of empty tubes, which are as numerous as the empty bottles in the corners of the rooms after a dinner or soirée, as Zola describes it for instance. Well, if there can be a little extra this month, that will be delightful. If not, it will be all right, too. I shall work as hard as I can. You inquire after my health, but how is yours? I am inclined to believe that my remedy would serve you also—to be in the open air, to paint. I am well, but when I am tired I still feel it. However, it is getting better instead of worse. I think it a good thing that I live as sparingly as possible, but painting is my special remedy. I heartily hope that you are having good luck and that you will find still more. A hearty handshake in thought and believe me,

Yours,
Vincent

You see how in the sketch of the beach there is a blond tender effect, and in the wood there is a more gloomy serious tone. I am glad both exist in life.

VINCENT VAN GOGH
Letters, 1882

DUTCH PATRIOTS, NAZI COURTS

There are many personal chronicles of the Nazi occupation of the Netherlands, including one—the diary of Anne Frank—that is unquestionably the most widely read document of the Holocaust. What follows is an impersonal document—a list of sentences handed down by German courts in The Hague and elsewhere during the occupation. It appeared as an appendix to an anti-German broadside, Holland Fights the Nazis, *that L. de Jong, a former editor of* De Groene Amsterdammer, *published in 1942. In a way, this brief roll indicts the Nazis far more effectively than de Jong's overheated text, for it reveals in chilling detail the ruthless caprice of Holland's captors, who thought nothing of sentencing schoolboys to ten months in prison because they had "played football with a German officer's cap, which was detrimental to the honor of the German armed forces."*

It must be borne in mind that the following list is far from complete. It includes only the few cases which, probably as a warning to the general public, were made known by the German controlled Dutch News Agency and published in all Dutch papers. Therefore the list merely intends to give an idea of the kind of "offences" and punishments. Convictions on charges of sabotage, spying, etc., are not included. The list shows at the same time, that all classes of Dutch community are taking part in the bitter undergound struggle against German tyranny.

August, 1940—The German *Landesgericht* at The Hague sentences an inhabitant of The Hague to eighteen months' imprisonment. He had publicly "said that he wished England out soon kick the Germans out of Holland."

11th October—The German *Landesgericht* at The Hague sentences an inhabitant of Utrecht to fifteen months' imprisonment and his wife to six months' imprisonment. They were accused "of having listened to foreign broadcasts."

November—The German *Landesgericht* at The Hague sentences a lecturer at the Agricultural University of Wageningen to three months' imprisonment. He was accused "of having used foul language in connection with prominent German statesmen."

November—The German *Landesgericht* at The Hague sentences Professor C. W. de Vries, of the Economic University of Rotterdam, to eighteen months' imprisonment. "The accused had in an address to 300 students declared that he had listened to the forbidden broadcast of Princess Juliana on the 31st August."

December—The German *Landesgericht* at The Hague sentences three schoolboys from Tilburg to ten months' imprisonment. "They had played football with a German officer's cap, which was detrimental to the honor of the German armed forces."

December—The German *Landesgericht* at Enschede sentences a 36-year-old baker from Zwolle to four months' imprisonment. He was accused "of having used foul language in connection with the highest German authority in the Netherlands."

December—The German *Landesgericht* at Enschede sentences a 52-year-old factory-manager from Enschede to four months' imprisonment; a 20½ year-old student from Hengelo to three weeks' imprisonment; the manager's 17-year-old son and a 16-year-old friend to two weeks' imprisonment. They were accused "of having demonstratively turned their backs in the cinema when Seyss Inquart appeared on the screen."

December—The German *Landesgericht* at Enschede sentences a 36-year-old butcher from Enschede to four months' imprisonment. He was accused of having "said that he wished the Reich's Commissioner would crash into smithereens into the windows of a corner-house." . . .

December—The German *Landesgericht* at Enschede sentences a 28-year-old navvy from Enschede to eight months' imprisonment. "The accused who had worked for seven weeks in Germany and who had returned upon his own initiative had told other unemployed 'Do not go to Germany, because you will starve there. Nobody can live in Germany.'"

December—The German *Landesgericht* at The Hague sentences two brewery workers to fifteen months' imprisonment. They were accused of having "thrashed two brewery foremen of German nationality." The defendants had pointed out that the thrashing had nothing to do with the fact that the foremen were Germans.

17th December—A German military court sentences a 26-year-old man to eighteen months' imprisonment and a 60-year-old woman to six months' imprisonment. "They had spread the stupid and mean report that the bombing of Dutch towns and the laying of mines in front of the Dutch coast had been the work of the Germans. This was foul slander of the German armed forces." . . .

December—A German military court sentences three young men to ten months' imprisonment. "They had stolen and torn to pieces some German officers' caps."

December—The German *Landesgericht* at The Hague sentences a typist to eight months' imprisonment. She had "distributed a poem of anti-German tendency."

December—The German *Landesgericht* at The Hague sentences a carpenter from Groningen to six months' imprisonment because he "had used foul language in connection with the Germans."

December—The German *Landesgericht* at The Hague sentences a 21-year-old office-clerk to twelve months' imprisonment, because "he had listened to foreign broadcasts."

December—The German *Landesgericht* at The Hague sentences a 39-year-old skipper to six months' imprisonment. He was accused "of having said in a café at Haarlem: 'The Germans are bombing us in order to incite us against England.' The accused defended himself by saying that he had recognized the German machines with his own eyes."

Streets in The Hague

January, 1941—The German *Landesgericht* at The Hague sentences a sergeant of the Reconstruction Service to eighteen months' imprisonment. "Accused was found in the possession of thirty copies of a poem on the bombing of Rotterdam which was highly offensive to the German *Luftwaffe.*'...

January—The German *Landesgericht* at The Hague sentences a lunchroom dish-washer to six months' imprisonment. "He had listened to foreign broadcasts and was found in the possession of a poem detrimental to the honor of Germany's armed forces."

February—The German *Landesgericht* at The Hague sentences a Dutch police-constable to eight months' imprisonment. The accused "had openly asked in a train whether there were any members of the NSB present. If so, he would like to throw them out of the window." Furthermore he had declared "that there were secret weapon-depots in the Netherlands and that the moment would come when we would make a final settlement with the Germans."

February—The German *Landesgericht* at The Hague sentences a 19-year-old man from Utrecht to eight months' imprisonment. "He had used foul language in connection with the *Führer* and the German *Reich.*"

February—The German *Landesgericht* at The Hague sentences a 49-year-old fitter from Rotterdam to fifteen months' imprisonment. The accused had "refused to go and work in Germany. When a Dutch woman tried to sell a flag of the Winter Relief to him, he had said: 'It is a shame! Why don't you go to Hitler?' The woman had asked him why *he* didn't go to Churchill. After that the accused had said that the money spent for the Winter Relief would disappear to Germany, one way or the other."

February—The German *Landesgericht* at The Hague sentences the brothers Baron B. to four months' imprisonment. They had "distributed a poem offensive to the *Führer* and Germany."

February—The German *Landesgericht* at The Hague sentences a 34-year-old butcher from Helmond to three months' imprisonment. The accused "has stated that the bombing of Helmond had been carried out by German planes as he had seen with his own eyes."

February—The German *Landesgericht* at The Hague sentences a 21-year-old man from Koudekerke to three months' imprisonment. "He had fixed a pamphlet on a neighboring house which referred to the broadcasts of *Radio Orange.*"

February—The German *Landesgericht* at The Hague sentences a nurse from The Hague to twelve months' imprisonment. "She had chalked words offensive to the *Führer* on trees in the Hague Forest."

February—The German *Landesgericht* at The Hague sentences a retailer from Haarlem to eight months' imprisonment. The accused "had listened to British broadcasts."

February—The German *Landesgericht* at The Hague sentences an office clerk to four months' imprisonment; a housemaid to three months' imprisonment; her sister to two months' imprisonment. The office clerk "had given a poem, highly offensive to prominent German statesmen, to the housemaid. The housemaid had made a copy of it and given it to the typist. The typist's sister had shown it to fellow pupils of her school."

L. DE JONG
Holland Fights the Nazis, 1942

In Auprès de ma Blonde *Nicolas Freeling does something that all successful writers of detective fiction are tempted to do but few have the courage to carry through—he bumps off the detective-hero of this and several previous stories. More astonishing, Freeling allows this catastrophe to occur at the book's midpoint, after which* Auprès de ma Blonde *becomes a tale of revenge, not routine police work. As the story opens Piet Van der Valk, Freeling's Sam Spade, is transferred from active duty in Amsterdam to a purely bureaucratic post in The Hague, a change that both Van der Valk and his French-born wife, Arlette, find hard to adjust to. Restless, Van der Valk takes to strolling, every evening, "through the wooded outskirts of the town where The Hague slithers out to the sea and Scheveningen."*

MURDER ON THE SCHEVENINGEN ROAD

Huis ten Bosch

It was the evening of March 3rd.

There was a smell of rotted dead leaves from last autumn, of rain-slimed and exhaust-blackened tree trunks, of sodden muddy grass alongside the pavements. The street lamps had a depressed droop like undernourished tulips: the shimmering halo of light, reflected off raindrops, hung around them like bad breath. But this is part of it, thought Van der Valk, not discontented; without this there would be no spring, no hairy pussy willows reminding him of the scent of mimosa far down in the South. He had bought some mimosa that morning for his wife; it had been in cellophane, already desiccated from the long weary voyage that Arlette, too, had made, the wonderful scent long departed. Just as well, she had said, pleased, smiling at him—that way she would feel no homesickness. His wife's smile and the scent of mimosa, vividly pictured and for one instant recaptured, would be almost the last things in his life. That, and the moisture on his loden coat, and the dead leaves, and a wet leather glove: the smells of Holland.

There was nothing in the sound of a car to make him turn: a relaxed sound, of a car idling along under no pressure; a contented sound, of a motor turning easily in the moist air. There was no instinct of danger to make him turn—it was the idlest of curiosity when the car slowed behind him. Probably some out-of-season tourist checking whether the road really did lead to Scheveningen. In a years-old police automatism, he did bring his back foot round to narrow the target and start going down to look for cover. There were four shots, and two missed him altogether, but he had no interest in that. He had no interest even in the face: distorted, rigid with fear, with terror at what it was doing, and the complete inability to stop. The pistol had commanded its owner to shoot and there was nothing else for it. An actor for many years, Van der Valk would have been interested in this piece of theatre, but he had a new part to study, the most important of his parts. In the words of the seventeenth-century actor, he was on the way to study a long silence.

So that he had no interest in the rough clash of the transmission and the squeal of the tires pulling away in haste. He was down on his face in the dead leaves. He knew that he was dying and was pleased that he knew, and could say the words he wished to say—very simple words.

And a few simple thoughts. He had never been afraid of dying, and least of all now. He had had a life, married a wife, raised children, dug ground and planted a tree, sailed a boat and skied down hill, eaten and drunk and made love. He was ready for what came next. He felt his life spilling out on the ground and turned his head a little. Bereitsein ist alles. He thought of Arlette without disappointment and without pain.

It wasn't a bad place at all to die. With a last flicker of recognition for this world, he remembered Stendhal saying there was no disgrace in dying in the street, when not done on purpose. And he had . . .

Van der Valk began to study his long silence but was interrupted. He was dead.

"The trouble with public-spirited witnesses is that they're such infernal busybodies." Arlette would remember the phrase. Others, too; light-hearted or disillusioned, even slightly soured. "One definition of aristocracy is a person who does not stop to gawk at a street fight." In one of the villas to the side of the road, beyond the strip of sodden poached dog-infected grass, beyond the cyclepath and the row of leafless trees, lived a public-spirited person. He had been in a first-floor front room, and he hadn't had the television on, being absorbed at the moment in his stamp collection. The coppery bonk of pistol shots at thirty meters, however dulled by the saturated air, had startled him, and he had run to his window and jerked the curtain—but he had not seen much through the wavering fine rain which coarsened the grain of the air, so that what he had seen was a worn old gangster movie of the early thirties, made by Warner Brothers. Van der Valk had enjoyed them greatly. George Raft and James Cagney, Paul Muni and Edward G. Robinson; the young Bogart. A man lying face down in the rain, and the dark-colored car accelerating away. Probably with Peter Lorre and Sydney Greenstreet in the back.

Arlette was not a woman of much imagination. She saw the scene quite differently, because she had lived through it as a girl of fifteen, while stopping to drink a cup of coffee on her way home from school. A street corner in Toulon in blinding dusty sunshine, deserted. The spit and snap of an automatic pistol and the squeal of a car furiously driven. Running police and a white képi fallen off and rolling through the heavy lazy air. Most vivid of all, the café owner with the big belly ducking with such unexpected agility.

"A plat ventre tous—on est en train de se faire flinguer." The young girl, as well as everyone else, à plat ventre in a heap; these episodes sometimes involved unpleasantly indiscriminate machine-gun fire.

Most ironic of all, for twenty-five years she had steeled herself for that telephone call from a potato-filled police mouth embarrassed into lumpish incoherence. Since the beginning of the desk job—in the civil service as it were; in The Hague, of all places (that most civil-service-minded of all prim Dutch towns)—she had told herself that at least there was no longer that to be afraid of. And fatally the call had come, and fatally she had not followed the rules she had long rehearsed that would govern her behavior. The car started as though it had been waiting whetted for this moment, and she had driven ridiculously, convinced of her sedate sober mind, congratulating herself on behaving well. The deux-chevaux braked, skidding, to a stop. So silly to have hurried; of course she was much too late, she knew that perfectly, for a lot of time had passed and there was not just a policeman gesticulating in the rain but a whole knot of cars. And the ambulance. And a group of careful middle-aged gentlemen in raincoats, with their hats on because it was still raining. The body was still in place. She did not worry about that or think anything silly like,

He'll get wet! She knew about the measurements and the photographs and the conscientiousness displayed by all, even the press. Everyone made way for her politely, and she did not do anything in the least absurd like going down à plat ventre.

But, being in shock, she did not remember properly anything much of what happened, and her next accurate recollection was of sitting in her flat in daylight, dried, dressed, combed, politely pouring a drink for the district commissaire of police. She could not place the time very well, but thought it must have been about midday. So silly a feeling . . . almost as though she were pouring the usual midday drink for her husband, but in that case why was she being so formal and polite?

"I needn't tell you how I feel," he was saying. "Thanks, Mevrouw, no more for me. And, if I may permit myself the remark, you shouldn't be drinking whisky.". . .

"That's as may be."

"Yes. Er—I need hardly say . . . when we lose a man . . . we don't give up."

"No," said Arlette, knowing that this meant they had found nothing.

"We have—er—the skid marks, which will tell us what kind of car it was. And—er—ejected cartridge cases, which will give us the gun. When we recover the bullets . . ." He had better not dwell on that detail, he was thinking plainly.

"Yes," said Arlette, knowing that the car would have been stolen and the gun ditched.

"We are, of course, going to examine everyone with whom he may have had—er, dealings and who might have—er, felt a grievance. It may take a long time. We will neglect nothing."

"Quite," brightly. "When can you let me have my husband back?"

"We were thinking, er, the funeral . . ."

"I don't want to seem rude, Commissaire, or ungrateful. He didn't belong here. He came from Amsterdam, but he has no family left there. I know that you will be extremely kind, and that you will want to come, and send big wreaths and everything—forgive me, please. I'm afraid I don't want that. I'm sorry but I want to leave as soon as I can, which is as soon as you'll let me."

"But where will you go?" asked the commissaire, worried. "If it's the press . . ."

"No. He had, you see, a little house in France—for retiring to, you understand? And that is where I'm going, and that's where he's going, and I want to ask you only one thing, which is that you'll please help me with that and see that I have no trouble, with the customs or whoever is responsible for taking dead people across frontiers. I feel sure that *they'll* be very worried about whether the proper taxes have been paid."

"Try not to be bitter," gently.

She drank some more whisky and grimaced. "You're quite right. I promise I won't be tiresome or troublesome at all."

He found this humility touching; he also felt uneasy. A frightening woman, in a sense; one didn't know what she mightn't be capable of.

"We won't let you down," he said, and really meant it.

NICOLAS FREELING
Auprès de ma Blonde, 1972

160

REFERENCE

Chronology of the Netherlands

A.D. 800 Charlemagne becomes Holy Roman Emperor; Netherlands inhabited by Frisians in north and west, Saxons in east and center, Franks south of the Meuse River (see inset map, page 164)

843 Division of Charlemagne's empire, with the so-called Middle Kingdom, which includes the Netherlands, going to Lothaire

c. 1000 First dykes built on Zuyder Zee; central authority in the Netherlands badly fragmented

1076 Pope Gregory VII, attempting to reassert Church's right to appoint bishops, excommunicates Henry IV

1122 Concordat of Worms resolves church-state dispute in favor of diocese

c. 1230 Floris IV begins construction on site of what is now the Binnenhof (see map, page 165)

c. 1250 William II, count of Holland, builds a manor house on rise of land once occupied by a hunting lodge belonging to the lords of Wassenaar; this complex is known as 's-Gravenhage, "the count's hedge"

c. 1260 Floris V, William's son, orders construction of the Ridderzaal, or Knights' Hall, at center of the Binnenhof

1300 Population of The Hague reaches 1,200

1397 Margaret of Cleves founds the Kloosterkerk, the first brick church in The Hague

1402 Fire destroys fourteenth-century Church of St. Jacob, known as the Grote Kerk; it is rebuilt on a grander scale

1420–23 Six-sided bell tower added to Grote Kerk

1433 Jacqueline of Bavaria, last independent countess of Holland, cedes country to her cousin Philip of Burgundy

c. 1450 Philip requisitions the mansion of the Brederoes and razes it to build The Hague's town hall

1479 Ministers' Turret erected in southwest corner of Binnenhof

1539 Steeple of Grote Kerk damaged by fire and replaced; bells ring out from new wooden spire for first time in 1565; Kloosterkerk extended to south with addition of aisle, side chapels

1548 Charles V annexes the Netherlands

1555 Charles abdicates in favor of his son Philip II

1564 Construction of Oude Raadhuis, a masterpiece of Renaissance workmanship, is begun

1567 Philip II sends the Duke of Alva to the Netherlands at the head of a 20,000-man army; creation of Council of Blood; execution of Egmont and other prominent Dutch patriots

1568–1648 Revolt of the Netherlands, also known as the Eighty Years' War

1572 Capture of Brill by the "Sea Beggars," first major victory for the rebels

1576 Pacification of Ghent signed; Dutch provinces agree to set aside political and religious differences pending expulsion of Spanish

1578–92 Duke of Parma, the duke of Alva's successor, subdues south

1579 Union of Utrecht ratified by seven northern provinces—a de facto declaration of independence from Spain; William of Orange, known as William the Silent, elected *stadtholder*

1580 Infamous Edict of Blood promulgated, making heresy an offense not only against Church but against state as well; William officially "banned" by Philip II

1581 Dutch officially declare their independence of Spain in a ceremony held in The Hague

1584 William the Silent assassinated at Delft; his seventeen-year-old son, Maurice of Nassau, succeeds him

1588 Duke of Parma organizes Great Armada to punish England for coming to Dutch rebels' aid; disastrous setback for Spain virtually ensures rebels' eventual victory

1591 William's widow, Louise, princess of Coligny, and her seven-year-old son, Frederik-Henry, move into Het Oude Hof; grounds later expanded to incorporate the Princessetuin

1602 Dutch East India Company founded

1609–21 Twelve Years' Truce between rebels and Spain

1613 Prince Maurice orders a moat dug around the Binnenhof

1616 Heilige Geesthofje, residence for indigent elderly, constructed

1617 Kloosterkerk becomes a Protestant house of worship

1619 Johan van Oldenbarnevelt executed in courtyard of Binnenhof

1633–34 Grenadierpoort built to replace former east gate of Binnenhof

1633–44 The Hague's most splendid private residence, the Mauritshuis, built for Johann-Maurits, count of Nassau-Siegen, by Pieter Post from designs by Jacob van Campen

1636 Work completed on St. Sebastiaansdoelen

1640 Frederik-Henry commissions Post and van Campen to design Noordeinde Palace on site of Het Oude Hof

1645 Post and van Campen design Huis ten Bosch for Amalia van Solms, Frederik-Henry's widow, as memorial for her husband; the Orange Hall of "House in the Woods" is specifically intended as a gallery for paintings commissioned by the *stadtholder*'s widow

1648 Treaty of Westphalia ends Eighty Years' War

1649–55 Nieuwe Kerk, with its splendid wooden vaults, erected from designs by Pieter Noorwits

1652 Work begins on two major projects designed by Pieter Post: the Johann de Witt house in the Noordeinde and the so-called Stadtholder's Quarters enclosing the Binnenhof

1653 Johann de Witt becomes grand pensionary of Holland

1654 First Anglo-Dutch War, a direct outgrowth of the English Navagation Act of 1651, concluded by Treaty of Westminster

1667 Treaty of Breda ends Second Anglo-Dutch War

1669 Death of Rembrandt van Rijn, greatest painter of the Golden Age of Dutch painting

1677 William III weds Mary, daughter of James II of England; Benedict de Spinoza, greatest Dutch philosopher, dies

1689 "Glorious Revolution" proclaims William and Mary joint rulers of England

1696	Daniel Marot, a Huguenot émigré, converts former apartments of Charles V in Binnenhof into the Treveszaal, the most splendid Louis XIV room outside France; here the Republic's leaders receive foreign ambassadors
1702	William III dies childless, bringing an end to the direct line of the House of Orange
1702–13	War of Spanish Succession proves ruinous to Dutch economy
1709–95	National lottery held in the Ridderzaal
1715	Hotel van Schuylenburch, Marot's masterpiece, completed
1717	Construction of Kneuterdijk Palace begins
1733	New wing added by Marot to Oude Raadhuis
1734–36	Marot designs the Hôtel Huguetan, since 1819 the Royal Library
1748	William IV, grandson of William III's cousin, proclaimed *stadtholder*; title made hereditary
1751	Death of William IV; his widow, Anne, appointed regent for their three-year-old son
1755–56	Three major commissions undertaken by Pieter de Swart transform the Lange Vijverberg into The Hague's most elegant street
1760	Pieter de Swart creates a palatial residence on the Lange Voorhout for Anthony Patras; now Queen Beatrix's working palace, it is known familiarly as the Palace of the Golden Balconies
1766	William V buys the Vijverhof, a building on the Hofweg, to house his personal art collection; William's ineffectual reign will last until 1795
1777–90	South wing of the Binnenhof completed by Ludwig Gunkel
1777	Anton Lyncker opens porcelain works in The Hague, which will become famous for its *pâte-tendre* ware, hard-paste porcelain, and silver in the last decades of the eighteenth century
1782	John Adams arrives in The Hague as first ambassador from the newly independent United States to the Netherlands
1793	France declares war on the Dutch Republic; country overrun; William V flees to England
1795–1806	Batavian Republic; Netherlands governed by the Patriot Party, whose leaders sympathize with the French
1804	Only completed wing of the house designed by de Swart for Duke of Nassau-Weilburg converted into Royal Theatre
1806–10	Louis Napoleon, emperor's brother, rules as king of Holland
1810	Kingdom of Holland incorporated into French empire
1813	Dutch liberated from French domination
1816	William I of Orange-Nassau buys Kneuterdijk Palace as a residence for his son and heir
1820	Mauritshuis opened as a museum
1821	William I designates renovated Noordeinde Palace his official residence
1843	Rail lines link The Hague to Amsterdam and Rotterdam
1848	Baron van Westreenen dies, leaving his house, book collections, and estate to the nation; this handsome patrimony is now known as the Museum Meermanno
1850	Population of The Hague estimated at 70,000
1858	Baron van Brienen, owner of Clingendael, an estate on the outskirts of The Hague, begins construction of what will be the city's most sumptuous private residence; sold by the baron's heirs, this building was converted into the grand luxe Hotel des Indes in 1881
1862	Binnenhof moat filled in
1869	Monument unveiled on 1813 Plein to commemorate liberation from French
1872	Birth of Piet Mondrian, most famous modern Hague artist
1880	Hendrik Willem Mesdag commissioned to create panorama of Scheveningen harbor, completes work in four months
1882	Van Wijk and Wesstra's Passage opened; subsequent additions made in 1929 and 1972
1884	St. Sebastiaansdoelen converted into a municipal museum; William III dies without male heir and is succeeded by his daughter, Wilhelmina
1885	P.J.H. Cuyper's monumental neo-Gothic fountain installed in Binnenhof square
1887	Rebuilt Kurhaus, gutted by fire two years earlier, opens at Scheveningen
1898–1904	Restoration of Ridderzaal includes complete rebuilding of its vaulted wooden ceiling
1900	Population of The Hague reaches 200,000
1907–13	Construction of the International Peace Palace
1912	Municipal council meets for first time in its new quarters on Javastraat
1918	Bronze statue of Johann de Witt unveiled in Plaats; Mata Hari's house on Nieuwe Uitleg opened to public
1923	Buitenhof cleared to ease vehicular traffic
1935	Berlage's Gemeentemuseum, designed in 1920, finally opened
1943	Large section of Hague Woods destroyed in preparing German lines of defense
1945	Allied bombers mistakenly strike Bezuidenhout in city's center
1948	The Hague celebrates its seven hundredth anniversary and Queen Wilhelmina's golden jubilee; she abdicates in favor of her daughter, Juliana; fire ravages Noordeinde Palace
1950	Madurodam, The Hague in miniature, is dedicated to the memory of the Maduros' son, who died in a concentration camp
1950–56	Restoration of Huis ten Bosch
1955	Clingendael, with its splendid gardens, opened to the public
1957	Extensive renovations of Grote Kerk completed
1969	Congresgebouw, by J.J.P. Oud, inaugurated
1973–76	Construction of The Hague Central Station and Babylon Complex
1975	Oude Raadhuis reopens after extensive six-year restoration
1976	Queen Juliana presides at the rededication of Portuguese-Jewish Synagogue in The Hague
1980	Queen Juliana, following her mother's example, abdicates in favor of her daughter, Beatrix
1981	Queen Beatrix and her consort, Prince Claus, take up residence in Huis ten Bosch

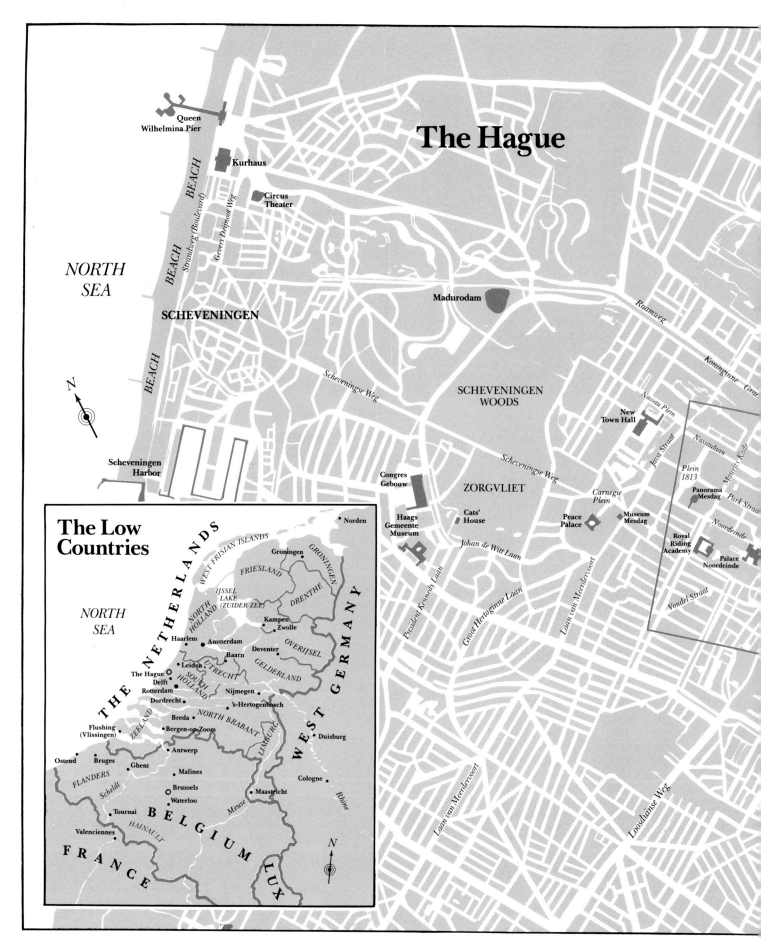

The Hague

Queen
Wilhelmina Pier

Kurhaus

Circus
Theater

Strandweg (Boulevard)

Gevers Deijnoot Weg

BEACH
BEACH
BEACH
BEACH

*NORTH
SEA*

SCHEVENINGEN

Scheveningen
Harbor

Scheveningse Weg

Madurodam

Raamweg

SCHEVENINGEN
WOODS

Scheveningse Weg

New
Town Hall

Nassau Plein

Java Straat

Koninginne Grac

Nassaulaan

*Plein
1813*

Maurits Kade

ZORGVLIET

Congres
Gebouw

Haags
Gemeente
Museum

Cats'
House

*Carnegie
Plein*

Peace
Palace

Museum
Mesdag

Panorama
Mesdag

Noordeinde

Park Straat

Royal
Riding
Academy

Palace
Noordeinde

Johan de Witt Laan

President Kennedy Laan

Groot Hertoginne Laan

Laan van Meerdervoort

Vondel Straat

Laan van Meerdervoort

Loosduinse Weg

The Low Countries

THE NETHERLANDS

WEST FRISIAN ISLANDS

• Norden

NORTH SEA

• Groningen

GRONINGEN

FRIESLAND

*IJSSEL
LAKE
(ZUIDER ZEE)*

NORTH
HOLLAND

DRENTHE

• Haarlem

• Amsterdam

Kampen •
Zwolle •

OVERIJSSEL

• Leiden

• Deventer

UTRECHT

• Baarn

• The Hague

• Delft

SOUTH
HOLLAND

GELDERLAND

• Rotterdam

• Nijmegen

• Dordrecht

• 's-Hertogenbosch

ZEELAND

NORTH BRABANT

• Breda

LIMBURG

• Bergen-op-Zoom

Flushing
(Vlissingen) •

Duisburg •

WEST GERMANY

• Antwerp

• Ostend

• Bruges

• Ghent

• Malines

Cologne •

Scheldt

FLANDERS

• Brussels

• Waterloo

• Maastricht

Meuse

Rhine

LUX

• Tournai

HAINAULT

B E L G I U M

• Valenciennes

F R A N C E

164

Guide to The Hague

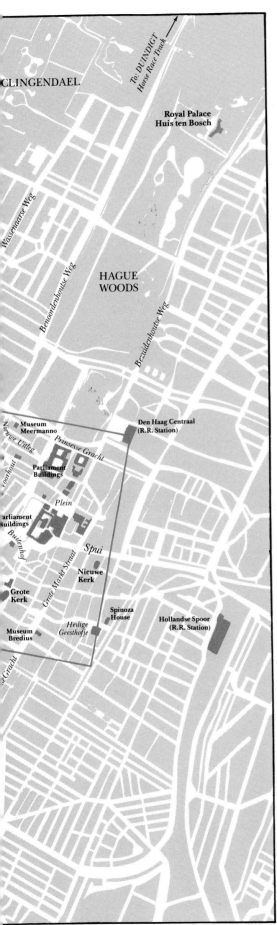

The Hague, little more than fens and dunes when William II, Count of Holland, first visited the area in the middle of the thirteenth century, has grown exponentially in the last seven hundred years. It has done so without losing its essential character, however, and William and his descendants would have little trouble recognizing the city that served as their administrative capital and chief residence. The Hague today is a true metropolis, part of the populous and productive urban corridor that stretches from Haarlem to Rotterdam (see inset map, "The Low Countries," at lower left). But the modern city that has grown up around William II's man-or house—a residential compound known as 's-Gravenhage, or "the count's hedge," from which The Hague derives its name—retains its small-town ambience. There is, in everything from the scale of the public buildings to the affability of the residents, a sense of intimacy and amicability about The Hague that is unmatched by any other major governmental seat. A visitor to the administrative center of the Netherlands will encounter this special quality in any part of the city, but he is likely to feel it most intensely in the oldest quarter, the Centrum or center of The Hague, which shown in detail on the map found directly below.

Center of The Hague

Wilhelmina Reyinga

A walking tour of The Hague might begin almost anywhere, but the logical place to start is at the **Ridderzaal**, or Knights' Hall, which rises from the middle of the **Binnenhof** (center right, below). The Ridderzaal is not only the oldest extant building in The Hague, it is also the largest secular Gothic structure in Western Europe. Built by William II's son, Floris V, toward the end of the thirteenth century, it has served successive *stadtholders*, or rulers, in various capacities. It was the first home of the Estates General of the Netherlands following the new nation's liberation from Spain, and it is visited each autumn by the ruling monarch of the Netherlands, Queen Beatrix, who formally opens Parliament under the Ridderzaal's arched wooden roof.

The Binnenhof itself, once open to the surrounding countryside, is now enclosed by a three-story structure known as the Stadtholder's Quarters. Built in the first decades of the seventeenth century—an era that has come to be known as the Golden Age of the Netherlands—this dormered and shuttered brick structure, set upon a graceful arcade, contains the so-called **Eerste Kamer**—the First Chamber, or senate, of Parliament. In a slightly newer wing is the **Tweede Kamer**, the Second Chamber—roughly equivalent to our House of Representatives.

There are three entrances to the Binnenhof, the most elegant and imposing of which is the **Grenadierspoort**, built in 1633–34 by Joris Cornelisz Faes to replace the old east gate. Originally the Grenadiers' Gate gave onto a drawbridge, but that bridge was replaced in 1862 when the moat around the Binnenhof was filled in; today one exits through the gate onto a cobbled street that leads directly to the **Mauritshuis**, once the home of Johann-Maurits, Count of Nassau-Siegen, and now a major repository of Dutch artworks. Count Maurits built his neoclassical mansion in the 1630s, and it is filled, not illogically, with paintings by contemporary Dutch artists. As it happens, the Golden Age of Dutch commerce was also the Golden Age of Dutch art, and consequently the Mauritshuis Collection includes works by Vermeer, Fabritius, Hals, and Rembrandt. The latter's *Anatomy Lesson of Dr. Nicolaes Tulp* occupies one wall of a first-floor salon; Vermeer's *View of Delft* and *Head of a Girl*—two of the greatest canvases ever painted—hang in a small corner room.

If you turn left as you leave the Mauritshuis you survey the **Plein**, a cobbled square dominated by an equestrian statue of William the Silent, founder of the Dutch nation, and ringed by government ministries. Another left leads you along the Korte Vijverberg, past the **Hofvijver** on the left. Various theories exist about the origins of the Hofvijver, or Court Lake, a placid pond whose central island is home to a large flock of swans. Some suspect that a lake of some sort existed on the site at the time William II built his manor house on the dunes that once rose where the Binnenhof now stands. Others contend that the site was excavated under William's direction—to provide landfill for his various building projects—and filled with water thereafter. In any case this flat sheet of water serves today to mirror the outer façade of the Stadtholder's Quarters, giving Pieter Post's legacy a fairytale quality.

Cross the Tournooiveld, a maze of tram lines, traffic arteries, walkways and flower beds, and you come to the Lange Voorhout. At its eastern terminus is the **Palace Lange Voorhout**, also known, in deference to its most striking decorative feature, as the Palace of the Golden Balconies. It serves today as a working palace for Queen Beatrix and her closest advisers. At the opposite end of the Lange Voorhout is the **Klooster Kerk**, the oldest brick church in The Hague. The central nave and choir of this severe Northern Gothic structure were originally part of a Dominican monastery, built at the beginning of the fifteenth century. In between the palace and the church is the **Royal Library**, once the private residence of Adrienne de Huguetan. Like the palace on the Lange Voorhout and the Hotel Schuylenburch on the nearby Lange Vijverberg, this austerely elegant structure dates from the first decades of the eighteenth century, a period when the genius of Daniel Marot, architect, interior designer, and landscape architect, was transforming the center of The Hague.

Marot was not responsible for the **Hotel des Indes**, which dominates the northwest corner of the Lange Voorhout; that distinction belongs to another local architect, A. Rodenburg, who gave his patron, Baron Willem van Brienen, exactly what the baron wanted—the most imposing private home in The Hague. Completed in 1859 at a reported cost of 150,000 guilders—one and a half tons of gold—the van Brienen mansion was luxurious beyond anything Haguenaars had ever seen: every doorhandle bore the family crest, which was also set into the façade of the building itself, and the design featured a covered central rotunda that visitors could reach without alighting from their coaches. Today that rotunda is fully enclosed, and it makes a perfect place to stop for tea or a meal along the route.

The Denneweg, which runs north from the Hotel des Indes to the Maurits Kade, is a singularly convivial agglomeration of boutiques, antique shops and ethnic restaurants, its pace frenetic by comparison with that of the warren of cobbled lanes and canals that lies just to the east. To the west, along the Maurits Kade, is the **Panorama Mesdag**, certainly worth the slight detour one takes to reach it. Step into this huge cyclorama, almost 300 feet in circumference and 30 feet high, and you step back into another century. Commissioned from Hendrik Willem Mesdag in 1880 and executed by Mesdag and three other local artists in a mere four months, it provides the visitor with a panoramic view of the fishing village of Scheveningen as it appeared in the nineteenth century.

From the Panorama Mesdag it is but a short walk down Noordeinde, the most fashionable shopping street in The Hague, to the **Palace Noordeinde**, one of the town's most imposing structures. Jacob van Campen and Pieter Post, the talented partnership responsible for the Stadtholder's Quarters in the Binnenhof and Huis ten Bosch, the royal residence in the Hague Woods, created this neoclassical palace for the *stadtholder* Frederik-Henry in 1640. Sumptuously furnished, it served successive *stadtholders* for more than a century before being abandoned. By the end of the Napoleonic era the palace had fallen into serious disrepair, and it was necessary to mount a major renovation effort in 1815 to make Noordeinde habitable again. At that time two new wings were added to the back of the palace and the roof was raised to accommodate another story. Fire severely damaged this section of the palace in 1948, and those charged with repairing the structure chose to eliminate the added floor, restoring both the original roofline and van Campen and Post's seventeenth-century façade.

At its southern end the Noordeinde empties into a large, irregularly shaped square that contains two public buildings of particular interest. The first of these is the **Oude Raadhuis**, or Old City Hall. Used today for official receptions and civil weddings, this building once served a more serious purpose. Its oldest section, a triumph of Northern Renaissance design and craftsmanship, was erected in the 1560s to house the mayor of The Hague; a subsequent addition, completed in 1733, provided added office space for the growing administration of a growing town.

Looming over the Oude Raadhuis is the bell tower of the **Grote Kerk**, as the sixteenth-century Church of St. Jacob is commonly known. The hexagonal tower, finished in 1423, is unique in the Netherlands: massive as any fortress, it lacks the airy grace we associate with the Gothic. It also lacks its original Gothic spire, destroyed by fire in 1539 and replaced with a finial of more contemporary design. The interior of the Grote Kerk, all whitewashed stone, arched wooden ceilings, and stained glass windows (some dating from the reign of Charles V), is an especially fine example of the interior design style known as the *Haagse Halletype*.

The **Buitenhof**, or Outer Court, is an open plaza today, clearly visible from the Grote Krek and Oude Raadhuis to the west. But until 1923, when a number of surrounding structures were razed to ease vehicular congestion, the Buitenhof was accessible only through the **Gevangenpoort**, or Prisoners' Gate, on the Outer Court's western perimeter. The gate itself was built in the 1300s, with the prison that gave the gate its popular name added a century later. Today, appropriately enough, the Gevangenpoort serves as a museum of medieval instruments of torture.

Even at a leisurely pace it takes less than half a day to complete this circuit of The Hague's historic center. The tour omits two small museums, the **Bre-**dius and the **Meermanno**, that merit an art lover's consideration—and two noteworthy houses of worship, the great drum-shaped **Nieuwe Kerk**, just west of the Spui (far right center, below), and the tiny **Portuguese-Jewish Synagogue**, up the street from the Meermanno Museum (top center). Also of interest is the **Heilige Geesthofje** (lower right corner), an especially felicitous seventeenth-century example of a uniquely Dutch institution: a public housing project for the indigent elderly, built around a well-tended garden court and entered through a street-side portal.

Other points of interest, at varying distances from the center of The Hague, include two splendid residences in the Hague Woods. One of them, **Clingendael**, was once the country estate of Baron van Brienen, builder of the Hotel des Indes. Its early-nineteenth-century gardens, credited to J.D. Zocher, favor the open leas and the natural-looking groupings of trees and shrubs favored by English landscape artists of the period. An exception is the Japanese Garden, which features plants, rocks and a small teahouse, all imported from the island kingdom itself.

Huis ten Bosch, the official residence of the royal family, is not open to the public, but its elegant symmetry is evident from the front gate. The central portal and flanking wings of the palace are attributed to Daniel Marot, the greatest of eighteenth-century Dutch architects; the house itself, to Marot's illustrious seventeenth-century predecessors Jacob van Campen and Pieter Post. Although modest in scale by European standards, this royal residence boasts a remarkably fine collection of seventeenth-century artworks, displayed in the Oranjezaal, or Orange Hall.

Madurodam, due west of Huis ten Bosch, is perhaps Europe's most remarkable memorial to the Holocaust. Dedicated to the memory of a young soldier from Curaçao in the Dutch West Indies who died in a concentration camp in 1945, it is anything but solemn; at the Maduro family's insistence, it celebrates life as firmly as it celebrates the past. Designed by the architect S.J. Bouma, it recreates, on a scale of 1:25, the principal buildings of The Hague, among them the Ridderzaal, the Heilige Geesthofje, the houses of Parliament, the Oude Raadhuis, and the Grote Kerk. Expanded several times since its 1952 opening, Madurodam now includes scaled-down models of tourist attractions from across Holland: Amsterdam's Palace on the Dam, for example, and the city hall of Gouda; famous Dutch factories and department stores, motorways and seaports—even the main terminal of Schiphol airport.

The Vredespaleis, or **Peace Palace**, which lies across the Scheveningen Woods from Madurodam, is a hulking neo-Gothic structure of no particular architectural distinction but great symbolic significance. Built in the first decades of the twentieth century by men determined to uphold the tenets of the first International Peace Conference, held at Huis ten Bosch in 1899, L.M. Cordonnier's Peace Palace was completed just before the outbreak of World War I. The spirit behind that 1899 conference lives on, however: today the Peace Palace is home to the International Court of Justice.

Far more interesting from an aesthetic point of view is the **Haags Gemeentemuseum**, or Municipal Museum of The Hague, located directly across the Zorgvliet from the Peace Palace. Designed by H.P. Berlage and officially opened in 1935, it represents a major advance in museum architecture over its predecessors. Airy, open and well lit, it offers the visitor a rich sampling of Dutch art and artifacts, among them silver and porcelain made in The Hague and works created by Hague artists from Steen to Mondrian. Of special interest is the museum's collection of musical instruments and a section devoted to the early history of The Hague.

This brief list by no means exhausts The Hague's attractions. Visitors with a yen for bright lights will want to visit the **Kurhaus** in Scheveningen, for example, while those with a serious interest in modern dance will want to consult the performance schedule of the **Circus Theater** in that same city, now home to the Netherlands Dance Theater under the direction of Jiri Kylian, one of his generation's most promising choreographers. The Hague has something to offer virtually every taste, and many of its pleasures—quiet byways, still canals, eccentric architectural details—are on no tourist map.

Selected Bibliography

Bailey, Anthony. *The Light in Holland.* New York: Alfred A. Knopf, 1970.

Beckman, Bernard. *The Hague and Scheveningen.* The Hague: W. Van Hoeve, Ltd., 1956.

Boxer, Charles R. *The Dutch Seaborne Empire: 1600–1800.* New York: Alfred A. Knopf, 1965.

Currie, Donald. *Holland: The Land and the People.* New York: A.S. Barnes and Co., 1974.

Elias, E. and A. Menalda. *The Hague as It Is.* Amsterdam: Lankamp and Brinkman, 1949.

Haley, K.H.D. *The Dutch in the Seventeenth Century.* New York: Harcourt, Brace, Jovanovich, Inc., 1972.

Hoffmann, Ann. *The Dutch: How They Live and Work.* New York: Praeger Publishers, 1971.

Huggett, Frank E. *The Modern Netherlands.* New York: Praeger Publishers, 1971.

Moore, Richard, ed. *Fodor's Holland 1981.* New York: Fodor's Modern Guides, Inc., 1981.

Nelson, Nina. *Holland.* New York: Hastings House Publishers, 1970.

Pevsner, Nikolaus. *An Outline of European Architecture.* Baltimore: Penguin Books, 1970.

Rogers, James E. *The Story of Holland.* New York: Gordon Press, 1977.

Rosenberg, Jakob, Seymour Slive, and E.H. ter Kuile, *Dutch Art and Architecture 1600–1800.* New York: Penguin Books, 1979.

Schuchart, Max. *The Netherlands.* New York: Walker and Company, 1972.

Shetter, W.Z. *The Pillars of Society: Six Centuries of Civilization in the Netherlands.* London: Heineman, 1971.

Slatkes, Leonard J. *Vermeer and His Contemporaries.* New York: Abbeville Press, 1981.

Slive, Seymour and Hans Hoetink. *Jacob van Ruisdael.* New York: Abbeville Press, 1981.

Sitwell, Sachaverell. *The Netherlands.* New York: Hastings House Publishers, 1974.

The Hague: Mirror of History. The Hague: Netherlands Government Information Service, 1949.

Toth-Ubbens, Magdi. *Mauritshuis The Hague.* Trans. J.J. Kliphuis. Munich: Knorr & Hirth Verlag, 1969.

Wilson, Charles. *The Dutch Republic and the Civilisation of the Seventeenth Century.* New York: McGraw-Hill Book Company, 1968.

Acknowledgments and Picture Credits

The Editors would like to express particular appreciation for the assistance provided by John Bertram and Hank Fisher of the Netherlands National Tourist Office, New York; Bernard E.N. Felix, Director of the Hotel des Indes, The Hague; and Margaret F. Stickney, Public Relations Director of KLM Royal Dutch Airlines, New York. The Author and Editors are especially indebted to Julika Baan, Press Officer of the VVV Tourist Office in The Hague, without whose many kindnesses, large and small, this volume would not have been possible. In addition, the Editors wish to thank the following individuals and institutions:

Ambassador of the Federal Republic of Germany and Mrs. Fischer, The Hague

Hon. Jonkheer Leopold Quarles van Ufford, Consul-General of the Netherlands, New York

Andreas te Boekhorst, Consul for Press and Cultural Affairs, Consulate of the Netherlands, New York

Haags Gemeentemuseum—Th. van Velzen, Director

Mauritshuis, The Hague—M. W. van Bohemen

Netherlands National Tourist Office—Jean van Zuiden, Photo Dept.

Gabrielle Wolohojian, New York

Tom Shay, Fuji Photographic Corporation

The cover subject for this volume was obtained through the generous efforts of Ursuline Prior, The Hague. The title or description of each of the other illustrations appears below after the page number (boldface), followed by its location. Photographic credits appear in parentheses. The following abbreviations are used:

(AH) —American Heritage Picture Library
HG —Haags Gemeentemuseum
MH —Mauritshuis, The Hague
(NS) —Nicolas Sapieha
(VVV) —VVV Tourist Office, The Hague/Scheveningen

ENDPAPERS Delft tiles. HG (NS) HALF TITLE Symbol designed by Jay J. Smith Studio FRONTISPIECE Weelinck Plein. (NS) **9** Statue on Lange Voorhout. (NS) **10–11** Skaters on the Hofvijver. (NS) **12–13** Dirck van Delen, *The Great Hall of the Binnenhof,* 1651. Rijksmuseum, Amsterdam

CHAPTER I **15** Official crest of The Hague (VVV) **16** (Guus Rijven) **17** Both: (NS) **18** top *Chronicle of Otto von Freising.* Deutsche Fotothek, Dresden (AH) bottom (NS) **19** (NS) **20** (NS) **21** *Phillippe Le Bon,* Ms. Fr. 9087 Fol 1. Bibliothèque Nationale, Paris (AH) **22** *Tres Riches Heures de Duc de Berri,* Fol 3 v. Musée Condée, Chantilly (AH) **23** Jan van Eyck, *Ghent Altarpiece.* St. Bavo, Ghent (AH) **24** Robert Campin, *Altarpiece.* Metropolitan Museum, Cloisters Collection **26–27** Bruegel, *Children's Games.* Kunsthistorisches Museum, Vienna (AH) **28** left Erasmus, *In Praise of Folly.* (AH) **28** right and **29** Hans Holbein drawings from Erasmus, *Folly.* Kupferstichkabinett, Basel (AH) **30** *Salomonis Tria Officia . . . Caroli V,* 1520. Bibliotheca Escorial **31** Titian, *Charles V,* 1548. Prado

Willem van de Velde, perhaps the most talented of all Dutch seascape painters, actually sailed out with the fleet to record moments like this one, a naval clash during the Netherlands' intermittent war with Great Britain in the latter half of the seventeenth century.

Index